FOR ME and MY GAL

D1409193

Robbi McCoy

Bella
BOOKS

2011

Bella Books, Inc.
P.O. Box 10543
Tallahassee, FL 32302

Printed in the United States of America on acid-free paper
First published 2011

Editor: Katherine V. Forrest
Cover Designer: Linda Callahan

ISBN 13: 978-1-59493-228-1

Other Bella Books by Robbi McCoy

Not Every River
Something To Believe
Songs Without Words
Waltzing At Midnight

Dedication

With much love, to my grandmother Arlie Dale McCoy and all of the women like her who stepped out of their traditional roles as wives and mothers during World War II to come to the aid of their country.

Acknowledgments

I owe a great deal to the adventurous women of generations past who forged a path for me to follow, who changed forever the roles and expectations of women by showing us that possibilities continue to exist where they didn't exist before as long as we are willing to recognize and fight for them.

I want to thank a very special woman, Marilyn York, one of the first U.S. Navy WAVES and the current president of the Alameda Naval Air Museum, for sharing her stories of WWII and her vision for the preservation of California Naval history.

As always, I'm grateful to my life partner, Dot, for her enthusiastic support of my writing and for dropping everything to help when I'm in despair over a sticky plot point or flat bit of dialogue.

Thanks also to my deserving editor, Katherine V. Forrest, for her remarkable skill in knowing exactly where to prune, where to fertilize and where to plow under. Under her guidance, the garden flourishes.

About The Author

Robbi McCoy is a native Californian who lives in the Central Valley between the mountains and the sea. She is an avid hiker with a particular fondness for the deserts of the American Southwest. She also enjoys gardening, culinary adventures, travel and the theater. She works full-time as a software specialist and web designer for a major West Coast distribution company.

CHAPTER ONE

"What are the specials tonight?" Shelby asked as she pulled a cropped black jacket over her stiff white blouse in the employee lounge. As long as she didn't remove her jacket, nobody would notice the spaghetti sauce stain on the left shoulder. Dabbing at it last night with a cold washcloth had merely spread it and she hadn't had time to do laundry because at the moment her life was in total chaos.

Oh, wait, she thought, we don't say "spaghetti" at Cibo. There's no such thing as spaghetti or spaghetti sauce. There's *bucatini alla Puttanesca*. There's *capellini pomodoro*. And there was her favorite—to eat, not to say—*Pappardelle Bolognese*.

Todd shoved a clipboard at her, then finished tying his bow tie and began fussing with his black, heavily gelled hair, making pucker lips at himself in the mirror. She read the printed list out loud to help herself memorize it.

"Fish of the day—seared Mediterranean *Branzino* with mint gremolata, served with fresh Maricopa Farms English peas and herbed farro."

She looked at Todd with a deliberate grimace. He was used to this routine, but he sighed in his typical exaggerated exasperation, thrusting out his left hip, and said, in a deadpan voice, "*Branzino* is sea bass. *Gremolata* is a condiment made of mint, lemon zest and garlic. Farro is wheat, so it's a side dish like rice."

As a student at the Culinary Institute of America, Todd knew this stuff. Without him, Shelby would have to ask one of the other waiters who would dismiss her with disdain. Todd was good-natured about it. She didn't mind looking like a no-nothing around him. But she couldn't afford to look like a no-nothing in front of customers...or Francois, the manager. The corncob up his ass was so tight it would take a jackhammer to budge it.

She turned back to the list to check the soup du jour. "Free-range Napa Valley capon with handmade *tagliatelle*, roasted *cippolini* onions and organic Thumbelina carrots."

Before she could make her face, Todd leaned down and whispered, "Chicken noodle soup."

Shelby laughed, then squelched it quickly. The mood here was serious. Serious food, serious mood. Todd raised one eyebrow and looked sideways at her. He was, as usual, putting the gay on for Cibo. He knew tips were better for gay men, so he went all out for his customers in a way he didn't do in private life. His hips never had this much swing in them away from the restaurant. It was expected by the patrons, or so restaurant traditions held, that the best upscale restaurants in the San Francisco Bay Area had the best waiters, and the best waiters were gay men. That did not hold true for the females, however. They could be straight or gay, it didn't matter, as long as they were professional and efficient. Shelby knew she was only one flying oyster away from being replaced by a gay man, for no matter how hard she tried, she would never match their *savoir faire* and elegance. In fact, she saw herself as a natural-born klutz, so her objective from one night to the next was simply to avoid disaster.

Where better to demonstrate klutziness, she mused, than as a waitress in an upscale restaurant? She knew she wasn't cut out to wait tables, but the schedule fit in nicely with school and tips at Cibo were great. If people were willing to pay nine dollars for a cup of chicken noodle soup, you'd expect that. She was lucky to have landed this job, since her only prior experience as a waitress was at the local Denny's. Now if only she could keep a straight face as Todd sashayed his way between the tables.

She took her order book and started her shift.

In addition to generous tips, one of the best things about this job was the west-facing wall of picture windows that gave her and the diners an unobstructed view of the Bay and the city of San Francisco beyond. At night you could look out at the length of the Bay Bridge sparkling with a white ribbon of headlights and red stream of taillights along its entire length as it hopped to Yerba Buena Island and then into the lap of the City. Beneath the bridge, lumbering cargo ships inched into port, loaded with chemicals from Russia, electronics from Japan and textiles from China. At the far end of the bridge, the outlines of San Francisco's downtown buildings glowed in a series of staggered rectangles, shapes relieved only by the cylindrical Coit Tower and the Transamerica Pyramid.

Shelby especially enjoyed her job on nights when the temperature was warm enough to open up the outside deck to diners. The deck was built on pilings, so it hung out over the rip-rap which lined the edge of the entrance to the Oakland Harbor. Seated there, you heard the gentle lapping of waves below and sometimes the sound of fog horns in the distance. In the early evening, the sunset and the cries of gulls made this one of the most romantic dinner spots in the East Bay. Tonight was such a night, mild and clear, giving patrons a view south to the regular comings and goings of the airplanes dipping low over the San Mateo Bridge on their approach to the San Francisco Airport. In the daytime, if there was no fog, you could even see the delicate orange strands of the Golden Gate Bridge at the entrance to the Bay.

Though none of this was new to Shelby, she still never took it for granted. On any day of her life, she had been able to travel a short distance from her Alameda home and look across the water to one of the most beautiful cities in the world. That view never failed to draw her eye and it still had the power to take her breath away.

The restaurant was busy tonight. It was a Friday at the start of the summer, so Shelby was sure it would be like this all night. More than once during the evening she felt the vibration of her phone where it was clipped to her waistband. She checked the number the first time to verify what she already suspected. It was her mother. When her break came, she made a dash to the restroom and listened to her voice mail in the bathroom stall. Multitasking both the phone and the toilet tissue was tricky, but she managed to avoid dropping her phone in the toilet. As she heard her mother's voice, full of exasperation and weariness, she let her head roll limply back on her shoulders.

"Shelby, will you please call me?" her mother said. "I want to give you an update. The doctor released your grandmother this afternoon. An ambulance took her to the rehab place. She'll be there several weeks like we thought. It's called Piedmont Gardens, on the east side of town."

Shelby stood and yanked up her black slacks by the waistband with one hand while her mother talked on.

"I hope you can move into her house like we talked about. It would give her so much peace of mind. And it's such a good plan for you too. You're just wasting money on that apartment anyway."

Shelby pressed the speakerphone button and set her phone on a shelf while she washed her hands. There was a second message, also from her mother.

"Did you remember to go over to your grandmother's house today to feed Oscar and water the plants? She's worried about them. Especially the weeping fig because it dries out fast."

Shelby wiped her hands on a paper towel while inspecting herself in the mirror. She looked better than she felt, she decided. A few strands of honey-colored hair, too long for bangs and too short to stay in her ponytail clip, hung limply on either side of her face. She tucked them behind her ears, knowing they wouldn't stay there. She gave herself a small, encouraging smile.

"Call me and let me know," her mother continued, "or I'm going to worry all night."

Shelby shut her phone and clipped it back on her waistband, then left the bathroom and collided with Todd in the narrow hallway. He grabbed her shoulders to keep her from falling sideways.

"Whoa!" he said, releasing her. "Watch it."

"Sorry. Just feeling a little stressed. And hungry. I never did get a chance to taste that ooh-la-la chicken noodle soup. I was hoping to get a snack this break."

Todd reached into his pocket and pulled out a Snickers bar. "I heard somewhere that if you give a girl a Snickers, she'll follow you anywhere."

Shelby snatched the candy bar from his hand. "I think that's an elephant, not a girl."

Todd followed her to the makeshift employee lounge, really a cluttered storeroom, where she fell into a faded chair with threadbare armrests, someone's castoff that properly belonged at the dump. She ripped open the candy bar, throwing one leg over the arm of the chair and revealing the small dolphin tattoo above her ankle. "Thanks," she said.

"What are you so stressed about?" he asked. "Finals getting to you?"

"No. Finals I can handle. Mostly it's family stuff."

Todd sat in the chair next to her. This was the first time she'd seen him this week, so he didn't yet know about Nana.

"Tell me." He sounded concerned. Todd was a wise-ass most of the time, but he was capable of breaking out of that persona to be a nice guy when required. His dark eyes regarded her steadily and patiently.

"My grandmother's in the hospital. Well, I guess she's not anymore. I've had two messages from my mother since I got here. Nana fell and broke her hip on Tuesday. They put an artificial one in on Wednesday."

Todd winced. "That's lousy."

"I've been over at the hospital a lot and running back and forth to Nana's house. With studying for finals, I haven't had much sleep." Shelby took a bite of the candy bar as Todd looked at her with wordless sympathy. "Now they've taken her to a rehab place. My mom wants me to move into Nana's house to take care of stuff there. She's got a dog. And plants. She's worried about her plants."

"Are you gonna do it?"

"It's fine with me. It's just the way she asks. I mean, the slams that come with it. Like, your cousin Rachel can't do it, of course. She has a family and a home of her own to take care of. You, no husband, no kids. No responsibilities at all."

"She didn't say that," he accused.

"Not exactly. But she did say I was wasting money on the apartment. Obviously, she meant the chunk that's her money."

"But you're a student. And you're about to graduate and start your illustrious career at Pratt and Rutherford. Two more weeks and you'll be an architect. She must be proud of you for that."

"My dad's proud of me for that, even though it took me seven years to get through college. My mom, I don't know. She has very traditional ideas about, you know, marriage, family, all that stuff. That's what's important to her. I'm twenty-five, still single, with nothing on the horizon. I'm causing her grief, stress, whatever."

"Maybe you should tell her you're gay," Todd suggested. "Then she'd quit complaining that you don't have a husband."

Shelby snorted and bit off another hunk of the candy bar. "Somehow, I don't think that would be better news to her."

Todd was one of the few people who knew Shelby was gay. Being closeted hadn't been her choice, though. Lori had insisted on it. Lori had never acknowledged her lesbianism even to herself. Considering how it had turned out, maybe that made sense after all. The entire five years they were together, Lori had always been terrified that someone would guess they were lovers. So they had pretended to be roommates and best friends. That was just as well for Shelby's mother's sake, though. Her mother had been the main reason Shelby had never put up much of a fuss about living in the closet. She was sure it would destroy Vivian to know her daughter was anything less than the perfect Barbie stereotype, especially coming so soon after the enormous disappointments of her own divorce and her son's less than model behavior.

That was Vivian's opinion, not Shelby's. She thought her older brother Charlie was doing just fine. Dropping out of college and having a child out of wedlock didn't strike her as the earth-shaking disaster their mother maintained it was. But if Charlie's indiscretions could cause her that much anguish, Shelby assumed her own revelation would bring about nothing less than Vivian's personal apocalypse. No, she thought with a private smile, she would not be going there any time soon.

"Besides," Shelby said, picking two peanuts out of the empty candy wrapper, "there's nothing to tell. I'm not dating anybody now, male or female."

"You mean you might be open to some straight action?" Todd's eyes widened in mock horror.

She shook her head. "Nope. I mean I'm nonsexual at the moment. After all these years of hiding it from my family, this would be a strange time to come out."

"I love irony," Todd gushed.

"I'd better get out there. You too. Thanks for the snack."

As they entered the dining room, Todd whispered, "Lesbians at table seven."

Shelby followed his gaze to see two women reading menus. They both looked around thirty years old, one with reddish-brown hair and the other a brunette. The redhead was dressed casually in jeans and a button-down cotton shirt. Her companion was wearing a lightweight business suit. Shelby nodded her agreement at Todd, then picked up a bread basket and bottle of olive oil. She made her way through the crowded restaurant to table seven and placed the basket on the table between the two women.

"Hello," she said cheerfully. "I'm Shelby. I'll be your waiter tonight."

Before she turned up the bottle to fill their oil dish, she tested the spout to make sure it was firmly in place. Last weekend, she'd tipped over one of these bottles and the stopper had popped out, flooding the table and a man's lap with oil. Not her best night. Francois nearly blew a gasket.

"Do you have any questions about the menu?" she asked after the oil was safely dispensed.

The redhead looked up and smiled. She had a friendly round face, wide mouth, large luminous brown eyes and thick, rust-colored eyebrows. "What's the soup tonight?"

Shelby started to answer, then realized she couldn't remember the menu version of the dish at all. All she could remember was Todd's sarcastic joke. She glanced furtively around to assure herself that Francois wasn't nearby, then lowered her voice and said, "Chicken noodle."

The redhead's eyes held hers for a moment, looking amused. Then she peered over the menu at her companion and asked, "Melissa, are you ready to order?"

The brunette, Melissa, nodded shortly and spoke in a husky, confident voice. "Yuzu-marinated halibut."

"How do you want that cooked?" Shelby asked. "Fried, grilled or broiled?"

"Broiled." Melissa handed over her menu, looking satisfied with her choice.

Shelby turned to the redhead.

"What kind of salmon is in the salmon salad?" she asked.

"Wild-caught Alaskan," Shelby answered confidently. "All our fish is on the eco-friendly list."

"Then I'll have that." She folded her menu and looked up with a naturally warm smile. "And why don't you bring me a cup of that chicken noodle soup. It sounds refreshingly unpretentious."

The woman laughed lightly. She looked refreshingly unpretentious herself, Shelby thought, noticing her large, unadorned hands and long fingers as she handed over the menu. These two might be out on a date, even a first date, she speculated.

"Would you like something from the bar?" she asked. "Or a bottle of wine?"

"No, thanks," the redhead replied.

"Actually," countered Melissa, "I'd like a vodka mojito."

Shelby nodded, then left, dropping the food order off with the kitchen staff and heading toward the bar to get the drink. After delivering a bottle of pinot noir to table twelve, she swung by table seven where the two women were engaged in a serious-looking conversation, which abruptly broke off as she approached. She set Melissa's mojito on a paper napkin and departed. The next time she visited their table, to deliver the soup, she caught a bit of dialogue before they stopped to wait out her presence.

"Look, Gwen," said Melissa, her tone decidedly irritated, "I don't know why we can't just enjoy a meal together once in a blue moon without—"

Shelby picked up the empty mojito glass, then said, "Did you want another drink?"

"Yes," snapped Melissa.

Shelby hurriedly left. Apparently this was not a first date. Must have been together awhile, she thought, remembering that the redhead's name was Gwen. *Gwen, Gwendolyn, that's a nice name.* It suited her. She had a fresh, casual look, like a girl from the Welsh countryside.

When Shelby returned with the second drink, Melissa said, "Her soup's cold."

"No, no," Gwen said with a wave of her hand. "It's fine."

"You said it was cold," Melissa accused.

"Well, it's not exactly hot."

"Sorry," Shelby said. "Let me get you another cup and I'll make sure it's hot."

Between setting the "not exactly hot" soup down on the busboy's cart and picking up Gwen's and Melissa's entrees, Shelby was pulled in several directions, taking orders and delivering drinks and food. Table seven was no longer on her mind, not until she carried the tray over with the halibut and salmon salad. She noticed, on her approach, that the two women were now sitting sullenly across from one another, not looking at each other. No, it was not a good night for them.

"Here you go," Shelby said as brightly as she could to counter the strain. She set the plates on the table.

"What happened to the soup?" asked Melissa.

"Oh!" Shelby said, inwardly cursing. "Sorry. I forgot. I'll go get it right now."

"That's okay," Gwen said. "Don't worry about it. Now that the entrée's here, I'll skip the soup."

"I'm really sorry," Shelby said.

Gwen gave her a reassuring smile, her quiet eyes conveying a genial lack of concern.

"This isn't right," Melissa said, staring at her plate.

"That's the halibut," Shelby replied, certain she'd gotten the order right.

Melissa poked the fish with her fork. "Yes, but I said I wanted it broiled. This is fried. It looks fried to me."

Shelby examined the fish, seeing that she was right and feeling a sense of helplessness.

"I can't eat this," announced Melissa flatly.

"Okay. I'll take it back." Shelby reached for the plate.

"No. I don't want to wait another half hour for it either. Can you find out what this was fried in? Is it butter or corn oil or what? I'm trying to avoid certain types of fat. That's why I ordered it broiled in the first place."

"I'm pretty sure it's canola oil," Shelby said.

Melissa stared at her for a second, then said, with a condescending smile, "I'd like you to check on that to be sure. At this point, I really don't think I can trust you."

Oh, boy, Shelby thought, *no tip for me from this pair!*

Francois, who had an uncanny ability to smell trouble, was suddenly standing directly across the table from Shelby, one of his murky eyes open wide with curiosity and the other narrowed at her with suspicion. He stood at attention, his suit perfectly pressed, his left arm bent at the elbow, his right arm straight at his side, posed as if he were a mannequin. Of course, he had been waiting, watching her, expecting her to screw up. She thought she could even see a hint of glee in that wide-open eye.

"Is there a problem, ladies?" he asked, smiling his counterfeit smile under his ridiculous little mustache.

"She's gotten everything wrong," Melissa complained.

"Not everything," Gwen corrected. "Nothing, really. Everything's fine."

"No, everything is *not* fine."

"Melissa," Gwen pleaded, "please."

But Melissa persisted. "The chicken noodle soup was cold. We sent it back and she forgot to bring a replacement."

Oh, no! Shelby thought as she heard that damning phrase.

She clenched her eyes shut for just a second before opening them to see Francois staring at her, his face pallid with horror, as if...as if—Shelby remembered another of her mistakes—she had shaved Parmesan cheese on crab! She was sure she had by now committed every last one of the seven deadly sins on the restaurant commandment list.

Melissa continued her litany of Shelby's failings. "And my halibut was supposed to be broiled, but it's fried."

"Everything else is fine," Gwen maintained, smiling reassuringly at Shelby. "And the halibut may not be her fault. Obviously, it's very busy here tonight and—"

"Chick...en noo...dle soup?" Francois repeated laboriously, glaring accusingly at Shelby.

I'm in really deep shit now, she thought.

After an exaggerated sigh, Francois hissed, "Go tend to your other customers and I'll take care of this."

Shelby obediently turned and left, hearing him say, "Ladies, I'm so sorry for all the trouble. Let me get you a complimentary beverage."

CHAPTER TWO

Melissa took a tentative bite of her halibut, chewed it thoughtfully, then took another.

"That girl's an imbecile," she said after swallowing.

"That's a little harsh." Gwen cut a piece of salmon in half with her fork. "They're pretty busy. She's probably brutally overworked."

"You're just saying that because you think she's cute."

Gwen's fork stopped halfway to her mouth. "What?"

"Seems like your type. Tiny little ditz with a button nose."

Gwen frowned, keeping her thoughts to herself. She did think the waitress was cute, but didn't want to give Melissa the satisfaction of getting that right. The fact that Melissa was nothing like a tiny little ditz with a button nose was yet another reason to avoid this subject. Not that it really mattered anymore. What had gone wrong with them had nothing to do with physical appearance. Gwen tried to stop her mind from running yet again down the mental list of everything that had contributed to her breakup with Melissa. The way she sucked her teeth after eating. She could have lived with that. The way she chopped all the roses off the bushes before they were halfway spent. She could even have lived with that. What she couldn't do was live in the closet. And Melissa couldn't live out of it. She had a deep-seated, fundamental shame that she couldn't overcome. She always claimed she was closeted so as not to damage her career at that conservative law firm she was so proud to work for, but as time went on, Gwen came to realize that Melissa wasn't even privately comfortable with her homosexuality. She didn't identify with the gay community. While they were together, there'd been no pride parades, no Olivia cruises, no rainbow-colored bumper stickers, no political signs on their lawn. Not even any lesbian potlucks. Melissa didn't feel a need to be around "those people" or to embrace their "political agenda." Living like that had injured Gwen's spirit and eroded away her love. She had vowed never to live that way again. Not for anyone.

"The halibut's good." Melissa looked up from her plate. "This restaurant usually has pretty good service. The food's great. And you can't beat the view. I don't know why you don't like it."

"It's too expensive. Everything's overpriced. Way overpriced."

"If you'd get a real job, you wouldn't have to worry about money all the time. You're a college graduate, for Christ's sake, although what possessed you to major in history, I'll never understand, instead of going for a marketable skill. Even so, you could make three times as much, even to start with, almost anywhere."

"I have a real job," Gwen said, regretting the direction this conversation was going.

"I'll admit you work very hard at it, which is just one more reason to quit. Why not work that hard at something that pays a living wage? It's idiotic to give yourself away like that."

Gwen felt frustrated. "I enjoy my job. Let it go."

Melissa frowned, setting her fork on her plate. "Okay, fine. It's none of my business anyway."

That's right, it isn't, Gwen thought, but said nothing. She finished her salad silently. Is this why lesbians remain friends with their ex-lovers? she wondered. So they will be continually reminded why they broke up and not waste any time pining over what might have been?

A waiter came to take her plate, a young man with an affected air of chic sophistication.

"What happened to our waitress?" Gwen asked him.

He looked perplexed. "Not sure. I was told to take over your table. Maybe she's on a break. Would you like to see a dessert menu?"

"No, thanks. We'll just have coffee."

When the waiter was out of hearing, Melissa said, "I knew it. I knew you thought she was cute."

"Would you please stop? I just wondered what happened to her."

"I'm sure you're very concerned about her. You always did have a thing for blondes. Like that woman at Trader Joe's, that checker. You always went in her line, however long it was."

Gwen sucked in an exasperated breath. "I can't believe you're bringing that up again. You're in a pissy mood tonight."

Melissa stared across the table, her features calm. "You're right. Sorry. I'm really stressed. I had a lousy day."

"Next time you ask me to dinner, how about making it on a good day?"

Looking chastened, Melissa nodded. Gwen knew Melissa's real problem was that she wasn't seeing anyone at the moment. She was the sort of woman for whom the ordinary stresses of work and family were greatly amplified by being alone. She couldn't be happy when she was alone. When she was coupled, however, she was the sweetest, most agreeable person in the world. Gwen hoped, for the sake of their friendship, she would soon find someone who would make her happy.

Unlike Melissa, Gwen was comfortable on her own. She'd been single since they'd broken up almost a year ago. She hadn't even been on a date. She was fine with that. She'd never been one to go actively looking for a mate. But if someone suitable happened to cross her path, she was open to whatever fortune had in store for her.

The young man who'd replaced Shelby as their waiter returned with their coffee, then silently withdrew.

"How's Skipper and the gang?" Melissa asked, clearly searching for a cheery subject.

"Good. Everybody's hanging in there. Last week was the third anniversary of Florence's death. Skipper brought in a bottle of champagne and we made a toast."

"Even you?"

"I had a glass, yeah. A special occasion. They were together fifty years."

"I remember." Melissa mixed the last bite of her halibut with some mashed potatoes and popped it in her mouth. "Fifty years. That's remarkable."

"Especially in their circumstances," Gwen added.

"You mean because they were career Navy?"

"Right." Gwen took a sip of coffee. "It must have created a tremendous amount of stress to keep that secret all those years."

"That's not as hard for everybody as it is for you, Gwen," Melissa pointed out resentfully. "Some people, no matter what their sexual orientation, have no problem keeping their private lives private."

Here we go again, Gwen thought, setting her cup down. "After all the discussions we've had about this, I can't believe you still don't get it."

"You mean you can't believe I still don't agree with you. No, I don't. It's nobody's business what I do in my bedroom."

"Being gay isn't just about what you do in your bedroom. Why can't you see that? You're a member of an oppressed class. You owe it to your brothers and sisters—"

Melissa dropped her fork in her plate and glared at Gwen. "I don't owe anybody anything! I'm not a soldier in your war. I'm just me." She shook her head impatiently. "Why are you so down on me and at the same time so supportive of Skipper and Florence who lived in the closet nearly their whole lives?

You've said yourself more than once that if all the lesbians in the military had come out altogether at any time in the past seventy years, they'd have thrown the whole system into utter meltdown. Well, they didn't. They hid. Including Skipper."

"You have no clue what it was like back then," Gwen said, attempting to remain calm. "They didn't have a choice. They hid to survive, literally. The few who tried to fight the system were pulverized by it. Things are so much easier for us."

"Easier, maybe, but not okay."

"Right, but how can we get there if we stay in the closet? No change was ever brought about through silence. These days, what are we afraid of? Somebody looking askance at us? Some kid putting flaming poo on our doorstep?"

"How about losing your job?" Melissa countered, speaking low but emphatically. "How about losing the respect of your co-workers and clients? For that matter, how about getting beaten, raped or killed? It still happens."

"It does," conceded Gwen, "but not as often. None of those things are very likely to happen to you, especially living here. And I don't believe you'd lose your job."

"Even if I wouldn't, I don't want flaming poo on my porch either." Melissa picked up her fork and stabbed at her green beans with a determination that told Gwen she was finished with the subject.

Gwen knew she should be finished with it too, but she couldn't resist the urge to have the final word. "These are all just excuses, a cover-up for your personal homophobia."

"Yeah, yeah," Melissa complained. "I've heard your accusations before. Can we please drop this? You know there's no point. Obviously, you think I'm a lousy lesbian and I think you're unfair and unreasonable and neither of us is going to budge. If there was any chance of that, we'd still be together, wouldn't we?" There was a slight tremor in her voice that hinted at emotional vulnerability. She put down her fork again, done eating, and proceeded to suck her teeth, looking out the window.

Gwen restrained herself from responding, hoping to end this meal without anybody crying. She knew Melissa's ultimate argument would be to burst into tears. Most of their arguments had ended that way. She was right. There was no point talking about it. All it did was dredge up a lot of old pain and neither of them had anything new to say.

Gwen finished her coffee in silence, calculating that it would be a month, maybe two, before Melissa felt friendly enough to try this again and possibly years before they quit attacking one another with recriminations from their past.

The irritating manager with the tiny mustache returned. "Ladies," he said, sounding like a Mafia don, "did everything work out okay for you tonight?"

"It worked out fine," Gwen said flatly. "I think we're ready for the bill."

"Very well. I have that right here. I took off for your drinks because of the unfortunate experience with your waitress."

On the way out, Gwen glanced around the restaurant hoping to catch sight of that waitress, but didn't see her. She and Melissa parted with a hug just outside the door. She walked out to the parking lot through the muted light cast by evenly spaced solar walkway lamps.As she pulled her keys out of her pocket, she saw a young woman sitting on the curb with her face in her hands in a posture of despair. She walked over to her and recognized the waitress, first by her blonde ponytail and then by her cute button nose in profile.

"Is something wrong?" she asked. As she remembered the young woman's name, she said it aloud. "Shelby, right?"

The waitress looked up, startled. In the light from the overhead lamps, Gwen could see her face well enough to tell she'd been crying. She frowned as she recognized Gwen.

"Just about everything's wrong," she said, her tone resentful. "My grandmother broke her hip, I just got fired, and my keys are locked in my car."

She motioned toward the pale green Buick she was sitting beside, a car that looked like it had seen a fair amount of history.

"You got fired?" Gwen asked, incredulously.

"Yeah." Shelby frowned even more forcefully. "What do you think happens when customers complain their waiter did everything wrong?"

"Oh, wow! I'm so sorry. Melissa and I weren't having such a good time tonight. I guess we took it out on you. You know, the kick the dog scenario."

Shelby stared, her somber hazel eyes unblinking, then said, "Is that supposed to make me feel better?"

"Sorry. That was stupid. I just meant—"

"I know what you meant."

Gwen knelt down so they were face-to-face. "By the way, I'm Gwen." She felt terrible about the chain of events Melissa's complaints had set in motion.

Shelby gave a begrudging nod, then brushed a strand of loose hair behind her ear.

"Did you call your auto club?" Gwen asked.

"Auto club?"

"Triple A or whatever?"

Shelby shook her head. "I don't have an auto club. And it's too late to call my dad. I'll get Todd to jimmy it open."

"Todd?"

"One of the other waiters." Shelby's tone was still bitter. "I sent him a text. He'll be out in a minute."

"Oh. That's good." Gwen stood and turned to go, aware that she was just one more irritant in Shelby's bad day. Then, having second thoughts, she turned back and said, "Why don't I wait here with you?"

"You don't need to do that. I'm fine."

"You seem kind of upset. And I feel responsible."

"You're not responsible for my keys being stuck in my car."

"No." Gwen sat on the curb beside her. "You were probably distracted when you did that...because of your grandmother."

"My grandmother?" Shelby looked confused, then seemed to remember she had mentioned that. "Oh, right. Maybe."

"That's serious, a broken hip. I mean, it can be. How did it happen?"

"She tripped over her dog. They put in an artificial one and now she's going to a rehab hospital to recuperate."

"How long will that take?"

"Awhile. Weeks. Months, maybe. I don't really know. They just moved her from the hospital today. I guess I'll be living in her house while she's away."

"Where does she live?"

"Here in Alameda. She's lived in that house since she was married. My mom was born there." Shelby appeared to be moving past her preoccupation with her problems. She was no longer doling out information reluctantly and her expression had relaxed, giving her face a much more appealing look. Sitting next to her, Gwen felt awkwardly overgrown. Shelby was petite, feminine and well-proportioned, but small in every way. Maybe it was her size that made Gwen feel protective and anxious to comfort, though the tears alone would be enough to bring out that instinct in her.

"Alameda's a nice place to live," said Gwen. "I love this town."

"Do you live here?" Shelby asked.

"No. I rent a place in Berkeley. I can't afford to live here. But I work here, on the old Navy base."

"For one of the environmental companies? Or EPA or something?"

"No. Nothing to do with the cleanup." Gwen pulled her wallet out of her back pocket and slid her card out of it. "I'm the director of the Naval Museum."

"Wow!" Shelby took the card. "That's really cool."

Gwen smiled, thinking about the contrast between Shelby's reaction and Melissa's opinion of her job. "It sounds more impressive than it is. Have you ever been there?"

"No. I mean, I've seen the building, but I've never been in it."

"A lot of history took place out there," Gwen said. "You should come for a visit."

"You're right, I should. I've lived here all my life. I used to ride my bike out by the base all the time. That place was so interesting, you know, because when I was really little, there were so many people working and living there. It was so alive. Then all of the sudden, it was empty. All those abandoned buildings.

I used to make up stories about what happened, why it became a ghost town overnight."

"I don't suppose your stories had anything to do with the BRAC Commission."

Shelby looked puzzled.

"Sorry." Gwen laughed. "That's the Base Realignment and Closure program responsible for shutting the base down."

Shelby nodded.

"Tell me what kind of stories you made up?" Gwen urged.

"Just kid stuff. Alien abductions. Things like that."

"Oh, sure! That's a natural."

Shelby smiled for the first time since Gwen had found her here. It was a slightly self-conscious, slightly askew sort of smile, but it was endearing, especially as it was accompanied by a lingering, less inhibited meeting of eyes.

"Well, come out for a visit if you get a chance," said Gwen. "We've got some cool stuff."

"Okay." Shelby slipped the card into her pocket. "You don't know how to jimmy a car door open, do you?"

"No, sorry."

Shelby looked around the parking lot. "Where'd your... friend go?"

"Melissa? She took off by now, I'm sure. Now *she* might have been able to get your car open."

"Oh. I thought you came together."

"I don't think we ever came together, actually." Gwen laughed shortly as Shelby raised her eyebrows. "Sorry. That was a bad joke. I'm feeling kind of snarky tonight toward Melissa. As you know, we didn't have a very pleasant evening."

"None of us did," Shelby pointed out.

"Right." Gwen felt guilty again, reminded of her part in getting this intriguing little waif fired. "Melissa's my ex, actually."

She watched Shelby's face closely, trying to see by her response whether she could be gay. She got nothing from her expression. Not that it mattered. She heard footsteps and looked over to see a young man coming toward the parking lot. He was nice looking with thick wavy black hair. Shelby jumped to her feet and ran to him as Gwen rose from the curb more slowly.

"Todd! Thank God!" She threw her arms around his neck. "Can you get my car open?"

Todd held up a wire hanger. "No problem with these old cars." He laughed as she released him, then walked over to her car and started unbending the hanger. Shelby was smiling freely now.

"Looks like your white knight has arrived," Gwen said. "You'll be okay now."

Shelby nodded and pushed her hands deep into her front pockets. "Thanks for hanging around."

"No problem. I wish I could have done something useful. I'm really sorry about your job."

Shelby shrugged. "Well, at least I'll be living rent-free for a while in my grandma's house."

"True. So I won't be worrying about you being homeless, living on the street or anything."

Shelby laughed. "Not yet."

"I guess I'll be going," Gwen said, feeling oddly reluctant to do so.

Shelby nodded and gave her a parting smile, then turned to join Todd at her car door. By the time Gwen drove out of the lot, she saw that the car was open and Shelby was again hugging Todd in gratitude. Maybe he was her boyfriend. Gwen sighed and headed home.

CHAPTER THREE

Shelby had all the drawers open in her grandmother's dresser and was shifting socks, underwear, nightgowns, shirts and sweaters back and forth, on the lookout for a turquoise sweater. That was what her grandmother had requested, a specific, favorite sweater that she could drape over her shoulders and slip off as needed. Shelby had made several trips already this week, running back and forth between her apartment, Nana's house and the nursing home as she moved her own stuff into this already cluttered little house and helped her mother get Nana situated in her new, temporary home.

She was now preparing for today's trip to Piedmont Gardens, hoping one trip would be sufficient. She laid a fistful of half-slips on top of the dresser, knocking over the wind-up ballerina which had been a fixture in this house for Shelby's entire life.

Setting it upright, she fearfully looked it over to make sure she hadn't broken it. She knew that wouldn't be an offense easily forgiven, as the tiny ballerina was a treasured possession. Shelby had learned at a young age that it wasn't a toy and she wasn't to touch it. She'd only actually seen it in action once. When wound up, the girl with the red lips and pink tutu had spun around on one foot, extending the other leg at a ninety degree angle and raising both her hands above her head. It was a remarkable little apparatus, obviously very old. Since it appeared unharmed, Shelby returned to groping through the dresser drawers. She held her phone to her ear with her shoulder as she waited for the woman at the electric company to look up Nana's account. When the woman returned, she said, "Okay, Mrs. Brewster, what can I do for you?"

"No," Shelby said, "this isn't Lucy Brewster. This is Shelby Pratt. I'm her granddaughter. I'm calling from her house. I want to know why the electricity is off."

Shelby was kneeling, casting about in the bottom row of drawers, one of which contained a pile of tangled beige and cinnamon pantyhose she was sure Nana hadn't worn in decades, left over from her years working in the doctor's office, before she went to pharmacy school. The pharmacy uniform had been a white smock, pants and comfortable flats. If she wore nylons at all in the pharmacy, Shelby was sure they would have been knee-hi's.

"Nonpayment," came the explanation over the phone. "Your grandmother hasn't paid her bill in three months. We sent notices."

Shelby directed her full attention to the phone call. "Really? I don't understand. There's no reason she wouldn't pay her bill."

When she'd arrived this morning at Nana's house, Shelby had flipped light switches one by one with no response until she finally realized that there was no power. The heater had not come on and the refrigerator was dark and silent. The partially-thawed contents of the freezer suggested the power had been off for a while. It could even have been off the day before when she and Charlie had dropped off a load of her stuff. In the middle of the afternoon, they had probably not even tried any lights.

"How old is she?" asked the electric company woman.

"Eighty-seven."

"Well, that's a possible reason right there. It's not uncommon for older people to lose track of things, get disorganized. They put things off and get overwhelmed. We see this."

"You mean it's common for old people not to pay their bill because they're absent-minded?"

"Yes, it's very common."

"If that's true, why'd you turn off her electricity without trying to talk to her or talk to somebody else, like me or my mom? Why not let somebody know there was a problem?"

There was a hesitation at the other end. Shelby's hand, rummaging in the drawer again, hit a solid object under the pantyhose. She got hold of it and lifted it out. It was an old cigar box with the words "El Roi-Tan" above an elaborate regal crest. Under that was the slogan, "The cigar that breathes."

"That's really not our place," the woman said, sounding defensive now. "Besides, all of this is automated."

Shelby was tempted to argue further but realized there would be no point other than to vent her frustration. She stood and set the cigar box on the dresser. "Okay," she said, "what do I have to do to get it turned back on?"

"You can pay the bill. If you have her bank account information, you can even do it over the phone. We can just deduct it from her account and we'll get power back on right away."

Shelby realized she didn't know where to find Nana's bank account information. "I'll have to call you back. Thanks."

She shut her phone and clipped it to her jeans. The house was cold and, in this room at least, dim. She took the cigar box and went to the living room where the midday sun was shining in through the front picture window. Nana's couch was hidden behind Shelby's furniture, but her own couch was sitting in the middle of the room, so she sat on that and opened the box.

The contents were old. She picked each one out of the box and examined it carefully. There was a union membership card from 1944 with her grandmother's name, "Lucy Brewster," written in. There was a metal coin with a small photo of her grandmother as a very young woman in the center. "Richmond Shipyard Number Two" was stamped around the outer edge of it. Some kind of ID badge, she guessed.

Shelby realized these were mementos from Nana's World War II employment with the shipyards, something she had heard of but knew almost nothing about. She knew her grandmother had worked building Liberty ships while her grandfather was overseas in the army. She'd been one of those Rosie the Riveters. The cigar box was a precious little treasure trove from the past.

Next, there was a yellowed card entitled "Notice of Termination" from the Kaiser Shipyards, Richmond, California, dated September 5, 1945. Her grandmother's name and occupation, listed as "Alum. Welder," were typed on the card in the irregular print of manual typewriters. Shelby laid each item on the coffee table as she removed it from the box. In the bottom were three photos, all black-and-white. One was a group picture of a squad of workers posed in three rows in front of a hulking concrete building, men and women, young and old, most of them wearing coveralls. The women had their hair tied in handkerchiefs. A few of them wore little caps instead. The second photo was of a small woman bent over a metal panel, a blowtorch in hand, a welder's helmet over her face. Shelby assumed this was Nana at work. *How cool*, she thought. The third photo contained two women. One of them was Nana wearing a dress, her long, dark hair hanging free, looking full of blooming youth. She had her arm interlocked with the woman beside her, a young woman with a lean face and confident smile, standing about three or four inches taller than Nana, looking down at her, not at the camera. That woman had short dark hair, cut just to the collar. She was wearing a light-colored suit, skirt and jacket with a white blouse under it. Both of them wore white gloves. They were standing in front of this very house between the square columns that framed the porch. Shelby tried without success to see a resemblance in the tall woman to any of her older relatives. She was some long ago friend or neighbor of Nana's, she supposed.

There was something about this photo that caused Shelby to stare into it intently. It was the look in Nana's face, a shining, innocent joy. Not just her smile, but her eyes, which were upturned slightly to glimpse her companion. There was a look of familiarity between them, an easy affection. Shelby turned the photo over. There was nothing written on the back.

At the startling sound of the doorbell, she jumped and knocked the now empty cigar box to the floor. She went to the front door as Oscar, Nana's dachshund, came running into the room, barking.

"Shsshh!" Shelby warned, putting one eye to the peephole. It was Lori, her frizzy head of hair easily recognizable. Shelby pulled open the door. Lori gave her a tentative smile. She had a look of distraction in her large, lazy eyes. Oscar had stopped barking and was wagging his tail in gleeful welcome.

"Hi," Lori said.

"Thanks for coming by. Come in."

Lori stepped inside and glanced quickly around the room. "I see you got all your stuff moved. Are you going to like it here?"

"Yes, I think I will. I'll get your things. Just a sec."

Shelby went to the dining room table where she had placed a box containing the last evidence that she and Lori had ever shared a life together. She handed it over. "Your bowling shoes are in there. Just ran across those this morning. And that's your rain jacket, I think. It's hard to remember about some things, but it doesn't matter. You keep it."

"Thanks," Lori said. "I thought I'd gotten everything."

"Me too. It was just when I cleaned out all the hidey holes, you know. I had to get everything out by today or pay another month's rent. So the apartment's gone." *Our* apartment, Shelby thought.

"I'm sorry about your grandmother. I hope she recovers okay."

"Thanks."

"Remember that time I cut my hand at your mom's house and she sprinkled pepper on it?"

"Yeah. That was always what she did when we got hurt. Pepper's a natural analgesic. That was something she didn't learn in pharmacy school, but back in Arkansas, I guess."

"I thought that was weird. For a pharmacist."

Shelby shrugged. "It works, so why not?"

Lori stood in the entryway as if she were waiting for an invitation to tea or something.

"I got my gown yesterday," she said, her eyes bright. "You should see it. It's amazing!"

Now why did she have to bring that up? She knew her impending marriage to Stephen was a sore spot between them. Anything to do with Stephen wasn't something Shelby wanted to hear about.

"Won't be long now," Shelby said uncomfortably.

"I know! You're still coming, aren't you?"

"I'll be there."

"I wish you'd agreed to be in the wedding."

Shelby had turned down the request to be a bridesmaid. Lori had seemed genuinely surprised at that, as if she still had no idea why Shelby would not be ecstatic for her. It was as if Lori had turned into a complete idiot the day she'd started dating Stephen. Their five-year relationship had metamorphosed in Lori's mind into nothing more than a friendship that had gotten carried away. Shelby hadn't known how to handle a situation like that. Her girlfriend, her partner, her lover was dating a man.

"But I love you," Shelby had said, shocked and heartbroken.

"I love you too," Lori had assured her. "But this is different. This is something more serious. Something more grown up."

It was true they'd been barely adults when they became lovers, but there was also no doubt that their relationship was serious right up to the day Stephen had burst into it. Lori had managed to make it seem like a childish indulgence. By the time she finally moved out of their apartment to live with Stephen, it was hard for Shelby to feel even a glimmer of affection for her. By then, Shelby was glad to see her go. Lori had diminished their relationship so completely that even Shelby had begun to wonder if there had ever been anything of substance there.

"I'm not a lesbian," Lori had told her. "It's just one of those things. Maybe you're straight too. You've never given boys much of a chance because of us."

In the end, Shelby had nothing but anger toward Lori, not just for falling in love with someone else, but for devaluing what the two of them had meant to one another. Lori had been patronizing, saying things like, "I know you'll meet someone too, like Stephen. You're such a cute, smart girl. I bet I'll be coming to your wedding by next summer."

Shelby did her best to pretend they were still friends, that they could somehow weather all the hurt that had happened between them over the last several months. But she had already resolved that attending this wedding would be the last gesture of friendship she would make. Their relationship would then come to its logical end.

"How's school going?" Lori asked.

"Okay."

"This is finals week, isn't it? Stephen took that computer class and they had their final last night."

Shelby nodded. She wasn't in the mood for conversation.

"Is this her dog?" Lori asked, looking at Oscar, who was now sitting placidly beside Shelby's feet.

"Yeah."

"What's his name?"

"Oscar."

"Oh, that's really funny, isn't it?" Lori looked expectantly at Shelby. "Because of Oscar-Mayer," she persisted, as if Shelby didn't get the joke. "Because he's a wiener dog."

"Uh-huh."

She bent down slightly, hugging the box to her chest. "Hi, Oscar. You're a little sweetheart, aren't you?"

Apparently she was trying her luck at conversation with him, since Shelby was so unresponsive. After making a sucky noise at Oscar, she straightened up.

"Well, I'd better be going," she said cheerfully, but with that tiny twitch of her upper lip that gave away her disappointment. Why did it matter to her that they remain friends? Shelby wondered. Guilt?

Shelby stood holding the door as Lori walked out to the street and her car. She took a deep breath and willfully pushed Lori out of her mind.

Returning to the bedroom, she did eventually find the turquoise sweater. The last thing on her list was Nana's Giants ball cap. This hung on a hook by the front door. It was shapeless and faded, black with orange letters: SF. She put everything into a large tote bag, placing the cap on top.

Shivering against the chill of the house, she pulled on her jacket and carried the bag to her car, thinking briefly about the rotting meat in the freezer. Thinking too that returning the last of Lori's possessions marked the end of a significant chapter in her life.

CHAPTER FOUR

Gwen looked up from her desk as Rusty banged his metal toolbox against the doorframe on his way in. A screwdriver jumped out and rolled a few feet in front of him. She could tell he hadn't noticed it. She had an image of him stepping on it, falling and killing himself instantly. A man his age probably confronted death several times a day, she thought, leaping to her feet.

"Stop!" she commanded, holding up her hand. "Don't move!"

He looked at her, wide-eyed, his ginger-gray hair blowing in the breeze from the overhead fan, his pale blue eyes staring out from under nearly invisible blond eyelashes. His broad face was a mottled field of ruddiness over a pale pinkish undercoat. Even his lips were blotched with freckles. His thick hands were similarly colored and his heavy forearms were fertile acreage for a dense crop of white hair.

Gwen retrieved the screwdriver, returning it to his toolbox. He nodded matter-of-factly, showing he understood that disaster had been averted.

"Put new hinges on that screen door," he said, too loud for the compact office area. "All squared away. She'll shut now."

"Thank you, Rusty," she said, giving his shoulder a pat. "You're a sweetheart."

"Anything else you want me to tackle?"

Gwen thought of the loose floorboards upstairs and the broken lock on the bathroom door, but dismissed these as quickly as they came to mind. At seventy-seven, Rusty was only good for one job a day, on a good day. He wasn't getting paid, after all. Like everyone who did anything around here, with the exception of Gwen, it was strictly voluntary.

"No, I think that'll do," she said cheerfully.

"I'll be topside for a bit."

She nodded as he shuffled into the elevator, banging the doorframe there as well, sending a loud metal-on-metal clang echoing through the narrow room. He grinned her way, deeply creasing his face, as the door closed. Gwen returned to the task at hand, sorting through the contents of another box taken out of storage.

Like most people who hung around the museum regularly, Rusty was retired from the navy. He was Korean War era, a widower who had nobody at home to talk to. But here, he and his friends met almost every day for card games and spirited conversation. He was on his way to join Grady and Skipper on the second floor where they'd fashioned their "wardroom" out of a corner of storage. Storage included everything that wasn't currently on display and everything that had been donated and remained under the layer of dust it had been accumulating ever since. Nobody, not even Skipper, knew what was in most of those boxes. If she had known once, she'd forgotten. She'd been collecting items for this museum for decades, storing them in her house and rented storage lockers until all of it was moved here when she'd leased this building nine years ago, finally realizing her long-time dream, a museum dedicated to preserving the history of the navy at Alameda Point.

Some of the items had found their way into displays. Many of them remained upstairs untouched. During the last decade since the museum opened, even more boxes had accumulated. People donated these things, typically when their parents died and they cleaned out their houses. Gwen had been going through some of the boxes in her spare time, to see what could be cleared out by auctioning off, putting on display or throwing out. But she also just enjoyed looking through this stuff. Most of it was predictable—papers, photos, uniforms, medals from someone's navy days, whatever era that happened to be, but you never knew what you'd come across.

She normally took a long time to go through one of these boxes, each one containing sketches of a life. Or several lives. This particular box, for instance, seemed to be full of unrelated objects. Mostly papers. She perused each object carefully as she always did, to make sure there was nothing remarkable, like a letter from Abraham Lincoln or a secret document proving a government conspiracy. Not that she'd ever come across such a thing, but she enjoyed a good novel of political intrigue now and then so her mind naturally traveled in that direction.

Most of this stuff was of little interest and less value. Donors didn't want to throw it out themselves. They thought something useful could be done with it. But, realistically, the best Gwen could do was to file the documents in the archives where they would probably never be consulted.

The archives were her creation. She'd set up several filing cabinets and folders for each veteran whose papers had been donated. She'd created a sort of historical society for the navy base here in the museum. Several people had benefited from this already, family genealogists trying to track down information about their ancestors. Sometimes they came in knowing nothing more than that Grandpa had been stationed on the base in the 1940s. Gwen was gradually compiling more and more detailed files on people like that. Occasionally, she'd been able to give someone some information they didn't already have. That made it worth the effort.

But, truthfully, Gwen didn't much care if anybody ever got any use out of these records. She enjoyed the process of assembling the pieces of an ever-expanding puzzle. She liked to do it for the sake of doing it. Just as she liked hearing the stories of the items on display in the museum. She liked all these old things, these relics of the past that sometimes spoke and sometimes remained silent. The objects without a story fired her imagination, like the German sword that hung in the weapons collection. Where it had come from was an unsolved mystery. Perhaps Gwen would solve it someday, tease its story out of the tangled past. History had always been her passion. Melissa had suggested to her once that her fascination with history grew out of her own lack of one. She'd been adopted as an infant and knew nothing of her biological family. Her own heritage was another mystery she might someday try to solve.

She heard chairs scraping on the floor above and a minute later the elevator started whirring. The doors opened and Skipper stepped out, her hunched frame reducing her height to four and a half feet. Gwen suspected she had once been at least five-two or five-three. She was a WWII vet, in her eighties, a bristling head of white hair framing a pale, lined face and deep-set, baby blue eyes. She held a glossy mahogany cane and employed it as she exited the elevator, a characteristically joyful smile across her face.

As career military, Skipper had been all over the world, but had managed to end her career back in Alameda. She'd retired twenty years ago right here. The idea of that, the long career with its beginning and ending in the same place, appealed to Gwen's sense of continuity. She liked things that fit together like that.

Not surprisingly, Skipper had a powerful sentimental attachment to the base. This museum was her vision. And her legacy, Gwen reminded herself, feeling again the weight of the responsibility she had assumed to keep this place alive.

"Hey, honey," Skipper said, leaning heavily on her cane, "I'm running over to Who's-its to get more pop. I need a break from those guys anyway. Lousy luck today. I just lost my pants in that poker game."

"You're not playing for money again?" Gwen asked.

"Land sakes, no! Can't afford that. Lost my pants, I'm telling ya. My skivvies." Skipper stood with her arms widespread, as if Gwen could tell somehow what she had on under her trousers. "Strip poker, that's what we're playing. But I'm still in the game. Grady's down to his socks."

Gwen laughed, which seemed to satisfy Skipper. She lowered her arms.

"Can I bring you something?" she asked. "Maybe one of those, you know, those doodlybops you like?"

"Corn dog? No, thanks. I brought my lunch."

Skipper made her way out the front door to the parking lot and her ancient Ford Fairlane. Gwen waited and listened for the roar of the engine, knowing it would take Skipper a good five minutes to get settled in the car with her seat belt fastened, get the key in the ignition and start it up. Skipper was proud she still drove herself wherever she needed to go. Gwen thought that maybe wasn't such a good idea, considering her compromised eyesight, compromised hearing and general state of fuzzy thinking. But the world Skipper drove in was a mere three-mile square, from her house to the base to the store to the doctor. After all these years, she could probably have done any of those trips completely blind.

Gwen heard the car start. She watched out the window as Skipper drove slowly off toward the front gate. If the museum were closed down, she wondered, what would these old people do day after day? Where would they go? They felt at home here, not just at the museum but on the base. This place embodied the most useful, often the most vital, phase of their lives.

It was disappearing, bit by bit, before their eyes. She knew it hurt them, this dismantling of their past. There was nothing that could be done about that, but Gwen was doing what she could to save this one building, to preserve it from being demolished along with the rest of the base. That wasn't going so well, though. She frowned, thinking about the intractable city officials and their thoroughly pragmatic vision of real estate.

She pulled her cheese sandwich out of its zippered plastic. As she ate, she lifted a slender leather-bound book out of the musty box. It was frayed around the edges and had a large water stain on the back. A once-red ribbon still tied it closed. She put her sandwich down to gently tug on the ribbon and it came loose immediately. She opened the cover of the book to the jagged remnant of a yellowed page that had been ripped out. On the next page, a journal entry began, written by hand in blue ink in a legible script that lacked flourish, but struck Gwen as feminine. There was no name on the inside cover. She didn't see a name anywhere and wondered what had been on that missing first page.

Journals did appear now and then from these donations, though they didn't show up often. A woman's journal was rarer yet, so Gwen forgot her sandwich and turned the desk lamp to shine directly on the pages. Excited, she read the first entry, dated January 10, 1944.

CHAPTER FIVE

January 10, 1944.

California, here I am! My new home, Alameda Naval Air Station, sits at the edge of the San Francisco Bay and the view is a doozy! San Francisco itself is right across the bay. I can't wait to get over there and see it up close. Frisco is right there in front of my eyes! Holy mackerel!

I'm trying to get settled in the barracks, get used to the way they do things here. I just got here yesterday and haven't met many people yet, other than the girls in my room and our "dorm mother," CPO Bricker. She's a sturdy-looking woman in her forties with a husky voice and a little bit of a mustache. When we marched in yesterday, she greeted us with, "Welcome aboard, Ladies. Stow your seabags and turn out for muster." All the new boots stood at attention while Chief Bricker looked us over. I hope she liked what she saw. I thought we looked like a million dollars.

The crew here is a bunch of wonderful gals from all over the country, all of us anxious to get to our posts and do our part now that basic training is over and we're stationed somewhere we can do some good. Six weeks ago, not a single one of us knew port from starboard. Was that really only six weeks ago? I can hardly believe it!

When we flew in on our transport, I saw a huge aircraft carrier at the dock and I thought what a kick it would be to be shipping out on that, but, of course, only the boys get to sail out for the real action. But we have plenty to do here at home. Our job is to keep the home front humming. Each one of us girls is here to free up a man to fight.

I was so lucky I got to go home for the holidays after basic. When my orders came in to report to California, Mama cried for hours. So far away, she said. I'll never see my baby again, she said. Don't cry, Mama, I told her, I'll be back to New York to visit every chance I get. But I was lucky to be there for Christmas. It was hard on all of us that Paul wasn't there, the first time we weren't all together for the holidays. Paul's somewhere in Europe right now, probably sleeping in a foxhole.

I know Daddy didn't want me to join the navy at first, but when I put on my uniform and said goodbye, he looked so proud. I think there may have even been a tear in his eye. He saluted me and said, "Steady as she goes, Seaman." I'll make sure he stays proud of me. I'm going to work hard and do what they need me to do to win the war. Giving my all for America, as the saying goes.

Grandpa gave me this journal. He said I'd want to write everything down so I'd remember it later because this was going to be the most exciting time of my life. And so far he's right! I just flew across the whole United States in an airplane! I have a feeling I'm going to want to remember every bit of what happens here for the rest of my life.

My quarters are not what I expected. They're nicer. I thought we'd be in one of those big open barracks with a hundred other girls like it is for the boys. But they've made it more private for the women. I'm in Barracks D. The rooms are all made up the same with four girls in each compartment. Two bunk beds and lockers. It's cozy. The head is down the hall and that's shared with girls from the other rooms. In my room there's Nettie, Cora Dell and Hazel. I'm on the top bunk with Nettie down below.

Cora Dell (on the level, that's her name) is such a doll. She's tiny and cute as anything with delicate features and skin like porcelain and these big, violet eyes that blink very slowly like a glass-eyed puppet. She talks with such a powerful accent we can't always understand her, what with her y'alls and honey this and honey that. I'm sure I'll get used to it in no time. She's from Alabama. She's already got photographs of her family and little dog all over her locker. She burst into tears last night when Hazel asked her what her dog's name was. "Tippy," she said. "I wish I could have packed her in my suitcase and brought her along."

"We all left somebody behind," Hazel said. "I said goodbye to my fiancé, and that wasn't easy. He's the dreamiest dreamboat you ever saw. But we all gotta make sacrifices."

"That's right," Nettie agreed, in a husky, put-on voice. "There's a war on, ladies."

We all laughed at that because that's what Chief Rinaldi at the Training Center at Hunter College said to us all the time, whenever anybody complained about anything. That was her answer to any grumble. "There's a war on, ladies." Nettie wasn't in my class, but she went through Hunter College too, a few weeks before me. She arrived here before me too, which is why she's got the bottom bunk and I'm on top.

Nettie, whose real name is Annette, is an aviation machinist's mate. She's a tall, broad-shouldered girl with the straightest white teeth you ever saw and wavy hair cut short like a boy's. She looks awfully strong. Nettie's kind of quiet, not in a shy way, but maybe just reserved. Holding back. She's a few years older than me, twenty-four, and she's from somewhere in California, so she's back where she started. I don't know much else about her. Nothing about her people. When the other girls were showing pictures of their family and sweethearts, Hazel asked Nettie about hers and she said she didn't have any pictures. "Why not?" Hazel asked her. "Don't you have a family?"

"'Course I got a family," Nettie grumbled. "Everybody's got a family."

That's when Hazel told us not everybody did, that she didn't. She grew up in an orphanage. I think Nettie felt bad about snapping at her then.

Hazel comes from New Jersey, so she's as far from home as I am. She's as skinny a thing as you ever saw, not a curve on her. She's got a long face and a thin nose and a pale complexion that makes her look a little sickly all the time. She doesn't like the outdoors. She's a bookworm. Whenever she has free time, she reads, mostly mysteries. She brought several with her. Another thing she brought is a Philco radio, which we're all happy to have. We've given it a place of honor on the little writing table against the wall.

There's a sad story with Hazel, I'm sure, her being an orphan and all, but now that she's in the navy, the sky's the limit. That's how I see it. So much opportunity for all us girls, regardless of where we came from or the color of our skin. Just like in basic training, there's all kinds. They treat us all the same here. We're all just another pair of boots, marching here, marching there.

There are these enormous airplane hangars on base. It seems like they go on for miles. That's where Nettie works, Building Five, the maintenance shop. They bring the planes in there and fix 'em up smart. Fast and smart. That's how we do everything in the Navy—full speed ahead!

Now I wish I was an airplane mechanic. That seems like a swell job and about as close to the action as we're going to get. One of the girls I flew over with has actually flown a plane! She's a bona fide pilot. They let the girls fly the planes from one base to another, like a ferry service. She flew an Electra from Virginia all the way to San Diego, which I understand is in Southern California. I'm hoping to hear more about that. Oh, there's lots of stories these gals can tell. We won't be bored here, ever. I know it!

The CO, Captain Blanchard, is coming through to meet the new girls in a half hour, so I have to stop writing now to get everything shipshape. I'm so excited to finally be here. I love the WAVES!!!

January 25, 1944.

I've been so busy getting settled, doing drills, learning how everything works here. There's no time to be blue or lonely or homesick. Not for me, anyway. Somehow, Cora Dell still manages to blubber anytime anybody mentions home, so now we make sure we don't mention it to her. She's a sappy little thing. In the mess hall yesterday she overheard somebody say, "You're not just whistling Dixie" and she burst into tears. I thought Nettie was going to slug her over that.

Of course, every letter from home makes her cry for hours. I can sort of understand that. I got a letter the other day from Mama and Daddy and I'll admit to a case of the weepies myself. The news from home was as usual. Daddy waited in line in the Rambler for an hour last week at a filling station. He did finally get his three gallons, but it's become a huge problem on the East Coast. He says people drive behind gasoline trucks in long lines, following them to their destination because the stations are always out of gas.

Mama made something called "ersatz meatloaf" for supper. She mixed some bacon grease with oats and onions and baked it like a meatloaf. She said she got the recipe from a new cookbook she got at church—"Victory Meals." Ersatz meatloaf doesn't sound very appetizing.

It makes me think I should quit complaining about the GI turkey we get here. That's what we call corned beef. At least it's meat. Same as the creamed chipped beef on toast we call S.O.S., which I kind of like myself, but you won't catch me admitting that to anybody. I had to ask somebody what S.O.S. stood for. "Shit on a shingle," she said. At first the rough talk embarrassed me quite a bit, but by the time I finished basic, it was just the way things were. I have to remember not to talk like that when I'm home with the folks. Mama would throw a fit! We get meat every day in the navy. They feed us so well here I've gained three pounds already. It's just the thing to do to complain about the food. Everybody calls the coffee "battery acid," but back home they're reusing their grounds to make coffee, so what have we got to complain about? It's just the way sailors are. Most of that comes from the men. Grumbling makes them feel more like men, I guess. Most of the women are not complainers. We're grateful for the opportunity to be here, to do something for our country. But there are still a lot of people who don't think women belong in the navy. We've got something to prove.

Other than the problems due to rationing, everything else is fine at home, but just thinking about the folks back there eating supper at the kitchen table without me and Paul, just the two of them, it kind of got to me. Because I know it's hard on them without us.

Hazel goes to mail call every day waiting for a letter from Andy, her beau back in Jersey. She's got a photo of him in a locket. He's a handsome boy but kind of a pipsqueak. He's 4-F because he's too short. He's helping the war effort by working in a Ford factory that's been converted to make tanks. Everybody's doing his part, even if he can't carry a gun.

Things are much less strict here than they were in basic. When we're off duty, we can do what we want and we can have more personal items in our rooms. It's definitely not the Waldorf-Astoria, but it's comfortable.

I've got to say I'm over the moon with my assignment. I'm the driver for the base commander, Captain Blanchard. He's a fine gentleman. Very polite and by the book. I'm to drive him everywhere he wants to go, on and off base, in a sleek black limousine. So no coveralls for me, not like Nettie. It'll be dress blues all the way, gloves and all, every day. Gotta look snazzy. I feel pretty lucky to have my dress uniform as my everyday duds. I look awfully good in that uniform, if I do say so myself. I'd go so far as to say I never looked better.

When the CO was introducing me to his clerk, Yeoman Stark, a fella walked by and he turned to him and barked, "Square your hat, Sailor!" By the book, like I said. He's going to want everything perfect, I know, but I wouldn't have it any other way. He won't catch me with my hat tilted. I memorized the Bluejackets' Manual first thing when I enlisted and I'm intending to follow all the rules to a T. They can call me A.J. Squared Away and I won't mind a bit!

Already a couple of the girls have gotten in trouble trying to get away with this or that. Usually there's a boy involved, which surprises nobody. No boy is going to jeopardize my career. Any sailor whistles at me, I just look the other way. A lot of these girls have no sense. Their heads get turned by the tiniest bit of flattery. Not me. I've got more important things to think about. I'm here for good, in the navy, as long as they need me. Someday they're going to get used to women in the military. Someday they're going to let us do more, especially if we show them what we're capable of now. Maybe someday we can even join the crew of a ship and sail off to some exotic land. I'm going to be there when that happens. You bet I am!

January 28, 1944.

I've got to say, she got me good today, that Nettie. This morning she turned on the Philco radio and got nothing but static. She said, "This thing's broken. But I think I can fix it." I said, "If you can fix an airplane, I bet you can fix a radio." Then she opened up the back and looked inside. "Yep!" she said. "Just like I thought. Why don't you run over to Building Five and see if you can get me an A-S-H Receiver. Just ask around. They'll know what you're after."

So I ran over and started asking people. The first guy said, "Nope, got none of those here. Why don't you go ask Seaman Schmuckatelli over in the machine shop." When I found the machine shop and asked for Seaman Schmuckatelli, the E-3 I was talking to started laughing. When he composed himself, he said, "Schmuckatelli? What do want him for?"

Thinking the first guy had set me up as the butt of a joke, I said, "I don't really care who it is, but I need an A-S-H receiver to fix a radio."

The E-3 started laughing even harder. An older man in the machine shop waved me over and said, "Hey, sister, I know who's got one." He told me to go to the office and ask Sparky.

"Sparky," I repeated, wondering if this was going to be another joke.

"Yeah, Sparky. He's an electrician, so we call him that. Name on his coveralls will be Lansing."

The sailor looked dead serious and it didn't sound like a joke, so I went to the maintenance office where three WAVES were doing clerical work and a man in coveralls was talking to one of them. Sure enough, his name tag said "Lansing." When I asked for the A-S-H receiver, he looked like he was trying to stay serious, but as soon as he started to talk, he burst out laughing.

One of the WAVES shook her head and came over to where I was standing. She picked up an ashtray from the desk and handed it to me. "Ash receiver," she said. "You been sent on a wild goose chase, honey."

Sparky was still snorting through his nose.

When I got back to the barracks with the ashtray, the radio was working just fine and Nettie was lying on her bunk, humming along to it and looking pleased with herself, a lit cigarette in her right hand. Hazel was sitting at the table brushing her hair. She turned to look at me and smiled with one side of her mouth.

"What d'ya think you're doing?" I asked Nettie, trying to sound sore.

"Just livin' the dream," she said before blowing a smoke ring.

I slapped the ashtray on her stomach. She flicked her ashes into it. "Thanks, kid," she said.

For the rest of the day, everybody razzed me about it. Even Cora Dell, this evening in the mess hall, said, "I just ran into Seaman Schmuckatelli and he said he has that A-S-H receiver for you."

"Very funny," I said.

By then, though, even I thought it was funny.

February 2, 1944.

Despite the ashtray incident, I think Nettie and I are going to be good friends. Though she isn't much of a talker, we've hit it off. I'm not a big talker myself and that may be why she likes me. Cora Dell talks nonstop and I know that makes Nettie feel like blowing a fuse some nights. Nettie only talks when she has something to say, so people listen to her.

Most of the other girls aren't serious about their careers.

They're thinking about getting married and starting a family. Like Hazel and Cora Dell. That Cora Dell is man crazy. We razz her about that, but it doesn't do any good. She's the flirtiest thing. Nettie works hard and plans on sticking with it, like me. She wants to be a pilot someday. She talks about airplanes like Cora Dell talks about her sister's baby. Nettie knows everything about planes. She's an ace mechanic already. A steady stream of planes come into that hangar, broken and battered in every way possible. They come out ready to fly in no time flat. Those girls in the shop are doing the navy a tremendous service.

Nettie comes into the barracks most days after her shift covered with sweat and grease. She works harder than I do. But I think she likes it better than she would putting on lipstick and stockings every morning to drive the brass hats around in a fine, clean car. I get my hands dirty too, though, when I put oil in the car and check under the hood. That's part of my job. I know my way around a car, but Nettie impresses me with her airplane skills. She says they're not so different. The engines, anyway. She started with cars too. Her brothers taught her how to rebuild a carburetor when she was just eleven and she knows four ways to start a car without a key. I want her to show me that sometime.

She's a swell gal. All the girls respect her. She's about the only one outside of Chief Bricker who can settle them down when they're in an uproar. She's got a confident voice and a presence that takes charge without even trying. I'd say she's becoming the unofficial leader of Barracks D and I don't think anybody minds that. I expect Nettie to distinguish herself very fast. I wouldn't be surprised if she was an E-3 by the year's end. I'll tell you what, when she's decked out in her crackerjacks, she cuts a fine figure. We had to turn out Monday for some visiting brass. I know Nettie prefers her coveralls, but I told her she looked mighty fine with her gams showing for a change. And she did too! I thought she was going to slug me there for a minute for giving her the business.

February 12, 1944.

Nettie and I took the ferry to Frisco today. After a month, I finally got to see the city. We walked all over, exploring, finding so many places I want to go back to, like Chinatown. Holy mackerel! It was so busy and crowded with all these little shops and chickens and ducks running loose. Like nothing I've ever seen. What a kick! If we'd had any money, we might have bought a souvenir. Maybe one of those beautiful silk robes. I'll try to save some money for next time.

It was windy and cold over there and my legs froze. Nettie wore trousers, which is technically against the rules for WAVES except when you have a very good reason for it, like safety on the job. She said she had a very good reason. It was too cold for a skirt. She was right about that!

A couple of the other girls wanted to go with us today. They're afraid to go on their own because they're from farms and aren't used to big cities, but Nettie said no. I don't know why she turned them down, but when Nettie says no, nobody argues. So it was just the two of us, walking for hours. There are a lot of hills in that town and my legs are sore from all the ups and downs. Nettie knew her way around the city. I asked her if she'd been there before. She said yes. Just yes and nothing more.

After we got tired of walking, we went to a movie, *For Whom the Bell Tolls*, with Ingrid Bergman and Gary Cooper. It was a hummer! After the movie, we rode a cable car up Market Street to the Ferry Building. While we waited for our ferry, Nettie started talking about her family. I don't know what got her talking. She's never talked about any of them before, so I didn't say a word, just listened. She has three brothers and her father is an engineer. She told me her parents live in a well-to-do neighborhood in San Francisco. She grew up there, which explains why she knew her way around. I also found out she went to Mills College in Oakland and majored in art. That's a top-notch women's school. She went for two years, which is more college than any other woman I know.

All of this was news to me. It put Nettie in a different light altogether. She was a rich kid from a privileged family who wanted to be an artist. And now she's an airplane mechanic in the navy. Even though she's stationed just across the Bay, she hasn't once been to visit her family since coming back from basic. She hasn't seen any of them for three years. I asked her why.

"We don't get along," she said.

"Don't you want to see them?" I asked.

"No. And they don't want to see me either."

She didn't explain any further. So here we were in the same city where her parents live and she didn't go see them. I felt sorry for her. I can't imagine being strangers with my mama and daddy. I think it would be the loneliest feeling in the whole world. After she told me about that, I hugged her.

Then she asked me not to say anything to anybody else about what she'd told me. She likes to keep her personal affairs private. It was just between us. And I said, sure, I understood, and felt happy she trusted me. I think I may be Nettie's best friend here. Maybe anywhere. I guess she's mine too, as I can't think of anybody I like better.

CHAPTER SIX

When Shelby stepped inside the nursing home, her nose was hit by the antiseptic smell of cleaning fluid, an unpleasant odor, but better, she supposed, than some of the imaginable alternatives. She walked down a wide hallway, passing several people inching along in wheelchairs across a shiny linoleum floor.

"Good morning," she said to a familiar nurse at the nurse's station.

The woman smiled at her, recognizing her from her many visits already this week.

"Your grandmother's in the activity room," she said, pointing down another hallway.

"Thanks." Shelby turned the corner, encouraged to think that Nana was feeling well enough to get out of bed. Of course, even in the hospital, they had her up and "walking" on her new hip right away. It seemed cruel, but supposedly was for the best.

She found Nana in a wheelchair in front of a computer screen in a room where four other residents were playing bridge. Piled on the counters around the perimeter of the room were games and jigsaw puzzles. In one corner was a huge birdcage where several green, yellow and blue parakeets sat on perches, twittering like an orchestra during warm-up. Nana was leaning forward, facing the computer monitor, her back to the door. Shelby easily recognized her by her cottony hair and the slope of her shoulders under a powder blue bathrobe.

"Hi, Nana," she said, approaching.

Nana turned to look at her, her hazel eyes focusing with exaggerated squinting. "Oh, hi, honey," she said in a tired voice.

"What're you doing? Checking your e-mail?"

"I'm researching my chances of survival."

"What?" Shelby took hold of the wheelchair handles and backed it away from the computer.

"Do you know that a woman my age who breaks a hip is likely to die of complications within six months?"

"Do you want to go outside for a little while?" Shelby asked, pushing the chair out into the hall.

"Okay, but not too long. It kills me to sit in this chair for very long. Do you know what they mean by complications?"

"No."

"They mean things like pneumonia, staph infections, taking another fall, strokes, heart attacks or just plain giving up."

"At least we don't have to worry about that last one." Shelby turned the chair around and pushed the door to the courtyard open with her backside, pulling the chair out behind her. "Nobody's giving up."

"Don't be so sure of that," Nana said. "You don't know the things that go on in my head here. I think giving up isn't such a stretch."

"Maybe for some people, but you're way too stubborn for that. And tough and courageous." Shelby leaned down and kissed Nana's cheek. "It will take a lot more than a broken hip to do you in."

Nana huffed good-naturedly.

It was a sunny day, warm enough if they stayed out of the shaded patio. Shelby parked the wheelchair in the sun beside a grape arbor where she could sit on a bench and rummage through her tote bag. She handed over the Giants ball cap, which Nana immediately put on, pulling the bill down close to her rowdy white eyebrows.

"How's that evil dog of mine?" she asked.

"He misses you. Otherwise okay. I'm officially moved in. It's a little cramped, but once I get things organized, I think I can make it work."

"Thank you so much for doing that, Shelby. It gives me real peace of mind to know someone's there."

"No problem. It helps me out too. Since Lori moved out, it's been kind of hard to make ends meet. Mom's been paying half the rent, you know, so she's thrilled about this arrangement." Shelby pulled the turquoise sweater out of the bag to show Nana. "I brought this. And some magazines and some of those mints you like."

Shelby noted how tired Nana looked, how pale. Her body, slumped forward, looked tiny and fragile. She'd always been a small woman, short and nimble. Shelby had inherited that body type. But Nana looked even smaller today than usual, diminished.

"Are you sleeping?" Shelby asked with concern.

"No, not much. It's impossible to sleep here. People come in all hours of the night to take my blood pressure and temperature. They wake me up to give me a sleeping pill, the imbeciles! And that roommate of mine is a lunatic. Dinky, that's what they call her, though I have no idea how she got a nickname like that. She's as big as a Volkswagen. She lies there moaning in her sleep, then hollering when she's awake. If she's not bellowing, she's listening to her TV at full volume because she's almost completely deaf. There's not a moment's peace around here."

Shelby, not knowing what to say, tried to look sympathetic.

"Maybe," Nana said, "one of the complications that kills people who are theoretically recovering from a broken hip is sheer madness at the indignities of being institutionalized."

"Maybe you could find something more entertaining to do on the Internet than reading about your condition."

Nana frowned. "Pretty grim stuff. But there's no point pretending, is there? Even if I make it through this patch of hell, they say chances are I'm going to break the other one within a year. A broken hip heralds the downward spiral to death. And, frankly, I'd rather be dead than live in a place like this."

Shelby looked at the ground. Nana was truly surly today. Who could blame her? She was a realist. Not one to sugarcoat anything. Not a sentimental sort. One of the first things she did after her hip surgery was call her lawyer to update her will and draw up a health care directive that put Shelby's mother in charge of all the medical decisions. Shelby had wondered at that decision. Aunt Vickie was the elder daughter and therefore the more likely choice, though Shelby wouldn't want either one of them making life-or-death decisions for her.

It was hard to believe sometimes that Vivian and Vickie were Nana's offspring. They were nothing like her. She was a very cool character—self-reliant and sharp. She wasn't prone to flights of fancy and she never felt sorry for herself. She accepted what came her way and tried to deal with it with ruthless common sense. Today, apparently, that meant stoically facing the reality that recovering her health was going to be a long and difficult process.

"Can you take me back to my room?" Nana asked.

"Sure. Are you cold?"

"Worn out. And the hip is hurting quite a bit."

When they arrived in the room, they found Dinky's bed vacant.

"She must be down in physical therapy," Nana guessed. "Good. A moment of quiet at last!"

After the painful ordeal of getting from the wheelchair to the bed was accomplished, Shelby taped a darling picture of Oscar to the closet door alongside the impromptu photo collage that was accumulating there. There were pictures of family members—Vickie and Vivian, grandkids, and great-grandkids on Vickie's side of the family. No grandkids were on the horizon on Vivian's side, which was Shelby's fault, as far as her mother was concerned, despite the fact that Charlie had completely screwed up the fatherhood attempt.

At twenty-five, Shelby knew she had already wasted several years that could have been devoted to fulfilling her mother's dream of the ideal family: successful husband and two model children, a dream Vivian herself had tried desperately to realize. She thought she had succeeded when she married Gary and had a son and daughter. But Vivian's dream had disintegrated in recent years, first when her marriage fell apart, and then when her promising son got a girl pregnant and dropped out of college. That had broken Vivian's heart, especially since Charlie was completely uninterested in the child he had fathered and the girl had moved out of state, taking Vivian's only grandchild permanently and completely out of her reach. Two big blows in one year had hurled her into a nervous breakdown. She had only recently stopped taking tranquilizers on a regular basis. Shelby was watching carefully for signs that she was cracking under the strain of Nana's accident.

One of Vivian's favorite photos was taped to the closet door, a picture of the four of them: Vivian, Gary, Charlie and Shelby, a beautiful family smiling in congenial unison, captured at a moment in time before that unity had been breached. That photo represented Vivian's view of what was right and valuable in the world. That she'd put it here was just one more indication she wanted to hang onto the way things were then, five years ago. But even then, though Vivian was unaware of it, the image of this perfect all-American family didn't reflect reality. The blonde twenty-year-old leaning affectionately against her father and smiling with her perfect set of teeth was already on a course that would shatter her mother's dreams. And probably her father's as well. Shelby would never be able to fulfill the promise this photo represented. She had no doubt she would be an even worse disappointment than Charlie.

She always thought her mother's quest for the model family was her response to being brought up in a broken home. Having divorced parents in the early 1960s wasn't common. It had embarrassed and saddened her. She was among just a few children whose mothers weren't home baking cookies while they were at school. It had made her different. Being different was the worst thing for a kid.

"Would you grab that newspaper off Dinky's bed for me?" Nana asked. "Just the sports and obits. I don't need the rest of it."

Shelby picked up the paper. "The obits? Why are you so morbid today?"

"I always read the obits. When you're my age, the obits take the place of the social column. You don't care who's getting married or having babies or shacking up with whom. All you want to know is who kicked the bucket."

Shelby handed over the sports section, then paged through to find the obituary page. "Do you see people you know in there very often?"

"Oh, sure. This is a small town. Working in the pharmacy all those years, I met a lot of people. You'd be surprised how many people you know turn up dead when you're old and have lived here most of your life."

"And it doesn't make you sad to see that?"

Nana shrugged. "Depends who it is. Sometimes it just makes me feel triumphant, like I beat them out, you know. It's the ultimate contest, life and death. They're dead. I'm not. I win. At least for today. Sort of like Russian roulette."

"Here are your mints." Shelby handed Nana the package, then scooted the visitor's chair up next to the bed and produced a black-and-white photo from her bag. "I found this in your dresser when I was looking for your sweater. In a cigar box with some other things from the war."

Nana took the photo and looked at it for several seconds, her expression unreadable.

"I don't recognize that woman," Shelby prompted. "Who is she?"

As Nana turned, Shelby saw the distant look in her eyes. It was a couple of seconds before she seemed to see Shelby. "Marjorie," she said softly, almost as if she were saying it to herself. Then, louder and more offhandedly, she said, "She was a friend of mine during the war. Lost touch decades ago."

She abruptly handed the photo back, then fumbled with the

plastic from the mint package. Apparently that was all she had to say about Marjorie. Shelby took the mints from her and pulled the package open, then handed it back. Nana put one on her tongue.

"How are things with you, Shelby?" she asked.

"Okay. Just finished up finals. I'm free as of last Friday. Free big time, actually. I lost my job."

Nana raised her eyebrows, her lips closed and puckered in the active sucking of the mint.

"Got fired," Shelby elaborated.

"You were too good for that job anyway," Nana pronounced. "Good riddance! Besides, you would have been quitting soon anyway to go work for your father."

"Yeah, I know. But it's no fun getting fired." Shelby draped the turquoise sweater over Nana's shoulders. "I want to set up your utility bills to be paid automatically out of your checking account. Where can I find your checkbook or a bank statement to get the numbers off of?"

"Is that safe?" Nana didn't look as though she had any idea there was a problem with the utilities.

"Safer than all that paperwork shuttling around town in the mail."

"That's all too complicated for me, but if you think it's a good idea, check the second drawer in my desk, left-hand side."

"It'll be a lot easier for you, once it's set up. You won't have to worry about writing checks. You won't have to remember to pay the bills."

There was still no indication Nana recognized any problem paying the bills, so Shelby decided to let it go.

"I've lost track of time," Nana said. "When's your graduation?"

"Next week. Tuesday."

Nana winced. "I'm going to miss it. I don't think I can sit through that."

"No, I know. Don't worry about it. Mom will take pictures and I can come and tell you all about it."

"But I did want to be there. My granddaughter graduating from college. That's a big thing. I can't believe I'm going to miss it. Maybe they could shoot me full of morphine and I could manage."

"If they shoot you full of morphine, you won't have any idea where you are anyway."

Nana chuckled, then took another mint. "You don't seem very happy lately, honey. You're always so serious."

"Really?" Shelby was taken off guard. "Well, my grandmother broke her hip and is in a rehab place with a bunch of lunatics."

Nana smiled softly. "Even before this, I mean. Since Lori moved out."

Shelby stared. She didn't know what to say. What did Nana know or think she knew about Lori? She was waiting, watching Shelby placidly while sucking gently on the mint. There was something about the expression on her face that told Shelby there was no point in pretending.

Finally, she said, "You knew?"

Nana nodded. "Not so difficult to see. I didn't know in the beginning, but the last couple years, I was pretty sure."

"Does everybody know?"

"Everybody?"

"I mean the family. Mom? Dad? Aunt Vickie?"

"I don't know. I doubt it. You were very careful, weren't you? Gave nothing away. Kept her out of sight. Showed up alone for Thanksgiving and Christmas. The entire time you were together, I think I saw her only a few times and spoke to her no more than to say hello."

"Then how did you know?" Shelby felt her hands growing moist. She was feeling a mixture of fear and relief. When she imagined coming out to her family, this was not how she imagined it. It was usually a nightmarish scene where her mother screamed hysterically and her father shook his head sadly, his spirit broken and his love for her tarnished beyond hope of recovery.

"Intuition," Nana answered.

Shelby lowered her head.

"Oh, don't worry," Nana said. "I've got no problem with it."

Shelby looked up. "You don't?"

"No! Not at all. I was glad to see you happy." Nana smiled

reassuringly, the bill of her cap nodding up and down. "Why'd you break up?"

Shelby hesitated, trying to determine if Nana really was okay with it, and decided she was. "She got involved with this guy. Actually, they've been dating for a year now. Since before she moved out. She's marrying him this summer."

Nana patted her hand. "That must have hurt."

"Yeah. It was just...a shock. After five years."

Nana raised her eyebrows. "Five years? You really did keep her to yourself, didn't you?"

"That's the way she wanted it. She was terrified somebody'd find out."

"That's tough. Hiding. Not being able to share your real self with people, especially your family. That's no way to live, Shelby."

"I've always felt you understood me better than anybody," Shelby said. "Better than Mom, for sure. You won't tell her?"

"No, I won't tell her. You will."

Shelby shook her head, feeling a sense of dread creeping up her spine. "No, I don't think so. I mean, it's over with Lori."

"You'll find someone else. You're young. You have so many options. So many possibilities." Nana smiled warmly while squeezing her hand. "Try to be happy, Shelby, however you can. That's the most important thing. And don't be afraid to be yourself. What's the point of having your mother's approval if she doesn't know who you are?"

It wasn't that she hadn't tried to come out to her mother, years ago when she and Lori were new and so happy to be in love and Shelby naively thought that anybody who cared about her would be equally happy for her. That was before Lori had become so paranoid and firm in her need for secrecy. That was also before Shelby had experienced the long-threatened nervous breakdown her mother had always predicted for herself. "If you don't stop that," she had often said, "you'll give me a nervous breakdown." An idle threat, that's what she and her brother had always thought. They weren't even sure what a nervous breakdown was. So Shelby wasn't as wary in those days. She had gotten as far as, "Mom, there's something I need to tell you about me and Lori." She'd gotten that far twice, in fact, and both times something had interrupted and her mother was off on another, more pressing topic. By then, Lori had decided no one could know about them and had made Shelby promise to never tell. Most of the time, that had been okay, but sometimes, as Nana said, it was tough.

Just then a loud bang made them both turn their attention to where Dinky was trying to maneuver her wheelchair through the doorway and had run into the wall. Shelby jumped up and dashed over to drive the chair safely in and park it beside Dinky's bed. Dinky wasn't quite the size of a Volkswagen, but she must have earned her nickname in a peculiarly ironic way. She was enormous, wearing a shapeless housedress that fell below her knees. Her face was small and round, buried in the midst of multiple chins and cheeks. She had tiny flashing eyes that peered hard in a way that felt like an accusation but was more likely near-sightedness.

After locking the wheels, Shelby left her to wrangle herself into bed. "What was your name again?" Dinky hollered.

Nana rolled her eyes as Shelby answered in an exaggeratedly loud voice. Then she turned back to Nana, kissed her cheek, and said, "Thanks for being so understanding. See you tomorrow."

She was out of the room and thirty feet down the hall when she heard Dinky roar, "She's a nice girl."

CHAPTER SEVEN

Deciding she wasn't done looking at the photo of Nana and Marjorie, Shelby stuck it on the refrigerator under a magnet. There was something intriguing about it, in Marjorie's expression and her stance. A subtle suggestion of protectiveness came through in the positioning of her arm and her upper body.

Shelby knew very little about her grandmother's youth, only that she had married Grandpa when she was nineteen, an innocent girl with no experience and no sense. That's how she described herself whenever she mentioned that time. "I got married because that's what you did," she had explained. Shelby also knew that Nana hadn't been in love when she got married, but had liked Grandpa well enough. He was a hard worker and a decent man, at least when she married him. That had seemed enough back when a woman's choices and imagination were strictly limited to what she could see in front of her nose.

Later, when Shelby's mother was twelve, Nana had divorced Grandpa and finished raising her kids by herself, working full-time as a medical receptionist. Some time later, when she was in her forties, she had gone to college to become a pharmacist. None of these things had been easy, not divorce, not a college education, not a career as a single mother. Shelby had always admired her grandmother, but she realized as she stared at the twenty-year-old in the photo that there were many facets of this woman she knew nothing about. That she would be comfortable, for instance, with her granddaughter being a lesbian. Shelby was surprised and relieved. Nana wasn't a particularly judgmental kind of person, but, still, she might have expected a little distress, or maybe just mystification. Someone from Nana's generation was often less familiar, less sympathetic with homosexuals than a younger person. Truthfully, though, Nana had never been the one Shelby worried about. The only person Shelby really wanted to protect from the truth was her mother.

The checkbook was in the desk right where Nana had said it would be. Shelby called the electric company to pay the back bills. Two hours, they said, and the electricity would be back on. While she waited, she began pulling thawed packages of meat, vegetables and old bits of bread products out of the freezer. Maybe it wasn't such a loss after all, she realized. Most of the stuff in there looked like it had been there forever. It was desiccated and stale smelling. When the freezer was empty, she moved on to the refrigerator, uncovering plastic bags full of slime and items years out of date. Several varieties of mold were thriving happily inside half-empty jars. She decided to throw everything away. Once the refrigerator was empty, she cleaned the interior out with soap and water until it gleamed inside.

When at last the lights flickered on and the refrigerator motor began to hum and the vents in the ceiling started pushing through warm air, she heaved a sigh of relief. She was eventually able to shed her outer layers down to a T-shirt. Then she sat at Nana's computer and set up online banking and automatic bill pay for all the household bills. When Nana gets home, she thought with satisfaction, everything will be humming along smoothly on its own. No more worries about forgetting to pay a bill.

Oscar sat on the floor beside her chair, looking up at her. She wondered if Nana would be able to keep him. It was Oscar, after all, who had caused her to fall. Oh, well, there was no need to make decisions like that now. Shelby patted his head reassuringly as if he might have been disturbed by her thoughts.

When the phone rang, she jumped up to answer to her mother's unconvincingly cheerful greeting. A tinge of hysteria seemed to always be running under Vivian's skin these days, as if she were only one thread away from completely unraveling.

"Hi, Mom," she said.

"How are you doing over there?"

"Okay, now, but when I got here this morning, the power was off. Turns out Nana hasn't paid the bill for three months."

Realizing she was hungry, Shelby searched the pantry for something to eat, settling on a can of vegetable soup.

"I don't understand," Vivian said. "Why would Mom ignore something like a utility bill?"

"I don't know. She just forgot, I guess." Shelby popped open the can with one hand.

"You mean you didn't ask her why she didn't pay the bill?"

"Nope. The woman at the power company told me it's a common problem with the elderly. They just don't get around to it or whatever. I mean, I doubt she'd have a good reason if I did ask. What do you think she'd say? Oh, I was wondering what it would be like to live like we used to, when I was a kid, reading by candlelight."

"There's no reason to be a smart-aleck about it."

Gee, I was just making a joke, Shelby thought. Or trying to.

"Anyway," said Shelby, "the bill's paid and I've got the power back on now. You know, Mom, there may be more wrong here than the broken hip. I mean, Nana may not be taking care of herself as well as we all assumed."

"Why do you say that?" Vivian sounded defensive.

"Just things in general. The bills, of course, and old, rotten food in the fridge. The house doesn't seem very clean either. I mean, you might not notice normally, but I'm living here now, so I'm seeing things."

"Do you think she's got Alzheimer's or something?"

"Well, no." Shelby wondered why her mother had jumped to that radical conclusion. "I think she's just having trouble tending to all the details. She might need a little help, that's all."

"But she never asked for help. She never said there was a problem."

"No, so there's no way you could have known." Shelby felt the need to head off her mother's attack of guilt. "Anyway, there's nothing seriously wrong. I'm getting things back on track here. I've found everything I need to take care of her business. And I don't have to worry about how to get into her online accounts because she's got a piece of paper at her desk, right by the computer, with all of her user IDs and passwords written out for anybody to see." Shelby laughed, then poured her soup into a bowl.

"Oh, for heaven's sake!" said Vivian, apparently not finding that funny.

"The main thing now is that she heals up, gets back on her feet. No point having her worry about things like this." She put her bowl in the microwave and punched the dinner plate button. "What'd the doctor say?" she asked, changing the subject.

"He said we'll just have to wait and see. At her age, there's the possibility for all sorts of complications. In the best-case scenario, she'll heal up and learn to walk with the artificial hip. She might have to use a walker for quite a while. She might have to use some kind of support for the rest of her life."

"That's the best-case scenario? What's the worst?"

"Shelby, there's no point thinking about that!"

So typical of her mother, Shelby thought, annoyed—always avoiding anything unpleasant, as though ignoring it would make it go away.

"But it could take awhile," Vivian continued. "I hope you'll be able to stay there as long as she's in rehab."

"Yeah, I'm settling in here for the long haul. Anything else, Mom?"

"Yes. While I'm thinking about it, I want to talk about Lori's wedding."

Shelby frowned and rolled her eyes at Oscar who looked up expectantly at her from the floor.

"I wish you'd have agreed to be a bridesmaid. You're her best friend. I know she's disappointed you won't be in the wedding. Would it have killed you?"

Maybe, thought Shelby.

Vivian didn't wait for her answer. "You're just not thinking ahead. When it's time to plan your wedding—"

"I'm not going to have a wed—"

"Oh, now wait just a minute, Shelby Ann! You most certainly *are* going to have a wedding. And your father's going to pay through the nose for it. My daughter is not getting married by a justice of the peace. Don't you even think about it. You're going to have a glorious wedding in our church with all your friends and family members present. Proud and proper."

Tell that to the California Supreme Court, Shelby thought, and then suppressed a giggle, imagining her mother doing just that.

"I think I'll get a new dress for Lori's wedding," Vivian continued. "Do you want to go shopping with me?"

"Why?"

"So you can get one too, of course." Vivian sounded exasperated.

"A new dress? Mom, I don't think—I haven't worn a dress in a long time. I think I'll just wear a nice pair of slacks."

"It's a wedding. What does it have to be to get you into a dress anyway?"

"Uh, I don't know. Maybe the Second Coming."

Vivian groaned. "Shelby, what am I going to do with you?"

Simultaneously, the microwave dinged and the doorbell rang. Oscar ran out of the kitchen, barking excitedly.

"Mom, I've got to go. Charlie and Todd are here with my stuff."

She ran to the door to find her brother on the porch and Todd at the curb with his pickup, the tailgate down and her mattress, bed frame and headboard inside. This was the last load. Todd waved.

"The movers have arrived," Charlie announced, grabbing

Shelby and tossing her easily over his shoulder so her head hung down his back. "Where should we put all this old junk?"

"Put me down!"

"Whatever you say, See-See." Charlie tossed her unceremoniously on the sofa.

Shelby sat up. "Until I can clear out the guest room, let's just move it in here."

Charlie looked around the already cluttered front room and shrugged his thin shoulders. He was slender and tall, six-three. His light brown hair hung limp over his ears and forehead, giving him a slightly scruffy look, a match for the day-old beard and favorite old pair of jeans with threadbare knees. Nobody knew why he was so tall. Nobody in their family was tall like that. When they were young, Shelby had teased him by calling him a "freak of nature." She didn't call him that anymore. She had become aware that there were people who would call her that as well for an entirely different reason.

The three of them moved her stuff in and packed it together on one side of the living room, mattress and bed frame standing on their sides to take as little space as possible. Then Charlie wandered into the kitchen, no doubt looking for something to feed his voracious appetite. Todd leapt into the air and landed in a prone position on the couch.

"How's Granny?" he said, propping himself on his elbow.

"On the road to recovery. Everybody keeps talking like a broken hip is a death sentence, though. It's scary."

"I guess you'll be here for a while, then. When does your new job start with your dad's company?"

"I think I'll take a little vacation first. Maybe take the summer off."

"Sure. Why not? You deserve a break." Todd reached down to pet Oscar. "You know, that woman was in the restaurant yesterday."

"What woman?"

"That woman who got you fired." He sat up. "The skinny, flat-chested one. The redhead."

Shelby stared at him, conjuring up an image of Gwen. "She wasn't flat-chested."

"Not compared to me, maybe." He stuck out his chest, looking down at his T-shirt.

"So, what about her?" Shelby asked impatiently. "Did she come in for dinner?"

"No. She came in to talk to Francois. She asked if I could take her to the manager. She wanted to ask him to take you back, to explain it wasn't your fault, what happened the other night."

"Really?" Shelby was impressed.

"Yeah, I know! I thought that was cool. She was in the back with Francois for about ten minutes. I was working a table, so I didn't get a chance to talk to her when she came out, but she frowned in my direction and shook her head before she left. Apparently she blew it."

"I don't think anyone could persuade him to take me back."

"You're right. I'd already asked him about it myself and he wasn't gonna budge."

"Ah, that was nice of you."

Todd shrugged. "I think he's been wanting to fire you for a while anyway."

"I know it! But Gwen couldn't have known that. She thinks it's her fault."

Todd pushed his black hair back from his face with both hands. "That's her name?"

Shelby nodded, touched to think of Gwen taking the trouble to plead her case to Francois.

"You know," Todd said, "his name is actually Frank."

"No!"

"Oh, yeah. Francois is an affectation."

"That's funny."

Todd leapt off the couch, stretching his hands up over his head. "I should go. It's getting late and I need to take a shower before I start work. And drop your brother off. By the way, when I stopped over there to pick him up, your mom was acting kind of weird."

"Weird?"

"She invited me in, gave me a tour of the house, showed me your old bedroom, asked me all these questions about my career plans."

"Oh, God!"

"I think she thinks I'm your boyfriend." Todd laughed.

"What did you tell her?"

"Nothing. I thought it was funny. I just said, 'Well, Mrs. Pratt, I'm currently in my final year of law school. As soon as I pass the bar exam, I'll be setting up my practice right here in Alameda.'"

"That was mean," accused Shelby.

"Oh, I don't know. Seemed to make her happy."

"Yeah! But you shouldn't mess with her like that. She's kind of fragile."

"Sorry. I won't do it again." He looked appropriately serious and contrite.

Charlie appeared in the kitchen doorway with a box of crackers in hand. "There's no food in this house," he complained. "The refrigerator's empty. I mean, *totally* empty. There's not even a Coke in there."

"Sorry," Shelby said. "I haven't got to the store yet. I'll have some next time."

With his mouth full of crackers, Charlie nodded.

After they left, Shelby sat in the living room amid her furniture, Oscar in her lap, and thought of Gwen confronting Francois to ask for her job back. That was really sweet of her to make the effort. Worth a thank you, anyway.

CHAPTER EIGHT

Shelby rode her bike down to old Main Street, a road that defined the eastern border of the Alameda Naval Air Station. On the right was a new residential area, rows of identical white and tan stucco houses, designed and built to pack the largest number of people into the smallest space for the lowest cost. On the left were the remnants of the military base. She passed the sagging commissary building with its peeling white paint, then swung westward toward the Bay, passing the parking lot for the ferry to San Francisco. The northern edge of the island backed up against the Oakland Inner Harbor. Huge cranes queued up at the loading dock across the channel, their rusted cables weighted down with grappling hooks taller than she was. Cargo ships lined up to unload, hulking vessels with variously colored railroad cars piled high like tightly-stacked Tetris blocks.

She rode through the old main gate. The guard shack now stood empty, its grimy front window shattered. Just inside the gate, a new skate park, an odd bit of modernity amid the dilapidated forties-era buildings, was occupied by a group of three boys on skateboards. The military complex was gradually morphing, bit by bit, into its new purposes. As she made her way across the huge expanse of the base, she passed corrugated metal structures with warped wooden doors and long banks of cloudy, small-paned windows, many of them broken. Some of the buildings, though ancient and decrepit, were still in use. The military had moved out for good fifteen years ago, but a few commercial businesses had moved in to take advantage of the bay front location and low rent, both of which were extremely rare in Alameda.

One of four airplane hangars along this road now housed the headquarters of the St. George scotch distillery. But many of the buildings she recalled from her childhood were now gone. Almost all of them would be, eventually. Despite the few businesses operating here, the base was quiet. It felt abandoned.

If you lived in Alameda, you knew the business of this base. It had once been the heart of the town, beating with the robust energy of the war machine. Even if people didn't know much about history, they knew this chunk of prime real estate on the San Francisco Bay was about to belong to the City of Alameda, and they all had opinions about how it should be used. Soon there would be plenty of fancy restaurants like Cibo lining the shore. *Lots of competition there, Frank*, she thought with a smile.

Gwen was right. There was a lot of history out here. Shelby suddenly wished she knew more about it. She'd been neglecting her history, even the personal part of it like the shipyards over in Richmond where her grandmother had worked, now just a rusty spot on the waterfront she'd driven past many times on her way to somewhere else. She'd never stopped there. She'd never even been to the Rosie the Riveter memorial park. In her defense, she told herself, Nana never talked about those days. It was easy to forget the family connection tucked away in a cigar box at the bottom of a dresser drawer.

But today Shelby was thinking about it, wondering how

important the war years had been to her grandmother. It was a brief span in a long life, but maybe not as inconsequential as its short duration would suggest.

As she rode toward the two-story building that housed the museum, she realized she didn't know if Gwen would even be there. For all she knew, the museum director had a swanky office downtown somewhere. But it was a nice day for a bike ride. Even if Gwen wasn't there, she reasoned, she could look around and pick up a little knowledge about naval history in her hometown.

She rounded a corner and found herself in front of the museum, a white Craftsman-style house with square, tapered pillars supporting the front porch. It was typical of the style, with a low-pitched gabled roof and overhanging eaves. An American flag was mounted on the right side of the wide porch. A sign that read "Alameda Naval Museum" hung on the clapboard siding of the second story. The sign was white with blue letters floating above a wavy blue line meant to represent ocean waves. The double-hung windows, with their hazy glass, were obviously original to the building. It didn't look like much had been changed at all since it was built.

This wasn't like the other buildings on base. It wasn't the same era and it wasn't the simple, practical style of military structures, all of them looking like they had been tossed up without any expectation of longevity. This building had more charm and more character. It was clearly older than everything around it. Where it sat on the eastern edge of the base, it must have been incorporated when the base was established, reclaimed from a pre-existing residential area. There were other homes nearby from the same time period and Craftsman homes were common around town. Nana's house, in fact, was one, on a much smaller scale.

She liked this architectural style. It was cozy and approachable. Nothing gaudy about it, but it had surprising touches of artistic flair. This building had the typical square pillars, but at the top of them and all along the porch cover was a unique and intricate scrollwork design. That was the hallmark of the style, the individual touches of fine detail work.

Three cars were in the lot. She rode up beside a Ford Fairlane, a car even older than her own, which prompted an involuntary nod of admiration. A "Retired USN" sticker adorned its rear bumper. Next to this was a silver hybrid with several bumper stickers: *Save Our Oceans, Green is a Way of Life* and *Celebrate Diversity* on a rainbow background. She smiled, more confident now that Gwen was here.

She parked her bike and walked up the stairs to the porch, examining the scrollwork more carefully. She tried the front door, which opened reluctantly after she gave it a firm shove. She stepped into a long, wide hallway, half of which seemed to be a makeshift office containing a couple of cluttered desks and filing cabinets. All the furniture, Shelby noticed, was old government-issue—battleship-gray metal desks, metal four-drawer filing cabinets, solid gray chairs with green vinyl cushions. The modern computer on the desk and the Xerox machine against the wall stuck out like anachronisms. The elevator to her right was also a poorly-integrated addition.

She took a few steps inside the room, noticing the Lucite collection box near the door. The wall opposite the office space was covered with framed posters, definitely old in style, mostly cartoon drawings with sayings like "Loose Lips Sink Ships" and "Buy War Bonds." Shelby scanned these, noticing one with an image of Hitler wearing swastika-covered boxer shorts and the slogan, "Let's catch him with his panzers down!" The familiar Rosie the Riveter "We Can Do It" poster was on the far wall, showing Rosie wearing her red and white bandana and flexing a bicep.

As Shelby stepped further along the hallway, eying model ships in glass cases, she heard footsteps approaching on the patchwork linoleum floor. She looked up to see Gwen rounding the corner at the far end, a stack of binders in her arms, her long legs clad in jeans as before. Seeing Shelby, she stopped abruptly, then recovered and continued her approach.

"Hi," she said with a friendly smile. She had a wide mouth that took up most of the lower portion of her face when she smiled. With her straight auburn hair and round face, she looked decidedly pixie-ish.

"Hi," Shelby returned.

Gwen dumped the binders on one of the desks, then faced Shelby. "You surprised me."

"Sorry."

The light streaming in from the high windows gave Shelby a better view of Gwen than she'd had at the restaurant. Faint freckles across her cheekbones were now visible and the red highlights of her hair caught the light, giving it a healthy sheen. Shelby found herself glancing at Gwen's chest to mentally dispute Todd's claim that she was flat-chested. There was nothing large about Gwen—she had a lanky frame, but, from what Shelby could tell, she was proportionate. Men, even gay men, are so peculiar about boobs, she reflected. They think it's normal for a woman with a size twenty-two waist to walk around with a size forty bust.

Suddenly realizing what she was doing, Shelby jerked her gaze back up to Gwen's face to see her watching with a look of curious amusement.

"Did you come to see the collection?" Gwen asked with a faint grin.

"Yes."

"Great. I'll show you around."

"Oh, you don't have to do that." Shelby felt unexpectedly nervous. "You're busy. I can just wander around on my own."

"I'd be happy to show you. You're the only visitor here at the moment."

Shelby had been hearing noise radiating down the walls from upstairs. She looked up as she heard it again.

"That's just the regulars," Gwen explained. "I'll introduce you when we get upstairs."

"Actually, I came by to thank you. I heard what you tried to do at the restaurant. That was really nice."

"The more I thought about it, the worse I felt about getting you fired. It was worth a try, but your boss was surprisingly inflexible."

"I'd have been surprised if he'd taken me back. I wasn't very good at that job. I'd already been warned a few times. It wasn't your fault. It was just a matter of time. And I would've quit soon anyway. Now that school's out, I'll be getting a full-time job."

"Oh, you're a student." Gwen leaned against her desk, regarding Shelby with steady interest.

"Yeah," answered Shelby, feeling inexplicably self-conscious. "Well, not anymore. Graduation is Tuesday night."

"Congratulations. What's your major?"

"Architecture."

"Really?" Gwen said. "That's fascinating. How did you end up doing that?"

"My dad's an architect. He works for a company that designs office buildings and parking garages."

"Parking garages? You mean somebody designs those?"

"Yes." Shelby laughed. "Anyway, I'll be going to work in my dad's company."

"Is that what you want to do, design parking garages and office buildings?"

Shelby shrugged. "For a while. Truth is, I'm a lot more interested in old buildings than new ones."

Gwen smiled and waved her hand at the room. "I'm interested in old things too."

Shelby nodded, transfixed by Gwen's presence. She watched her, her large hands, her freckled nose, the soft down on her jawline where the sunlight hit her face. There was something fascinating about her. Shelby didn't quite understand it, but she just wanted to keep looking.

"Okay," Shelby said, rousing herself, "so show me your museum."

Gwen led the way into the next room, which she called the "uniform room." It contained dozens of male and female mannequins wearing navy uniforms from different eras, starting with World War I up to present day. Most of them were varying patterns of white and navy blue with smart skirts, jackets and caps. As they went further into the room, Shelby heard music playing low, an old romantic ballad that conjured up an image of lovers dancing close and slow in a smoky room.

"What's that song?" she asked.

"That's 'I'll Be Seeing You' by Bing Crosby. Do you know it?"

Shelby shook her head. "No, but it's nice. My grandmother's nuts for Bing Crosby."

"A lot of people were back then." Gwen put a hand on Shelby's back to turn her toward the next room. "The next display is for the WAVES," she announced, leading the way to an alcove containing memorabilia from the navy women of World War II. On one wall was a poster of a proudly smiling woman saluting with a white-gloved hand, under the caption, "Enlist in the WAVES. Release a man to fight at sea."

"The WAVES were formed in nineteen forty-two," Gwen said in a practiced voice, "along with the WAC for the army, to take over noncombat jobs. Unofficially, though, women did end up in combat zones and many were killed and wounded."

Shelby read an old metal sign that said, "Remove Lipstick Before Eating."

"That's a funny one," she said, gesturing at the sign.

Gwen nodded, smiling at her with a twinkle in her eye. "Seems funny now, doesn't it? But lipstick was part of the uniform back then."

"I like all these old signs."

"Me too," said Gwen. "Look at this one. It's one of my favorites."

The poster on the opposite wall was an image of Mickey Mouse waving an American flag with the caption, "Come on, gang—all out for Uncle Sam." In smaller print was a plea to buy war bonds.

Shelby nodded her appreciation.

"We've got dozens of these," Gwen said. "Too many to display."

"In a way, they don't seem serious enough for the situation," Shelby observed.

"You're right. There was so much optimism and so much certainty that we were in the right. Things have gotten much more muddied up since then."

Gwen looked momentarily pensive and Shelby assumed she was thinking about Vietnam and more recently the "war on terror," neither of which were conflicts with the stakes clearly established. She waved Shelby over to a photo of one female and three male sailors standing in front of a machine gun. The woman was young and very pretty. The men appeared to be listening to her as she spoke and gestured.

"This is Skipper back in nineteen forty-three," Gwen said. "This is her museum."

"Her museum?" Shelby was surprised. "I assumed it was owned by some government agency. The navy, for instance."

"Might be better if it was. But, no, it's private. Skipper's dream. This is all her doing. She leases the building from the city. She was a gunnery instructor while she was stationed here. I'll introduce you when we get upstairs. She's one of the regulars I mentioned before."

Gwen pointed to another photo, a prominently displayed black-and-white print of two women in dress uniform saluting in unison. "This one was taken in nineteen fifty-five. That's Skipper on the left. That's her partner Florence on the right. They met here. They were together over fifty years."

Shelby peered at the photo. "Together? You mean as a couple?"

"Yes. And this is Skipper the day she retired." Gwen pointed to another photo, color this time, of an older woman wearing a similar uniform but with pants instead of a skirt.

"She was able to stay in the military all that time even though she was a lesbian?"

"She was very discreet. It happened all the time. Long before Don't Ask, Don't Tell, gays in the military were not asking and not telling. If you didn't cause any trouble or get on anybody's shit list, you might slide by. Plenty were kicked out, but plenty more weren't."

The background music changed to a male voice singing, "I've Got a Girl in Kalamazoo."

"There's a real focus here on World War II, isn't there?" Shelby noted.

"We have stuff from the entire history of the naval base, but, yes, heavy on that time period. It's the most interesting to people. And it was the most vital period for this installation. Let's take a look at the Rosie the Riveter exhibit."

"Rosie the Riveter? They weren't military."

"No, but there were women civilians stationed here during

the war. Just like at the private factories. They brought women in to meet the demand for labor."

Gwen led her to a small room containing photos and the paraphernalia of factory work—blow torches, riveting guns, protective gear. Many of the photos looked like the ones Shelby had found in Nana's cigar box. Several versions of Rosie the Riveter posters adorned the wall.

"I found some stuff the other day in my grandmother's house," Shelby said. "From World War II. She worked in the Richmond shipyards."

Gwen's eyes widened. "Really? You mean she was one of the Rosies?"

Shelby nodded. "She was a welder."

"Has your grandmother been interviewed by the oral history project?" Gwen asked eagerly.

Shelby turned from a display of welding equipment to face Gwen. "Oral history project?"

"For the Rosie the Riveter memorial. They're interviews of people who still live in the area, who lived here during the war. I did quite a few of those interviews myself a few years ago when I was a student at Cal. I still do them on occasion."

"You mean the women who worked in the shipyards?"

"Yes. The shipyards were the heart of Richmond during the war. They took over everything, redefined the town completely. It's fascinating, what those women did. Just ordinary housewives coming in and wiring, welding, assembling these huge warships. I'll tell you what, that story never gets old for me."

"You know, all of this makes me realize I don't know much about it, what Nana did during the war."

"You should ask her. She was part of a phenomenon. Those women just did what they were asked to do, what needed to be done for the war effort, but in the process, they started to bloom, to embrace independence, to become the seeds of change for all of us. Suddenly it was okay for married women to work outside the home. They could earn money. Money, as we all know, is the key to independence." Gwen's voice was impassioned, her expression intense, those thick eyebrows angled in toward one another. "It was the beginning of everything. Suddenly, women, millions of ordinary women, found out they could make it in the world without a man, make it in whatever they chose to do. It was the beginning of a revolution. It sparked the women's liberation movement."

Shelby was gripped by Gwen's sudden enthusiasm. "Was that really how women's liberation began?"

"Yes. I mean, it was pivotal." Gwen pointed at an enlarged photo of four young women in scarves and blue jeans, all smiling, their arms thrown around one another's shoulders. "It woke up millions of women to the possibilities a paycheck could create. It gave them dreams they never could have had before. All the rules that kept them in their places were revoked. It's ironic, isn't it, that gender roles were smashed by war. How long would it have taken otherwise? But the country had no choice. We had to have the manpower. Not enough men, so it had to be women. Win the war at any cost. Well, what it cost them was the liberation of women."

"I always thought of women's liberation as taking place in the early seventies."

"Yes. You're right. But the war was the beginning. They couldn't put Eve back in the Garden of Eden after she'd tasted the apple."

Shelby looked again, more thoughtfully, at the images of young, high-spirited women in dungarees.

"Let me show you the weapons room," Gwen offered. "The little ones always get a kick out of this. We have a torpedo they can sit on for photos."

As they were looking at a display of battleship ammo, the music changed to a song Shelby vaguely recognized, "You'd Be So Nice to Come Home To."

"Dinah Shore," Gwen informed her before she asked.

"The lesbian golfer, Dinah Shore?"

Gwen laughed. "Dinah Shore wasn't a lesbian."

"No?" Shelby felt insecure under Gwen's wide smile of amusement.

"No. Definitely not. But she was a golfer. Not her claim to fame, though. You should look her up. Or ask your grandmother. She can tell you about Dinah Shore. While you're at it, why don't you ask her if she'd be interested in being interviewed? We could add her story to the Rosie project. We've got hundreds already, but every one is special. Every one gives a more complete picture. I'd do the interview myself. I can do it in the nursing home, even."

"Okay, I'll ask her."

They slowly made their way through the first floor, then Gwen led her up a sturdy wooden staircase with intricately carved balusters. Shelby paused, running her hand along the round handrail, admiring its smooth golden brown sheen, polished by innumerable gripping hands over time.

"Who are these guys?" she asked, indicating the staggered row of photographs on the stairwell wall. "All these distinguished looking male officers?"

"These are the base commanders over the years. Starting when the navy took over in nineteen thirty-six up to nineteen ninety-six when the base closed."

They took the stairs slowly as Shelby looked into the serious faces of the parade of military men. At the top of the stairs was a black-and-white image of a young man in civilian clothes standing in front of the museum building. *Daniel Hebberd, 1911*, she read. "Who's he?"

Gwen shrugged. "I don't know. These photos were here when I came. I never paid that much attention. But that was taken long before the military came. That may have been when the building was new."

The name Daniel Hebberd was vaguely familiar to Shelby, but she couldn't place it. She looked up to see Gwen waiting for her at the top of the stairs, grinning.

"Lesbian golfer!" Gwen snorted and shook her head.

"Well," Shelby said defensively, "the Dinah Shore Golf Tournament is notorious for being a big lesbian event."

"True. Your assumption's understandable, since you're way too young to know anything about her. So how do you know about the golf tournament?" Gwen seemed to be trying unsuccessfully to hide a self-satisfied smile. "Are you a golfer?"

Shelby couldn't suppress a brief giggle. "No." She turned away from Gwen to avoid revealing the blush she felt coming on. When she turned back, she saw Gwen observing her with a meaningful gaze and a slow nod. Apparently they now understood one another. Shelby felt distinctly fluttery to think Gwen might be interested in her. She tried to think of some clever, flirtatious remark to let her know the feeling was mutual, but her brain was mush. *She can probably tell anyway,* Shelby decided, *by how red my face is.*

"Come on," said Gwen, laying a hand on her shoulder, "let me introduce you to the gang and get you out of here before the kids arrive."

"Kids?"

"There's a busload of them scheduled for one o'clock. You know, a field trip. We get a lot of that."

"Oh, sure."

"Believe me, you don't want to be here when they are."

Gwen's hand lingered longer than necessary on Shelby's shoulder. She didn't mind. She gazed up at Gwen to give her an encouraging smile.

CHAPTER NINE

The writhing, screaming mass of fourth graders was now making its way up the stairs to the second floor, which heralded the arrival of Grady and Skipper on the first floor. Right on schedule, they stepped out of the elevator. Skipper appeared wide-eyed, as if she'd just escaped with her life. They both silently acknowledged Gwen as they collected themselves after their close call with disaster.

Grady was Skipper's contemporary, a heavyset man in his eighties, with droopy, sad-looking eyes and a fleshy, clean-shaven face. On his forearm was an ancient blue tattoo of a Hawaiian girl in a hula skirt and lei, some remnant of a youthful night's drinking, no doubt. The hula girl had stretched and sagged along with Grady, so at first glance she looked more like the Liberty Bell with an ivy vine around it than a beautiful dancing girl.

Like Skipper, Grady was a WWII vet and retired navy. Unlike her, he had not spent his life in the military. After four years, he had left the service and become a civil servant, working on the base as a supply specialist for the next thirty-five years. He knew the base better than any of them and had witnessed the changes it had gone through over the decades.

"I'll see you tomorrow," Grady called, moving quickly, relatively speaking, to the front door. "Gotta go visit a buddy in the hospital."

Gwen waved from her desk. Skipper trundled to the nearest chair and lowered herself with measured care.

Breathlessly and disapprovingly, she said, "Rusty's got those kids all worked up."

"He's got a knack for making history come alive for them."

She nodded, training her bright blue eyes on Gwen's monitor. "What're you working on?"

"My presentation for the city council."

Skipper wrinkled her nose in disgust. "Damn bureaucrats! I can't see what harm this place is doing anybody."

"From their point of view, the harm is in the revenue they aren't realizing from this property until they can tear down the building and sell it to a developer."

"Money! That's all anybody cares about!"

Skipper didn't know or care much about the money end of things. Her idea of accounting was adding up the take in the donation box. That's why Gwen was here. But she made sure Skipper understood their fragile hold on this building. There was no point leaving her in ignorance. She didn't want it to be a surprise when—if—the museum was shut down. So now the city council members, in Skipper's view, were the arch villains, as if they were all in an old-time melodrama where some hapless girl was tied to the railroad tracks and some dashing hero might swoop in at the last minute and save the day. No such hero was on the horizon for this place, though. Arguing for the survival of the museum was solely on Gwen's shoulders and she knew her case was thin.

"I'll do the best I can," Gwen promised.

"Oh, I know you will, honey. I know you will." Skipper patted her hand reassuringly.

"But I might not be able to persuade them to let us stay. If they decide not to renew your lease, you should be prepared to move the collection."

"Move it?" Skipper's pupils shrank into hard little dots.

This wasn't the first time they'd had this discussion. The threat to the building had been going on for over a year. But Skipper wasn't yet able to deal seriously with the idea, so Gwen had continued to remind her, trying to acclimate her over time, so she could survive the blow when it came.

"It should be right here," Skipper insisted, agitated. "Right here on the base. This is where everything happened. This is where it belongs."

"I'll be sure to make that argument. But, as you say, it all comes down to money, ultimately. Perhaps we'll find a couple of sympathetic council members who have a soft spot for history."

Skipper frowned, then tilted her head like a bird to listen to the multitude of tromping steps on the ceiling above them. When she looked back at Gwen, she was no longer frowning.

"That girl, what's-er-name," she said. "The one you brought around today. Friend of yours?"

"Shelby. Yes. Well, I just met her."

"Cute little thing, isn't she?" Skipper grinned and arched her white eyebrows suggestively. "Hey? Hey?"

"I think she's a just a smidgen young for you, Skipper."

"Ah!" Skipper rocked back in her chair gleefully. "Yes! Yes, just a smidgen. But just about perfect for you, isn't she?"

Just about perfect, Gwen thought, amused.

"Do you like her?" Skipper prodded.

Gwen shrugged. "I barely know her." She observed Skipper's expectant, twinkling eyes. "Yeah, I like her. She's very nice. Seems grounded and sensible."

"Uh-huh." Skipper nodded knowingly. "That's what always got me sweet on a girl, grounded and sensible."

"Your sarcasm is noted. Now I'm officially changing the subject. What do you think of this early summer weather?"

Skipper's mischievous grin remained. "I'd say it's gotten a lot hotter in here in the last couple hours."

Gwen sighed, then chuckled. "Okay. You're very observant."

The noise from the fourth graders increased suddenly as they hit the landing at the top of the stairs and a few of them started spilling down. That was Skipper's cue to hoist herself out of the chair.

"I'm going back up," she announced. "You've got the helm."

As Rusty came down with his raucous group, Skipper slipped into the elevator to disappear back upstairs. Gwen stood to greet the kids and give them their souvenir, a gold-colored eagle wrapped around an anchor. As soon as they got their pins, they all jumped up and down frantically in front of the adults, begging for someone to attach them.

Skipper didn't dislike children, but a teeming mass of them intimidated her. They were all in motion and mildly out of control. She worried they would knock her over, which wasn't an unrealistic fear. Rusty was bigger and more solid, much less inclined to teetering. If they ran into him, they just bounced off harmlessly.

Gwen and Rusty pinned the eagles on one by one, saluting each child in turn. And then the kids marched out in single file like good little sailors, leaving a thunderous silence in their wake.

"I don't think I got a single recruit out of that bunch," Rusty grumbled. "All of them were 4-Fs. Most of 'em are too short."

"Then it's a good thing we're in the history business and not the recruiting business, isn't it?"

"Roger that," he said. "Skipper topside?"

Gwen nodded. When Rusty had gone, she sat back down at her desk, breathing, "Peace, at last!"

She took the WWII journal from her desk drawer and opened to the page she'd marked with a strip of cloth. She also placed a notepad beside her to jot down any pertinent facts, details that might help her identify the journal's author. So far, the page contained just a few lines:

??, Driver for Captain Blanchard, b. 1923, New York, brother named Paul (Army)

Nettie (Annette), aviation machinist's mate, from San Francisco, Mill's College
Cora Dell, Alabama
Hazel, New Jersey, orphan
Chief Petty Officer Bricker
Barracks D

Gwen made these notes out of habit, following the procedure she normally used for genealogical research. She wasn't yet sure what she would do with this information, if anything. But the fact that the journal was anonymous created an automatic mystery that begged to be solved. It was the sort of puzzle she couldn't resist.

CHAPTER TEN

February 17, 1944.

We were all talking today at chow about how we decided to join up. For a lot of the girls, it was the lure of travel and adventure. These girls are the spirited ones. Leaving home was a big step for most of them. Me too. Before I went to basic training, I'd never been outside the state of New York. And here I am on the other side of the country!

How it started for me was with a dream like a lot of them. My grandfather was a fisherman with quite an imagination. He used to tell me and my brother the most incredible stories of his voyages, including tales of mermaids and sea monsters. To this day, I have no idea if there was a shred of truth to any of it, but as a kid I believed it all. In high school I read *The Odyssey* and found out that's where some of Grandpa's stories came from. Like the Sirens. I felt awfully cheated when I learned it was Ulysses and

ps at a time. Most of the workers there are women!
overalls with scarves on their heads, welding, riveting,
l, building the guts of those ships bolt by bolt. Even
crane operators are women. I've never seen anything
w they were recruiting women for factory work, just
let us join the navy, but to see it, to see thousands
re going about their business, all competent and
that was something! Holy mackerel!
l them Rosie the Riveters, like on the posters. "We
That's their motto. And they can, too!
e CO was at his meeting, I stood out in the yard by
atched the crews work. Just in that one hour, a huge
hull got lowered into place by a crane and the rivet
firing and the welding torches started sparking.
noisy!
at I've seen the WAVES do on base and what I've
ian women do at the shipyards, it makes me wonder
thing a woman can't do. There are things they
lo, like fight, but it's the women that are training
that now. One of our WAVES is giving the boys
n how to shoot a gun. If she can teach them to do
e able to do it herself. I know what they say, about
ce and all that. And that's all fine and dandy for a
vants that kind of life (like Cora Dell and Hazel),
t the rest of us, women like Nettie and me with a
nture? Why won't they let us do it? Like the poster
it. So why not let us?

1944.

written anything here for a while. I've been very
y duties. Captain Blanchard has expanded my
s to the office. He said he likes the idea of having a
girl in the front office instead of Yeoman Giannelli,
nt secretary, but a man. I still drive, but I'm doing
o now. I have to say I prefer the driving. I thought
y from getting coffee and taking dictation. But
r the navy needs me. I'd rather get coffee for the

not Grandpa who lashed himself to the mast of his ship so he
could listen to them sing.

I suppose that's how it got started, my dream of the sea. The
idea of a girl being a sailor, well, it wasn't possible. The closest
I was going to get was when my grandfather took me out in
his boat. My parents sent me to secretarial school because they
realized, I guess, I wasn't going to do the usual thing and get
married right after high school. I've never been very interested
in boys. Sometimes I listen to Cora Dell and just sit there
wondering why boys make her go bananas and I have no feelings
about them at all. What's it all about? Love, I mean. Nettie
thinks Cora Dell is a fool, but there are girls like her back home
too and I sometimes wished I was like them, that I could flip my
wig over some guy. Maybe not like Cora Dell, but at least like
Hazel. She's in love with her Andy. She never gives another boy
the time of day. There's just one boy in the world for her. He's
not bad looking and maybe he's a sweet fella, but why him? It's
such a mystery! Whatever makes a girl like a boy and a boy like
a girl, it's never happened to me.

So I dreamt of some other kind of life like sailing around
the world, but it was just another cockeyed dream like so many
of my ideas. A few months ago, I was on my way to being a
secretary, an ordinary, boring office gal who brought coffee and
took dictation, about as far as you could get from adventures on
the high seas.

Then the war broke out and everything changed, all of a
sudden. Women could join the navy! It was like all this happened
just for me, so I could become a sailor. That's how it felt to me. So
I signed up as soon as they'd let me, as soon as I turned twenty.

And here I am. I miss my family, but I can honestly say I've
never felt so alive as I do now. This is where I belong.

February 19, 1944.

Like usual most evenings, Nettie and I are at the service club
tonight. Nettie's playing cards with some women I barely know
from Barracks B. We decided against going to the film tonight,
since it was an old Three Stooges and neither of us likes them.

Cora Dell is in the dance hall with the boys. I'm sitting by myself, writing in my journal, drinking a bottle of pop. Nettie and her friends are all smoking cigarettes and drinking beer straight from the bottles with no glasses. Not very ladylike, that's what the hostess said. None of Nettie's friends look like they're trying to be very ladylike. Two of them even look like boys with their short haircuts and coarse ways about them. When they're in work clothes, from behind, you wouldn't know they were gals at all.

I've heard people talking about these women, about how you want to stay away from them, leave them to their own kind. Queer, that's what people say. Nettie doesn't seem to care about that. She seems to be having a good time and they seem okay to me too. Nettie's friends with everybody and everybody likes her. She doesn't listen to gossip. She doesn't spread it either, which is why I can't ask her if those women really are queer. But I'd like to ask. Just to know, just out of curiosity.

I never knew there were queer women until I joined the WAVES. I'm not what you'd call in the know about such things. But one of the first talks they gave us at Hunter College was about homosexuals, telling us to be on guard against them, to prevent ourselves from falling prey to their wiles and to make sure we reported any suspicious behavior immediately. They defined suspicious behavior as two women spending all their time together, seeming to like one another too much, and, of course, any kind of physical intimacy. I remember at the time wanting to ask the Chief what two women did in bed together, but, of course, I didn't ask. I wonder if Nettie knows. I'm sure she knows more than I do about anything like that, about sex, since I know nothing. I wonder if I could ask her. Even asking, though, might seem like "suspicious behavior."

Involvement with homosexuals would not only put a swift end to your navy career, CPO Rinaldi warned us, but it would also ruin your reputation and destroy your life. "If you're caught engaging in homosexual activity, no normal, decent person will ever again have anything to do with you." Women like that are wicked, she said, and they will try to seduce you by any means possible, to make you one of them. That's their goal, to turn innocent, normal women to their purposes, and once you

succumb, your life will spiral into
might never recover. "Depravity,'
sounds very serious.

Even if Nettie's friends are hon
seem more interested in getting a
seducing anybody.

The idea of queer women is c
since hearing that lecture in basic.
live their lives without men, with
they happy? Can you be happy livin
Rinaldi didn't think so.

February 26, 1944.

I'm taking a few minutes to wri
the sack. Hazel's radio is on and al
to "Your Hit Parade." Cora Dell
letter she's writing because Fran
Low" and she's crazy about him. I
them. Men, that is. Her mouth is c
at the radio with a kind of dreamy
right at him.

Hazel's sitting on her bunk
Nettie's lying on her back with h
just looked over the edge of my b
Nothing. She winked at me and wh
doesn't come on that squawk box."

We both know what'll happen
scream and say, "Couldn't you just d
Nettie ragged her with, "What're
Cooper's twice as handsome as Nels
fell open in disbelief and she said,
Nettie kept a straight face through
that followed. So this is a typical
D. But my day was not so typical. I
fact.

Today was the first time I dro
Richmond shipyards. The place i

bunch of s
Women in
working st
some of th
like it. I kr
like they'v
of them t
determine

They
Can Do It

While
the car and
section of
guns start
That place

With
seen the ci
if there's
won't let
the men t
their cour
it, she mu
a woman'
woman w
but what
thirst for
says, we ca

Marcl

I have
busy witl
responsib
good-lool
who's an
clerical w
I'd gotten
I'll go wh

captain than some insurance agent or banker. It makes me laugh, though, to think that carrying a cup of Joe is how I'm helping to win the war. Chief Bricker has reminded us on many occasions that if we were not here doing our duty, which does include getting coffee, then an able-bodied man would be doing it and that'd be one less sailor manning his station, maybe even firing the shell that sinks a German U-boat. So that's what I think about when I'm pouring that cup or typing a memo.

Nettie and I've been going off base a lot whenever we're off duty. We go dancing, to movies or bowling. Nettie's such a hotshot bowler. We're going to start a WAVES league and she's going to handpick only the best for her team. She said she's going to pick me, of course. First choice. Nettie's my best friend here. She's a real swell gal!

Though I'm with her every day, there's a lot about her I don't know. And things I don't understand. It was her mother's fiftieth birthday yesterday. She said there was probably a big shindig for that. She seemed down in the dumps when she mentioned it and then spent most of the day drinking beer. I said they probably would've invited her if they'd known where to send the invitation. I thought she should at least call and tell her mother happy birthday. But she said her mother wouldn't want to hear from her.

"Why not?" I asked her, unbelieving.

She wouldn't explain. By then she was so drunk she could barely walk, so I helped her back to our room and her bunk. Sometimes she drinks too much, which I don't like to see because she's kind of mean when she's drunk. As long as you don't bother her, it's no big thing, but if you even ask her for a light, she's likely to say, "Drop dead!" when she's like that. So when she comes in loaded, the rest of us know to keep our distance.

I'm beginning to think she did something bad to be so cut off from her family, something she thinks is unforgivable. The way she looks so miserable whenever she talks about her parents, it nearly brings me to tears. But I can't believe she did something that bad, so bad that her mother wouldn't forgive her. Whatever it was, I'm sure it wasn't her fault. I wish I could think of some way to help.

March 19, 1944.

It's Sunday and I'm lying on my bunk recovering from last night. I've got a roaring headache. Nettie's gone out sailing with some friends. I'm surprised she's up and about at all today because she drank even more than I did. She seems fine, though. She even brought me a cup of Joe earlier. I guess she's more used to it than I am. I wasn't able to make it to breakfast. The room was spinning. I'm finally feeling recovered enough to sit up, but I can tell it's going to be awhile before anybody's going to see me in the chow line.

We went bowling in Oakland last night with some friends of Nettie's, Pug and Vera. Nettie knows people, civilians, in the area because she's lived here all her life. I'm sure Pug is a nickname. She does have a bit of a pug nose, but I didn't really want to call her that, so I didn't call her anything. Pug looks like a boy. She's small-breasted, slim-hipped and has a boy's haircut. Her complexion's the color of coffee with cream and her eyes are dark and exotic. She wore men's clothes and I couldn't stop looking at her, watching the way she walked, moved and the way she attended to Vera. Vera's a very feminine, round, curvy girl with long golden curls and puckery red lips. By the time we were done bowling, I'd figured out they were a couple.

Nettie and Pug act like old friends. They spent the evening joking around like true-blue buddies. Nettie said they went to college together.

We had beers at the bowling alley and then we went to their place. They room together in a ground level, two-bedroom apartment with another girl named June. She was there too. She was wearing a straight skirt and a tight pink sweater. I swear she looked just like Lana Turner in those pinups the boys have. Her face isn't as beautiful as Lana's, but she can fill out a sweater just as well. She was kind of a chatterbox, though, and I figured Nettie wouldn't want to be around her because of that.

Pug and Vera had a record player and a swell collection of records. We moved the furniture out of the middle of the living room so we could dance. After a couple hours and a few whiskey sours, I wasn't able to dance anymore. Nobody was. Vera and

Pug were standing in the middle of the room, slow dancing to "There'll Be Bluebirds Over the White Cliffs of Dover." They weren't really dancing. They were just hanging on one another and swaying. I could reach the record player from my chair, so when the record ended, I swung the arm back to the edge and started it up again.

Nettie was sitting in an easy chair, her jacket and shoes off, smoking a cigarette, when June came along and sat right in her lap. By then, that same record was on its third time around. June took Nettie's cigarette and took a drag from it, then they just sat there staring at each other like they were statues. Finally June leaned down and kissed Nettie right on the lips. If I'd been less drunk, I might have made some kind of noise or fallen out of my chair. But I just stared. Neither one of them was paying any attention to me.

Nettie pulled June closer and kissed her again, and they just kept at it, really romantic kisses like Humphrey Bogart and Ingrid Bergman in *Casablanca*. Strangely enough, it didn't strike me at the time as odd in any way, not even when Nettie felt June through her sweater. June arched her back and moaned while Nettie caressed her.

Then I watched Nettie's hand slide under June's skirt, up along her thigh. I felt so strange. I was hot, so hot I could barely breathe. June lay against Nettie with her eyes closed and her mouth open. I couldn't see Nettie's hand, but I knew what she was doing. Maybe not exactly, but I had a good idea.

I was so caught up watching Nettie and June I didn't notice the record was over again. All that was playing was the click-click-click of the needle. Vera and Pug kept dancing anyway as I watched two women, one of them my best friend, doing something I'd been taught was unnatural and disgusting. But it didn't seem that way to me. It was tender and lovely and they both seemed to enjoy it. When it was over, June lay on Nettie's chest, nuzzling under her chin while Nettie stroked her hair and puffed on a fresh cigarette.

It was just about then I passed out. I don't know what happened after that, but Hazel said we got back to the barracks at "oh-dark-thirty" and she and Nettie somehow got me up to my bunk.

Lying here this morning, I've been thinking about what happened last night. I feel like I understand a lot more about Nettie now.

Chief Rinaldi made homosexual women seem scary and cruel. But Nettie's nothing like that. Those were scare tactics, exaggerations. I think I know now why Nettie doesn't get along with her family. A lonely life, that's what the chief said.

From now on, I have to remember to hide this journal whenever I'm out of the room. What Nettie did last night, if anybody else knew, would get her kicked out for sure. It's good to know she trusts me.

I feel lousy. If it was Monday, I'd be on the binnacle list for sure. Fortunately, I can lie here in my bunk all day if I want. And I do.

CHAPTER ELEVEN

Gwen sat in a pool of light from the desk lamp, the journal open in front of her. Whoever this woman had been, she was providing a riveting view of a military woman's life in 1944. That her best friend was a lesbian was the cherry on top. No surprise there were lesbians in the WAVES, but she was surprised to find someone writing so frankly about them. And so sympathetically.

The elevator started humming. She waited for the doors to open, realizing she hadn't been paying attention to the comings and goings of the old folks and didn't know who was still in the building. It was Rusty.

"You still here?" he asked. "You should be getting on home."

"You're right. What about you? Why are you still here?"

He grimaced and said, "Fell asleep. Now my back's going to be out of whack for a week."

Gwen glanced at the fifties-style starburst clock above the door. "Sorry I didn't wake you. I've been so caught up in what I was doing, I lost track of time. I'll be out of here in a minute."

After Rusty had gone, Gwen packed a few things in her satchel, including the journal, deciding to take it home. She felt odd, distracted, so drawn into the story she was reading. She was beginning to feel like she knew this young woman and wanted more than ever to know her name. She also wanted to know how Nettie fared as a lesbian in the WAVES. Gwen knew how ruthless the military, and the world in general, could be for lesbians in those days. The lecture Chief Rinaldi had given them was an accurate representation of the public perception, and this woman was right to keep her journal hidden if she wanted to protect her friend.

Just as Gwen reached for the doorknob, the phone rang. She hesitated, then decided to grab it.

"Hi," said the voice on the other end. "This is Shelby."

"Oh, hi. You just caught me."

"I wasn't sure what time you left." Shelby sounded unsure of herself.

"We usually close at four thirty, so this is late for me. What's up?"

"I just got hungry and I was wondering—I mean, if you don't have anything planned—would you like to get something to eat?"

Gwen caught her breath, hesitating while she overcame her astonishment. "Oh, yeah, sure. I'd like that...a lot."

"Great. Do you know Ollie's Diner?"

"I do, yeah. I can be there in fifteen minutes."

"Awesome!" Shelby sounded relieved. "Bye."

Gwen hung up, smiling to herself. *How about that*, she thought. *That sweet little girl just asked me out on a date.*

Ollie's Diner was an Alameda mainstay, an old-time lunch

counter, now a local favorite any time of day. Gwen and Shelby sat in a booth on red vinyl seats, eating cheeseburgers and fries under bright lights.

"I really like this place," Shelby said.

"Me too. It suits me better than Cibo."

"The view isn't as good," Shelby pointed out, nodding toward the unobstructed view of the car wash across the street.

"Oh, I don't know about that." Gwen held Shelby's gaze. "I'd say the view is charming."

Shelby smiled with just a hint of embarrassment.

"Are you having a party or anything for graduation?" Gwen asked.

"No big deal. After the ceremony, we're having a family thing at my mom's house. Just my brother, parents and my aunt and cousins. It'll be a little awkward because my parents are divorced and my dad is bringing his girlfriend Bonnie."

"That will upset your mother?"

"Everything upsets my mother." Shelby laughed lightly. "I shouldn't say that. Divorce is a hard thing to deal with. She has every right to be upset. But my father seems to be thriving."

"Your father the architect," Gwen said, picking up her soda glass, "builder of parking garages."

"And office buildings," Shelby added.

"Speaking of buildings, what do you think of this one?"

"I love it. Classic American diner, built in nineteen fifty-one. And their hamburgers aren't bad either. I've been eating here since I was a tiny kid. It makes me feel good to see a place like this still here, still the same."

"It is nice to have some things that don't change," agreed Gwen. "It's comforting."

Shelby nodded. "Whenever my dad's company builds something in San Francisco, they have to tear something down first. I mean, there's no bare land left in the city. I know there are a lot of old buildings that can't be saved and maybe aren't worth saving, but they all have something interesting about them. If not architecturally, then at least historically. They've endured through time and collected stories. I always hate to see a building go down."

"You have a soft spot for buildings." Gwen shook some ketchup onto her fries. "That's sweet."

"It may be more of a liability than sweet for an architect. My dad, for instance, loves to see old buildings demolished. He likes replacing them with clean, efficient, high-tech, earthquake-proof new ones."

"Also a valid point of view, especially for someone in the business of designing new buildings."

Gwen took a bite of her burger, letting the juice drip out the back end into her plate. She glanced at Shelby, whose mouth was full. She smiled self-consciously.

"The city wants to tear down the museum building," Gwen said after swallowing.

"No way!"

"All part of the redevelopment. They want all the old stuff gone to make way for a shiny new planned community. Unless I can persuade them to change their minds, the museum will be history in a couple years when the current lease is up."

"That's terrible."

Gwen nodded. "That's really my main goal there right now, to save the place. At least, that's how I see it. I also have to keep it going, raise money, do the accounts. But what it needs more than anything is a dedicated advocate to stand up against people like your dad who can envision better uses for the land."

"Good luck. I hope you're successful, but in these cases, it seems people like my dad usually win."

"I won't be surprised." Gwen took another bite of her burger, watching Shelby with interest and amusing herself remembering their exchange about golf from earlier in the day.

"How'd you get that job anyway?" Shelby asked.

Gwen put down her burger. "It evolved out of the Rosie the Riveter project, the interviews I told you about. That was when they first started the national park, the memorial and all that over in Richmond."

"The oral history project," Shelby confirmed.

"Have you ever been to that park?" Gwen asked.

"I've been past it, but never stopped to check it out."

"You should. It's very moving."

"I will. I'm just beginning to realize what an impact that war had on everyone who lived through it."

"Exactly. That's what I noticed right away when I started the interviews. Everyone, absolutely everyone, was involved on a daily basis. It's like nothing we've lived through."

Shelby nodded, ignoring her food. "When I was a kid and heard about my grandmother being a welder in the war, I didn't think much about what it meant, what it must have been like for her. Honestly, I never thought that much about her life as a young person. She was just my Nana. Like she didn't have a life before I was born."

"You were a child. That's how children think."

"I guess so." Shelby looked serious and thoughtful.

No, she is not a ditz, Gwen thought, speaking to Melissa in her mind.

"Anyway," Gwen explained, "to answer your question, working on the Rosie interviews, I spent a lot of time at the museum with the files. That crew you met today, none of them want to run the place. They just want somebody, anybody, to run it. Skipper may be the vision behind the museum, but she's no businesswoman. She latched onto me as someone who was interested in the history and practical enough to take care of the business side of things. Before I knew it, I was over there all the time, organizing things, doing the books, even opening the place up in the morning and closing up at night. All volunteer stuff. Eventually, Skipper started cutting me a paycheck and before I knew it, it was my job. But I love it. I just love all the stories."

"That's what history is, right? Stories."

"Yes. Exactly. And every person who has ever lived has one. Like your grandmother."

Shelby looked pensive. "I wonder if the war changed her. Liberated from innocence and all that like you were saying earlier."

"What'd she do after the war?"

"She went back to being a homemaker. Grandpa came home and they had kids."

"Like the majority of them."

"Then she divorced him."

"Oh? When?"

"In the early sixties."

"Well, that was ballsy."

"I guess it was…back then. She went to work in a medical office. Then, later, she went to college and became a pharmacist. I'm pretty sure it was early seventies when she graduated pharmacy school."

Impressed, Gwen nodded. "Quite an accomplishment."

"Yes! You're right."

"I hope she wants to be part of the Rosie project. It sounds like her story would be an awesome contribution."

Shelby sucked the last of her Coke through a straw, carefully stopping at the point right before the sucking sound would start. She set her glass down and grinned triumphantly across the table.

"You're cute," Gwen said.

Shelby blushed. "Thanks."

Gwen then sucked up everything in the bottom of her glass, going well beyond the start of the sucking sound. When Shelby started laughing, Gwen let off her straw. Shelby had an easy laugh—easily provoked and easy on the ears.

"You're cute too," she said.

The waitress appeared and took Shelby's plate, leaving the bill.

Gwen finished her hamburger while gazing across the table, taking in Shelby's features, thinking how nice she was to look at…and how nice she'd be to touch. It had been a long time since she'd had the pleasure of that particular anticipation—first embrace, first kiss, first— *Ah*, Gwen thought, shaking herself gently, *I'm getting way ahead of myself.*

She barely knew this girl. But there was something about her that made it seem like it would be the simplest thing in the world to take hold of her small, graceful hand. Gwen willed her own ungainly hand to move toward Shelby's across the table, coming within an inch of her when a phone rang. Gwen pulled her hand back as Shelby grabbed for her phone and glanced at it.

"It's my mom. Sorry. I should answer this." She jumped up and went outside.

Gwen watched through the window while Shelby stood on the sidewalk talking calmly on the phone, her free hand shoved in her front pocket, her expression neutral. The call was over quickly and she returned with an apologetic smile.

"Is your grandmother okay?" Gwen asked.

"Yeah, she's fine. My mom's at Nana's house looking for some papers. I need to go help her. I've been organizing, so I know where everything is. Sorry."

Gwen nodded, standing. "No problem. Thanks for asking me out."

"You're welcome. I really enjoyed it."

"See you soon, I hope."

Shelby reached out to hug Gwen warmly. "I'll ask my grandmother about the interview," she promised before slipping out the door.

Gwen returned to her chair, realizing that first kiss wasn't going to happen tonight, as she had hoped. She tipped up the ketchup bottle over the few remaining fries in her plate, waiting for the sluggish red stream to emerge.

The thing about anticipation, she thought, was that the longer you waited for something, the sweeter the reward when it finally did come.

CHAPTER TWELVE

April 1, 1944.

Nettie and I went to San Francisco again today. We walked down the Embarcadero in the sunshine, arm in arm. It was such a glorious day—gay and festive. There were so many sailors in town, getting off ships or about to get on. Some of them saying hello and some of them saying goodbye. Lots of tears down there at the port. Lots of sweethearts kissing.

We stopped to get a hotdog from a street vendor. When we finished that, we shared a cigarette and were minding our own business when a couple of sailors on skirt patrol came up to us and started flirting. Both of them were second classmen, same as Nettie.

"Look out, Joe!" said the uglier of the two. "The WAVES are in and they're cookin' with the gas on." He had a nose like Jimmy Durante—huge—and he walked like he thought he was really something, his upper torso thrown back so his legs led the way.

"Hi, kitten," said the other one, looking at me, "what's knittin'?" He was thin, slack, a pale boy with round, surprised looking eyes.

"Take a hike," Nettie said dismissively.

We walked away, but they followed, bouncing around like puppies behind us.

Then the first guy said, "Do you think they're trying to give us the brush-off?"

"Naw," said his buddy. "They're just playing hard to get."

Durante-nose ran around in front of us. "Hey, girls, I've got a wad of smackers and nobody to spend them on." He pulled a stack of bills out of his pocket and flashed it in front of us, making like a hotshot. "Latch your lashes on this and give us a kiss."

The sailors were obviously drunk and Nettie was getting angry, so not a good combination.

"I said beat it!" she told them again, making a fierce face at them.

"Hey, don't snap your cap, sweetheart." Durante-nose stepped up to her face, then, and said, "What's with the slacks, Jack? Are you a dame or aren't ya?"

I could tell by the way her eyes were getting smaller that Nettie was about to get very serious. "You boys hit the road or I'm calling the SPs. You got it?"

Durante-nose stared at his friend, pretending to be afraid, then he turned back to Nettie and said, "Look here, doll face, all I want's a little smoocheroo. Ease up on the throttle."

The expression on her face must have finally convinced him she was steamed, so he turned his attention to me, giving me a wide-open smile. "How about you, sugar? You like the looks of this mug?"

Then he made a big mistake. He grabbed me and tried to kiss me, the smell of stale whiskey all over him. I pushed against him and turned my head sideways, so I didn't see what happened next. But all of a sudden he was gone and I was pushing against thin air. When I looked back, Nettie had him by the front of his jacket, pulled up straight on his tiptoes, his arms dangling at his sides. Her expression was fearsome. She held him like that for a few seconds, then she let go. As his feet landed flat on the ground, she hauled off with her right fist and popped him square on the jaw.

Nettie's as strong as most men and she knows how to fight. Nobody who knows her would ever pick a fight with her. That sailor went flying sideways and was down on the ground before he had time to blink. While his buddy ran over to check on him, Nettie grabbed my arm and pulled me away.

"Let's get out of here," she said, "before *they* call the SPs."

I was laughing out of control by the time we were out of sight of those guys. Nettie led me off the main street and through a loading dock area behind a tin building. When we finally stopped, she started laughing too. Then she checked her knuckles to see if her hand was okay.

"Does it hurt?" I asked, taking her hand in mine.

"It does, but I think it'll be okay."

I kissed her knuckles gently. We both stopped laughing. Nettie's hand rested in mine between us. I tightened my fingers around it and she did the same, moving closer, both of us looking silently into one another's faces.

"Is June your sweetheart?" I asked, voicing a question I'd kept to myself for two weeks.

"Naw," she answered quietly. "I don't have a sweetheart."

She took hold of my other hand and pulled them both up against her chest, under her open coat. I could feel her heart thumping under my hands, thumping from running away from the sailors, but it wasn't slowing down. I knew that when I looked up to meet her eyes, she would kiss me. I think she'd been wanting to for a while. And I'd been wanting her to ever since I saw her kiss another woman and knew it was possible.

She took off her hat and pulled her coat around us both so anybody passing by would think we were just another couple saying hello or goodbye. We stood by that tin building kissing one another for a long time. Her mouth was so warm and soft and smart, reaching down inside me, moving me like the moon moves the tide. Nobody's ever kissed me like that. I felt like I was floating or drowning. Something to do with water anyway. I can't describe what it felt like. But it felt good and I didn't ever want to stop.

April 7, 1944.

I couldn't wait to be alone with Nettie again after our day in Frisco, but it isn't easy to be alone on base. We have managed to steal a few kisses in our room while the others are out using the head or late coming in from work. But Hazel never goes out in the evenings. After chow, she lies on her bunk reading her mysteries.

The more Nettie touched me, the more I wanted her to touch me. I wanted her to touch me like she did June. She wanted it too, but until tonight there was no opportunity.

This evening I took my shower later than usual. It must have been after ten. I was the only one in the shower room and was nearly done when I heard the outer door open. I didn't pay any attention. I figured it was just another one of the women coming in for a shower. Though the men have to shower together in one big, open space, the navy has designed the women's showers with privacy booths. I never knew how much I appreciated that until tonight. My stall door opened and there was Nettie, wearing a towel. She touched her finger to her lips, removed her towel and stepped inside.

We'd seen each other naked before. We dress in front of one another every day. But there was something different about this. Her body seemed completely new to me. It was strong and soft at the same time as she took me in her arms and pressed herself against me, the warm water encasing us like a protective screen. Her skin felt like silk under my fingers. Her mouth took my tides in and out like before while her hands caressed me, touching me in ways I only poorly imagined before this.

What she did to me, it was like magic. I didn't know my body had feelings like that. What a surprising and marvelous thing to discover.

When we finally came back to the room, Hazel took a look at us with our wet hair and said, "Where've you two been?"

"Shower," Nettie said. "What's it look like?"

"It's nearly midnight," Hazel pointed out. "That's some Hollywood shower!"

The look of suspicion she gave us reminded me how easy it would be to trigger a rumor. But at that moment I didn't care. All I wanted was to lie down, close my eyes and remember Nettie's hands on my bare skin and how my stomach had flip-flopped when she pressed her tender, feminine flesh against mine.

April 24, 1944.

Nettie's friends Vera and Pug gave her a key to their apartment. We've been going there as often as we can. We leave the base separately and head off in different directions so the SPs won't suspect we're going somewhere together. Once I give them the slip, I get a bus to the apartment. After we make love, we return to the base the same way, separately.

It's very hard to be sleeping in the bunk above Nettie night after night when I want to be in her arms. But Hazel and Cora Dell are just a few feet away.

I didn't know it could be like this with another woman. Nettie says she loves me. Maybe she does. I don't know how I feel about it, exactly. It's wonderful and horrible all at the same time. Being with Nettie feels wonderful. Sneaking around and pretending is hard. But it would be a disaster if anybody else knew. Nobody can know about this.

April 30, 1944.

Cora Dell is pregnant. She broke down and told Chief Bricker yesterday. People were suspecting anyway because of the way she was getting sick so much and refusing to go to the infirmary. We have no idea who the father is. Nobody's telling us anything. Everybody's quiet and sad today. They're sending her home, of course.

I have to admit it's made me scared. If you break the rules, you're out. That's just the way it is. Obviously, Nettie and I are breaking one of the biggest rules.

You hear stories—women being beaten up, even killed for doing what Nettie and I've been doing. I keep remembering what Chief Rinaldi said: *If you're involved in even one incident of sexual perversity with another woman, you'll be out of the navy so fast your head will spin.* The worst thing, though, worse than being discharged, maybe worse than being killed, is how they say you'll end up, alone and despised by everyone, an outcast with no family and no friends. I know this is true because of Nettie, because of how she has no contact with her family. Everyone will know too because of the undesirable discharge. It will follow you all your life like the mark of Cain. That's what Chief Rinaldi said.

"Maybe we should stop," I suggested to Nettie this morning. "You know what would happen to us to if anybody knew." I sat beside Nettie on her bunk, holding her hand.

"You don't really want to stop, do you?" she asked.

I was torn. I just looked at her and didn't answer. She touched my cheek gently, then kissed me. Then she was kissing my neck and her hands were hot on my back as she lowered me to the bunk. I pushed her away.

"Not here. We can't."

"Hazel won't be back for a half hour at least," she said. "Plenty of time for a little necking."

"No. Not here. It's too dangerous."

"Tonight, then. Come to the apartment." Nettie's eyes flashed with hunger.

"I don't know. Hazel's already suspicious. All these nights we spend out together."

"Hazel won't tell. We can trust her."

"Maybe so. But you know what they say. You can't keep secrets from your shipmates."

Nettie looked troubled. "Don't you want to be with me?"

"Yes, of course I do." I kissed her to reassure her, trying to calm my own doubts. "Tonight, then. But let's not stay out too late this time."

The fear of discovery, the constant looking over my shoulder and searching the faces of everyone around me for suspicion, is weighing me down. It's taking away my joy and my desire. Maybe it isn't worth the risk. Cora Dell's empty bunk is a constant reminder of what happens when you break the rules.

May 12, 1944.

Nettie's been so angry she hasn't said a word to me the last couple days. That really hurts. I tried to explain to her. I thought she'd understand because she's serious about her career, like me. It's not that I don't love you, I told her. It's just too dangerous. She said if I loved her, I'd be willing to take the risk, that nothing would be able to keep us apart. I didn't know what to say to that.

Now she's lying in her bunk below me like a corpse. When I leaned my head over and said good night, she didn't move, didn't even look at me. Last night about three in the morning when I was sound asleep she hauled off and kicked my bunk as hard as she could. I nearly flew right out of it. I hope it made her feel better.

I feel just awful.

June 2, 1944.

Captain Blanchard has put in for a promotion for me. He thinks I'm doing a swell job and I'm ready to be a second classman. I'm flying high today and can't wait to tell my folks. I invited all the girls down to Flanagan's for drinks. When you're buying, everybody's your friend. So we had a big crowd. Nettie came too. She's friendlier now than she was for a while. She let me buy her a drink. I wouldn't want her to have a grudge against me. I think maybe she's feeling better about everything because of Gina. She's a new girl, transferred from San Diego, machinist's mate, third class, in the repair shop, so she works with Nettie. Nettie's been showing her the ropes and they seem to have gotten close. Gina's a knockout. I'm not surprised Nettie's falling for her. It makes me a little sad to see them together, but I'm trying to be happy for them.

We all had a great time tonight at Flanagan's. We played the jukebox for hours and danced with some boys who came in. Danced with each other too. Nettie even asked me to dance once. So I guess she's over being mad at me. I'm over the moon about that. It was lousy having her sore at me.

It was a good night. Now I'm gonna get some shut-eye.

June 6, 1944.

We all sat around the radio, listening as reports came in throughout the day of a major Allied offensive into France. We've been waiting for such an invasion, hoping for it, but the thought of so many men being killed and wounded has left us full of fear. Every one of us has some relative or friend serving overseas.

Just yesterday we had the thrilling news of the liberation of Rome. There was lots of celebrating last night and now this. It seems we're moving forward now, fast and furious, so everyone's tense with mixed feelings, thrilled and horrified at the same time. If we, who are so far removed from battle, have such conflicted emotions, I can't guess what it must be like for the men at the front.

This evening, as a big crowd of us gathered around the speakers in the service club, the president made an announcement, asking all Americans to pray with him. Of course we did pray, all of us, bowing our heads all together, completely silent, while Mr. Roosevelt spoke in his clear, unhurried voice about the brave men storming the coast of France. "Some will never return," he said, and I felt a chill at the back of my neck. "Embrace these, Father, and receive them, Thy heroic servants, into Thy kingdom."

I kept thinking about my brother Paul, wondering where he was and if he was unlucky enough to be part of this invasion. At the end of his prayer, Mr. Roosevelt said, "Amen," and a reverent chorus of echoed amens sounded through the crowd of sailors around me.

June 9, 1944.

I drove Captain Blanchard over to the shipyards this morning. They were christening a ship at sunrise. The shipyard band was playing and they had a singer there too. It was a big shindig.

We got back around two in the afternoon. Because we'd had to go over so early, the CO let me knock off early. I was looking forward to having my home sweet home to myself for a couple hours before the other girls got back from their duty shift. Hazel had loaned me *The Lady in the Lake*, the latest Philip Marlowe detective novel, which she'd barely been able to put down for a minute until she finished it.

My dogs were killing me, so I kicked off my shoes as soon as I got in the building and carried them to the room in my stocking feet, hoping Bricker wasn't around to put me on report. Bricker will put you on report if you've got an eyebrow hair out of place.

I was trying to be quiet slipping into the room, which is why Nettie and Gina didn't hear me come in, I'm sure. They were on the bottom bunk, both of them naked from the waist down. Nettie was on top, moving against Gina, who had her eyes closed and was moaning, her arms locked around Nettie's broad back. I was so surprised I just stood there, frozen in place, watching.

Finally, I decided to back out. As I took my first step, Nettie turned her head and saw me. She didn't say anything and she didn't stop what she was doing. She just watched me coolly as I silently left the room. When my thoughts cleared a little, I kept thinking how lucky they were it was me who had happened on them and not somebody else. That was such a dangerous thing to do, I thought, still in shock.

I slipped my shoes back on and went over to the service club for a snack. When I came back, they were gone. I found out from another girl at mess tonight that Gina had gotten sick at work and Nettie had offered to take her back to her room. Apparently that was a ruse they'd cooked up to be alone. There's no way they could have known I'd knock off early. But it was still a reckless thing to do.

Tonight, Nettie acted the same as usual, like nothing had happened. So I did too. We all went to the club to dance and have a few drinks. Nettie seemed to be in a wonderful mood. She bought all us Barracks D girls a drink, including me. I'd say she's definitely over me.

June 10, 1944.

A new recruit showed up today to take Cora Dell's place in our room. Her name's Maria. She's from Arizona. She's small and shy, very quiet with large, deep eyes and long black hair she wears wound up in a bun. She'll talk when you ask her a question, but she doesn't go much beyond a simple answer. Nettie barely says a word that isn't necessary and Hazel has her nose in a book most of the time, so our room has gotten really quiet with Cora Dell gone. As irritating as she seemed before, I miss her now. I guess she was the glue that knit our little group together.

June 14, 1944.

Today was a bad day. It started early in the morning when two Shore Patrol officers came into our barracks and put Nettie under arrest. As she was being led out, she looked back and stared hard at me, right into my eyes, accusing.

I wanted to tell her I didn't say anything. I wouldn't say anything. It wasn't me. But, of course, I couldn't say a word with the SPs there. Gina was arrested at the same time in the same way in her own room. This afternoon, someone came and cleared out Nettie's belongings. Nobody told us anything. The rest of the day everyone was whispering and speculating, and some of the others have guessed correctly what's behind this. They've gotten the feeling, even if they haven't seen anything suspicious, for what kind of friendship Nettie and Gina have.

I just keep thinking about the way Nettie looked at me when she left, how she must think I was the one who ratted on her. As I sat at my desk typing today, I kept looking up every time the door opened, thinking they'd be coming for me next. I was so nervous I jumped every time the typewriter dinged at the end of a line. My heart was in my throat all day.

I don't know where they took Nettie. People are speculating the brig. Or maybe she was turned over to ONI for questioning. I hope she's okay. I feel miserable.

June 16, 1944.

Nobody's heard a word about Nettie or Gina. It seems like they just disappeared into thin air. I finally asked the chief about it. "Mind your duties, seaman," she said. That was all.

This episode has really shaken me. For the first time since I enlisted, I'm feeling truly homesick.

I think I'll write a letter to the folks before I turn in tonight.

CHAPTER THIRTEEN

Looking at herself in the mirror, Shelby thought she looked both dorky and impressive in her cap and gown. The school colors, black and red, created a bold contrast. She tilted the cap slightly and gauged the effect in the mirror. The silken tassel hung down on the right. She reached up and flipped it over to the left side, practicing.

When the doorbell rang, she briefly considered throwing off the gown, but then changed her mind and went through to the living room. The door swung open before she reached it to reveal her mother, who smiled in delighted surprise from behind unfashionably large sunglasses, her keys in her hand.

"Oh, my God!" Vivian cried. "Look at you!"

She embraced Shelby tightly, shaking her a bit before letting go. Then she stepped inside, removed her sunglasses and stood gawking for a moment while Oscar made fast and tight circles around her legs. She'd had her hair done for the graduation, Shelby noticed, but hadn't had it colored this time. Vivian's thick head of wavy hair was almost completely gray, a gunpowder shade that suited her complexion. Shelby was glad her mother wasn't a platinum blond or ash brown today. At her age, a full complement of gray hair was a flattering blessing. It looked right.

"I'm so proud of you," Vivian enthused, then headed rapidly toward the kitchen.

Shelby followed, the fabric of her gown swishing against the denim of her jeans underneath. "What are you doing here, Mom?"

"I'm going to visit your grandmother. I thought I'd take her some things. Something to remind her of home. I got them to put up a little shelf, a curio shelf, you know. So now I need some curios."

Vivian stopped short and stood staring at the kitchen table. It was covered with a collection of Scotch tape dispensers with their signature red and green plaid inserts. There were twenty-seven of them in various stages of use, running the gamut from brand new to totally empty with everything in between. Shelby knew, in fact, that there were three empty dispensers and nine so new the little plaid tab was still in place at the start of the roll.

On the other side of the table was a cardboard box full of safety pins, all sizes, gold and silver, that Shelby had not counted. But out of curiosity, she'd weighed the box. Three pounds, five ounces.

"Need some tape?" she joked.

"What is this?" Vivian sputtered.

"I found these around the house. I've also got a monster pile of paper clips and those bread wrapper plastic thingies. Right now, I'm just putting everything together, sort of an inventory. Gathering all the like items together. I haven't started throwing anything out yet."

"I don't understand. Where'd you get this stuff?"

"All over the house. In drawers, in shoe boxes, sitting on shelves and windowsills."

"But why would she need all these rolls of tape?"

"I don't know. I think maybe she just bought them when she was in the store, if they were on sale or something. Maybe she didn't realize how many she already had. I found one roll in a paper sack in the sewing basket with the receipt still in the bag. It was from four years ago."

Vivian scratched her head. "Well, I know this house is cluttered, but—"

"You wouldn't really see it unless you started pooling them like this. I can sort of understand the tape, but the plastic tabs from the bread sacks, I don't get that at all. Why would she keep those?"

"She probably thought they were useful."

"I found this in the oven." Shelby pointed to a coffee can on the counter. "It's full of grease. I think it's bacon grease."

"I didn't know she'd started saving that again."

"Again?"

"She used to always save bacon grease, but I hadn't seen her do that for decades. That was something people used to do. It got to be common practice during the war for everybody. You saved all your cooking fat and took it to the meat market to turn in, for the war effort."

"Really?"

"They recycled all kinds of stuff then. People went through their attics and basements looking for anything to turn in, any metal or rubber. Practically everything was in short supply. But even my grandmother saved bacon grease, long before the war. It was just something people did. They cooked everything in bacon grease, like fried potatoes." Vivian's face lit up. "Potatoes fried in bacon grease in a cast iron skillet. You can't beat that!"

Shelby laughed. "That's a big can of grease. I'd say she's been accumulating it for a while."

"People who lived through the Depression and the war do stuff like that. Cathy was telling me awhile back that her mother never throws away Zip-Loc bags. She washes them and dries them and then puts them in a drawer to reuse. She even uses paper plates several times if possible and never uses a whole paper towel. She tears little bits of it off, like a small corner and uses that to wipe up a spot of something."

"Nana doesn't do that."

"No, she doesn't!"

"But she collects tape and safety pins."   Shelby gestured toward the table.

Vivian gazed at Shelby, looking helpless. "It's not a crime."

"No, of course not. A harmless obsession. But the other things, the bills, checks, the disorder there is more serious."

"Did you find more unpaid bills?"

"I've found a lot of random piles of papers. Like a cable TV bill next to a drugstore receipt, unopened junk mail, a birthday card, and it's all together in a box. A lot of these things are really old. I found a fifty-dollar rebate check for her computer, for instance, that was never cashed. She went to the trouble to send in the forms for the rebate, which they always make a lot harder than it should be, but then she didn't cash the check. Expired now."

Shelby thought of the piles of useless objects she had gathered from all the nooks and crannies of the house. The further she went, the more she discovered, and the more she worried about Nana's state of mind. There were the many boxes of paper she'd been sorting through, several months' worth of mail. Some of it had been opened and some of it hadn't. She'd found two notices from the power company about the nonpayment of the electric bill. There was a similar notice from the city about the water and sewer bill. Nana must have acted on that one. The water was still on, after all. There were late charges on her credit card bill, as she was paying that sporadically. Shelby was dismayed to see there were a couple of checks too, one of which was written to the power company, filled out but never mailed. The situation was troubling. Nana didn't seem feebleminded. She seemed sharp, in fact. But here was plenty of evidence she was losing control of the details of her life.

Vivian sank into a kitchen chair, staring at the tape dispensers. "I didn't realize—she's always saying how she's got to get her life in order, get organized, throw some junk away, but everybody says that. Everybody's a little out of control. Even me."

"Yeah. Like that upstairs bedroom. I think my old stroller is still in there somewhere."

Vivian frowned. "Yes, like that. But this is—"

"I'll keep at it," Shelby said, recognizing her mother's increasing anxiety level. "I'll get her organized if I'm here long enough."

Vivian smiled weakly at her. "You're a good girl. So level-headed and responsible. And about to be a college graduate too."

Shelby, remembering she was wearing her gown, looked down at the expanse of black cloth. When she looked up again, her mother was crying. She opened her purse and took out a tissue to wipe her eyes. Shelby put her arms around her, giving her a tight squeeze.

Shelby wasn't sure what had brought on this burst of emotion, but there were so many possibilities she didn't bother to ask. It could be the thought of her daughter's maturation or her mother's incapacitation. Or maybe it was because of Shelby's father, who'd left two years ago and, even Vivian must realize by now, was never coming back. It could have been any of these things or a combination. Shelby felt a deep sense of sympathy and, as always, the urge to protect her mother, as if they had, at some point, swapped roles.

Vivian's cry was brief, a momentary loss of composure. Thankfully, she wasn't going to melt down today. She stood and took a deep breath, smiled reassuringly at Shelby, then noticed the photo on the refrigerator. "Oh, look at that," she said, brightening. "That's Mom. In front of this house, isn't it? And who is this woman? I don't recognize her."

"She was a friend of Nana's back in the Forties. Her name was Marjorie."

"I don't recall her mentioning a Marjorie."

"They lost touch after the war, I think. It was before you were born."

"Well, it's a good picture of Mom. Look how young she was!" Vivian turned from the refrigerator, picked up one of the tape dispensers and put it in her purse. "I'll just take one of these since there are plenty."

"Sure," laughed Shelby. "Some people think you can never have too much tape."

Vivian looked askance at her. "I'll see you tonight. No goofing around after the ceremony. Come straight to my house."

Shelby decided not to ask what she meant by "goofing around."

"Did you want to invite Todd?" Vivian asked.

"Todd? No. It's just family, right?"

"Well, family and close friends. We can always cut an extra piece of cake for someone special."

Shelby was confused. "Todd isn't special."

"That's not very nice, Shelby." Vivian shook her head disapprovingly.

She remembered then what Todd had said about Vivian thinking he was her boyfriend. "Mom, Todd—"

"He seems like a nice boy. Good-looking too. And he's going to be a lawyer. That's impressive."

"He's not—"

"He's not going to be a lawyer?"

"No, he's going to be a chef. He's a waiter at Cibo."

Vivian frowned. "Then why did he tell me he was in law school?"

"He was just messing with you."

"Oh." Vivian shrugged. "Well, a chef isn't bad either. A man who can cook is a rarity. Your father could make only one thing his whole life."

"I know. Joe's scramble."

"So don't knock him for wanting to be a chef."

"Knock him?" Shelby felt exasperated. "No, I think it's terrific. He's going to be a wonderful chef."

"Good. I'm glad you feel that way. One of the most important things in any relationship is mutual respect."

Shelby opened her mouth to object, but Vivian had already pulled her into another hug. Then she gave her a look of wistful pride before leaving the kitchen in search of curios.

Shelby sighed.

CHAPTER FOURTEEN

Shelby felt Nana's absence keenly at graduation and even more so at her mother's house afterward. Nana's presence would have helped defuse Vivian's edginess. Vivian obviously thought it rude of her ex-husband to bring his girlfriend Bonnie to her house, *their* house. Dad, though, seemed oblivious to all this tension. He had probably just decided to ignore it, for there was no way he could really not see it.

"Congratulate your sister," Vivian commanded, pushing Charlie toward Shelby.

With typical goofiness, he hugged her with the sentiment, "It's about time you graduated, See-See."

Although he was teasing, he did have a point. It had taken her seven years to get through college. It had taken her awhile to get serious. The distraction of Lori had diverted her from her education. But she had recovered and it was done now. Good for me, Shelby thought.

"Are you ready for the real world?" asked her father, holding a scotch and soda.

"Yeah, Dad. I've been working in the real world for a few years now."

"I know," he said, chuckling. "But now you're going to be making real money. You're going to move up quick, too, angel. You're a smart girl. Serious and smart. I see you moving right up the ladder." He tapped the air three times, each time higher, punctuating each tap with a sound effect: "Boop, boop, boop."

At sixty, Gary Pratt was possibly more attractive than he had ever been with his solid, dimpled chin and crisp gray hair, receding in front, but still full on top. The wrinkles at the outer edges of his eyes tempered the seriousness of his countenance, hinting at the generous sense of humor. He had the look of a man at the top of his game. Her mother, on the other hand, was looking soft and a little dowdy. She was having to work harder than ever at looking good. The wrinkles around her eyes made her look tired and angry.

"We're all looking forward to having you on the team," her father continued. "I thought you'd enjoy working with Joe to begin with. He's young and sharp, like you. You've met him, right?"

Shelby conjured up an image of a geeky engineer with a pronounced gap between his front teeth, a guy who shrank into the corners and shadows of rooms when a crowd was present, but who might legitimately be called a genius.

"Yes, I've met him," she answered, wondering briefly if her father was pairing them up for more than work. She hoped not. She hoped it was enough for him that she had followed his blueprint for her career and he wouldn't be trying to plan her social life as well.

"Joe can teach you all the good habits you'll use throughout your career. He's working on a new office building in the Financial District. It'll be a beauty. I'll take you down and show you the location. Just a pile of concrete rubble at the moment, but that's the exciting part, to see that and then imagine this gorgeous new building soaring into the skyline like a phoenix rising from the ashes."

Shelby nodded noncommittally. She was still having trouble generating excitement for this next phase of her life. She didn't know why. She knew she was lucky to have this big step up into the profession. She even knew her father's vision of her rapid rise was likely accurate, unless she really screwed up. Even then, a certain number of mistakes would be forgiven as she learned the ropes. The way was paved for her, a glimmering yellow brick road to her personal land of Oz.

It was hard for Shelby to remember a time before she was going to be an architect. As a young child, she'd played with her father's models as if they were dollhouses. She and Charlie had put green plastic soldiers behind hedges and atop foot-high office buildings. They had moved cars and pink ponies around streets surrounding "green spaces," the planner's name for parks. She had positioned miniature people and farm animals in the windows of the rectangular multistoried buildings of her father's imagination.

Later, those very buildings, fully-realized in the downtowns of Bay Area cities, did almost nothing to inspire her. They were purposeful and fully functional. The wires and pipes coursing through them gave them life. Her father likened these buildings to living things with bone, sinew and blood vessels—powerful, flexible, majestic, throbbing with energy. It seemed the bigger they were, the more he admired them. There was nothing wrong with that. She was glad he enjoyed his work and took pride in his accomplishments. He built the sort of building a modern society needed, an efficient, sleek, often sterile structure whose innovations were technological rather than artful. Maybe they were pulsing with life, but, Shelby had often thought, they had no souls. If she had ever voiced that thought to him, he would have scoffed at the mere idea of buildings with souls. He was a practical man.

Although she had studied the same subject as her father, the buildings they admired were often mutually exclusive. Within the larger context of architecture, he was more of an engineer and she was more of an artist. She'd never told him that the beauty of his buildings was lost on her. After Charlie had shown no aptitude for math and no interest in architecture, and finally after he had dropped out of college, Gary had pinned all his hopes on Shelby, and she had been determined not to disappoint him.

Although her father's buildings failed to inspire her, she knew that someday when she had learned the ropes, she would develop her own style and design her own type of building, and that style would not resemble her father's, but that was okay. It would be okay with him too. That was what it meant to be an artist or an innovator in any discipline.

As she tried to imagine what sort of parking garage would spring from her personal vision, she smiled to herself, seeing Gwen's amused face in her mind.

"So when do you think you want to start?" Gary asked.

"Not right away. I was hoping to have this summer, you know. Just to hang out."

He nodded. "Sure, sure. You earned it. Enjoy yourself for a couple of months."

"And there's Nana. I'm house-sitting for her, taking care of things."

"Right. Your mother told me. Sorry to hear about Lucille. Probably by the end of summer, by September, though, it'll all be settled...either way."

"What do you mean, either way?"

He looked embarrassed and struggled with his answer. "Well, Shelby, she's an old woman. She may not recover. Statistically, it's not an optimistic situation. It's not nice to think about, but you need to be prepared."

Shelby resented the tone he'd suddenly taken, talking to her as if she were a child who couldn't face reality, as if she were her mother.

He squeezed her shoulder briefly, then said, "I hope everything goes great and she recovers completely, of course." He turned to smile at Bonnie, who had just appeared at his side. Shelby didn't know Bonnie well and had made no attempt to do so. She had assumed, perhaps based on comments made by Vivian, that Bonnie was inevitably temporary, so why waste time getting to know her? At the moment, looking into Bonnie's calm eyes, Shelby wondered how fair that was. She was ten years younger than Dad, not exactly a young woman, and didn't seem as flighty as Vivian had implied, or maybe hoped. Vivian wanted the worst for her ex-husband, at least romantically. It was a mean-spirited attitude, but Shelby knew she wasn't capable of anything else. Not yet.

Gary's request for a divorce two years ago had shattered Vivian's life and her image, however illusory, of their perfect happy family. It had come as a complete surprise to her, she claimed. It had surprised Shelby too, but she hadn't been married to him. He wasn't someone who voiced his dissatisfaction, at least not to his children, and in Shelby's opinion, that was an admirable trait. Shelby had tried not to resent it that he left like that, going off to fulfill his desires and leaving his devastated wife in the hands of her children, mainly Shelby.

That had not been a good year. Charlie was about to drop his own bomb on their shell-shocked family. His girlfriend was pregnant and he had no intention of marrying her. Vivian had pleaded with him to "do the right thing." He maintained that the right thing was not to marry someone he didn't love. Shelby had agreed with him. Vivian's ideas, the fantasies she tried so hard to mold her own life to, were old-fashioned and impractical. It seemed no one believed in them but her.

After two years of grief counseling and drug-induced tranquility, Vivian was almost herself again. She was just beginning to show some interest in her old pastimes—gardening, playing the piano, going to the theater. She seemed out of the woods. At least she was no longer sleeping through whole days. Things had been looking up. But then Nana had fallen and broken her hip.

Shelby had been watching her mother carefully, watching for any sign she was about to crash back into her post-divorce depression. So far, she was holding steady. Even tonight, with Bonnie in her house, she seemed to be coping surprisingly well.

Shelby wandered into the kitchen where Charlie was piling food onto his plate while Aunt Vickie poured herself a glass of wine. Charlie ate three times more than anybody Shelby had ever seen. She stood behind him, reached into his plate, and grabbed a black olive.

"Hey, get your own," he complained.

"Oh, I see. Now you have only nine, so one of your fingers will have to go without. Can't have that." She reached over to the relish tray, picked up an olive, and dropped it onto his plate.

"You're so funny, See-See," he said sarcastically.

"Hi, there, graduate!" Vickie said, putting her glass on the counter to give Shelby a serious hug. "So proud of you, baby."

"Thanks, Aunt Vickie."

Vivian appeared in a carnelian dress and pearls, holding a bulging plastic bag, which she thrust toward Charlie. "Take this out to the trash, will you?" she said.

"Aw, Mom," he groaned, "I'm trying to get something to eat here."

"It will still be here when you get back."

Charlie frowned, shoved an enormous spoonful of potato salad in his mouth, then took the bag.

"When are you starting your new job?" Vickie asked.

"I think we just agreed on September," Shelby said.

"What'll you do in the meantime?"

"Organize Nana's house. I want to get it really nice for when she comes home."

"It's a bigger mess than we imagined," Vivian said. "Mom's hoarding things like an old person."

Vickie laughed loudly, showing all her teeth. "She *is* an old person, Viv!"

"Well, I know, but she's never really seemed old to me. She's been so capable and independent. And now, all of the sudden, I find out she hasn't been paying her bills or cashing checks. She's gotten absent-minded."

Vickie nodded agreement. "I know what you mean. About three months ago, she called me from her car and told me she was lost."

"Lost?"

"Lost. She was in town and didn't know what to do. Just sitting in her car, helpless."

"Where was she?"

"Trader Joe's."

"Trader Joe's?" Vivian's eyes opened wide. "You mean here in town? Off of Park Street?"

Vickie nodded, then took a swallow from her glass.

"But, my God," Vivian said, "that's only two miles from her house."

Vickie nodded again. Charlie came bouncing back into the house and retrieved his plate, ducking past them on his way to the dining room table.

"What'd you do?" Shelby asked her aunt.

"I got Dan and we went over there and picked her up. I thought maybe it was some side effect of medication or something, so I took her to the doctor a few days later. She seemed fine then. The doctor said it might have been low blood sugar or any number of things. It hasn't happened again, but that day, she just went completely blank."

"Why didn't you tell me?" Vivian asked.

"She asked me not to."

Vivian shook her head. "This is just getting worse and worse."

"I don't think she eats right. But when I tried to talk to her about meals, she got defensive and waved me off. You know how she is."

"Yes," Vivian agreed. "Fiercely independent. She doesn't like us meddling. But it seems to me maybe we haven't been meddling enough."

The doorbell rang and Vivian turned to look at Charlie, who sat at the table hunched over his plate. He stared defiantly at her while shoving baked beans into his mouth. Watching him eat, Shelby couldn't help thinking of a starving junkyard dog.

"I'll get it," Vivian said, leaving the room.

"I probably shouldn't have told her that," Vickie said.

"No," Shelby countered, "I think you should. It's better to know. For Nana's sake, I think we need to know how things really are with her."

Vickie nodded uncertainly. Shelby turned to see Lori walking into the kitchen, followed by her mother. She stiffened as Lori approached and hugged her.

"Congratulations!" she said, her eyes beaming with goodwill.

"What're you doing here?" Shelby asked, realizing only after she said it how rude it sounded.

"I invited her," Vivian said, frowning disapprovingly.

Lori stepped over to Charlie and gave his shoulders a squeeze. "Hi, Charlie."

Vivian sidled up to Shelby and spoke under her breath. "What's wrong with you?"

"Why'd you invite her?" Shelby shot back.

"Why shouldn't I invite her. She's your best friend."

"No, she isn't!" Shelby said, glaring at her mother.

Vivian looked bewildered and Shelby left the room, realizing that her mother had no way to understand what had happened between Lori and herself. Not without knowing the nature of their relationship. She recalled Todd's advice, to come out to her mother. She did want to, but how could she? Vivian had one last dream for her family, that her daughter would marry a handsome prince and have a couple of happy, healthy, high-achieving offspring. Shelby's heart sank at the thought of her mother losing that dream. That wasn't happening today, she decided, resolving to be friendly to Lori.

"Get in the dining room, everybody!" she heard her mother holler with forced cheerfulness. "We're going to cut the cake."

CHAPTER FIFTEEN

June 27, 1944.

Today I met a gal named Lucy over at the shipyards. She's one of the workers there. I drove Captain Blanchard over for a meeting. It was a foggy day and everything was glistening. The gray hulls of the ships were darker than usual because the fog completely covered the bay, blocking out the sun. You could see the showers of sparks flying in the prefab yard where the welders were working. That place is always so busy. I understand they once built a ship in three-and-a-half days, the Robert E. Peary. That was in 1942 and the record still stands.

Exactly at noon, the lunch whistle blew. A startling silence fell as the cranes quit moving and the rivet guns quit firing. The clang, clang, clang of metal on metal from all around just stopped. Workers sat down with their lunch pails. Obviously, I was going to miss my own lunch. At least the fog was clearing. I could see a bright disk of the sun poking through. Just the sight of it made the day seem warmer. I decided to take a walk over to the dock and watch for sea lions.

Heads turned as I walked by. I knew I stood out from the other women, all of them wearing work clothes with their hair covered up. There I was decked out in my summer whites from head to toe except for my black tie and the brim of my cap. I lit a cigarette as I walked past the medical clinic. Behind that was a wooden dock, open to the water. As I reached it, I saw a woman sitting on the ground, facing the Bay, a black lunchbox open in front of her. Beside that was a copy of the company paper, *Fore 'n' Aft*. She was pouring coffee out of a thermos into its metal lid.

I walked up to her and said hi. I think I scared her a little. She probably wasn't used to seeing a woman in uniform. Quite a pretty little thing, I thought, as she turned her face up. A few wisps of dark brown hair showed around the edges of the handkerchief on her head. Her complexion was pale, clear and luminous and her eyes were bright and penetrating. She had a small mouth, but her lips were full, soft looking. A real beauty, even in coveralls.

"Patty and I usually have lunch on the ship," she said, "but she had cramps, so I came over to the clinic to get her some aspirin and decided to take advantage of the view. She's lying in the double-bottom, curled into a ball."

I laughed because I thought that was an odd greeting. "What's a double-bottom?"

"Oh, that's the hull of the ship. That's what they call it because it has two layers, two hulls in case the outer hull is damaged." She squinted, looking up at me against the brightening sky. "You want to sit down?"

"In this getup, I'd better not."

"You can sit on my jacket." She grabbed her jacket from beside her and spread it out on the dock.

I decided it would be rude to turn down that offer, so I sat down and we introduced ourselves to one another. It turned out I was talking to Lucy Brewster.

"I've seen you," she said.

"Oh? How's that?"

"Driving. I've seen you with the car. I said hello to you one day."

"You did?"

"Yes, but you didn't answer. I took it you couldn't answer. But you winked at me."

I had a habit of winking at the civilian girls, something I'd picked up from Nettie, so I knew that was probably true. It wasn't true I couldn't answer, though.

Lucy unwrapped a sandwich and picked up half while I took a drag from my cigarette, watching the fog thin. I caught her staring at me as she bit into her sandwich.

"You want the other half?" she asked.

"Oh, no, that's okay," I said, touched by her thoughtfulness. "You need your strength. They feed me great over there at the base. Too much, if you want to know the truth. The Navy gives you a good deal—a bunk and three squares."

"It's pimento loaf," she said, pulling back the bread to show me the lunchmeat, trying to tempt me.

This time when I laughed, she laughed too. Then she took another bite of her sandwich and washed it down with coffee.

"What do you do here?" I asked her.

"I'm a bucker."

"What's a bucker?"

"I work with a riveter." She put her sandwich down, balancing it on her Thermos lid. "We're a team. She's on one side of the sheet of steel and I'm on the other. She puts a rivet in with a kind of gun and I hold a board up against on the other side to flatten it out." She held up her hands as if she was holding a board to demonstrate.

"I guess you've got to work fast to get the ships out as quick as you do."

"Fast, sure. But do it right too. We wouldn't want to send them out in a leaker."

"No." I laughed.

"How about a peanut butter cookie?" she asked. "I've got two. I was going to give one to Patty, but she won't want it now, not with the cramps." She held it out to me with a white paper napkin folded around it.

"I can't turn that down," I said. "Did you make this?"

She nodded. "We made a batch last night to send to the boys overseas."

"This is wonderful!" I said with my mouth full.

She smiled as she picked up her sandwich, a smile that looked like a light coming on. I realized the sun had broken through the fog and we were now blinking into the bright afternoon. I tried not to hurry the cookie, but it didn't last long.

"You married?" I asked.

She nodded. We both looked at her bare ring finger, then she said, "We can't wear rings on the job. No jewelry of any kind."

"Your husband," I asked, "a GI?"

She nodded again.

"Kids?"

Lucy shook her head. "We were just married before he went off."

I took out another cigarette and lit it, then offered her one from my pack.

"I don't smoke," she said.

"I need to quit. Getting too expensive, especially these Pall Malls. All you can get at the commissary now are those awful knock-offs. When you can find these, some creep's charging you three or four times what they'd cost at the commissary, if they had them." I took a long drag. "So do you live in company housing here? What's it called? Atchison Village?"

"No. I have a house in Alameda. His mother lives there too. It's her house, actually."

"Well, that's nice for you. So we're neighbors."

"I guess we are."

I flicked the ash off my cigarette. "Do you go out after work—movies, dancing, that sort of thing?"

"Once in a while." Lucy broke a piece off her cookie. "I'm usually pretty tired."

"Hard work, is it?"

"It's physical. It's tiring, yes. But they have entertainers come here sometimes during lunch. We've had some really big stars." Her eyes lit up. "Last month Bing Crosby was here. Oh, you should have seen that!"

"You like Bing Crosby?"

Lucy shook her head enthusiastically. "Sure! Don't you?"

She looked so sweet, I just smiled at her. While she finished her lunch, we sat there watching the Golden Gate Bridge emerge from the mist.

I took my makeup bag out of my purse. Lucy watched as I put on lipstick, then pressed my lips onto the white napkin, leaving a bright red impression of my mouth there. I folded the napkin and put it in my makeup bag along with the lipstick tube, then snapped it shut.

"Do you go out much?" Lucy asked, locking the latch on her lunchbox.

"Yes, pretty regular. There's a place near the base, Flanagan's. Maybe you know it, since you live over there. Classy joint with a jukebox, dancing. Not so many sailors there. Mostly civilians."

"I went there once with my husband. It's not far from our house."

"I'm there most Fridays and Saturdays with a couple of the other girls. Come by sometime. I'll buy you a drink."

"I'm not old enough to drink. I just turned twenty."

"That's okay. You're old enough to dance. Besides, nobody cares. I just turned twenty-one myself and I've been drinking there for months."

The whistle blew, sounding the end of the lunch half hour and signaling Lucy to hop to her feet. I stood too, then picked up her jacket and shook it gently before handing it to her. She was shorter than I was by a few inches, a small woman altogether.

"Maybe I'll see you at Flanagan's, then, Lucy," I said. "Beats sitting around the house missing your fella."

"Do you have a fella?" she asked, as I started to leave.

I turned back and smiled at her. I shook my head, then walked back to wait for the captain.

She's a sweet gal. Seems very young, though we're nearly the same age. Maybe it's just me who's gotten quite a bit older all of a sudden. They say the navy will make a man out of a boy. Maybe it works the same for girls. Maybe it's turned me into a woman already.

June 30, 1944.

I went off base tonight to go to Flanagan's as I usually do on Fridays. I was by myself, as I was kept late in the office with some memos that had to go out, so the other girls had already left. It wasn't dark yet, just twilight. After walking down Main Street, I turned up a side street. Someone grabbed me from behind and I struggled, but was pinned to the ground, face down in the gutter. My attacker was sitting on my back bending back my arm at a painful angle.

It was Nettie sitting on me and I could tell by the way she was breathing that she was furious. She knew my routine. She'd been waiting for me. I hadn't seen her since the day she'd been taken out of our room over two weeks ago. I knew why she'd attacked me.

"It wasn't me!" I blurted out, feeling the hard pavement against my cheek.

"It had to be you," she said between her teeth. "Who else?"

"I don't know, but I swear—"

She cocked my arm roughly, sending pain through my shoulder.

"I should break your arm, you jealous bitch!" Her voice was low, but insistent.

Tears started in my eyes from the pain. I thought for sure she was going to do it.

"Please, don't!" I gasped. "I didn't report you, Nettie. I never said a word to anybody. They never even interviewed me. They never asked me a single question. There was no reason to. Nobody knew about us."

"Then who's the snitch?" she demanded.

"I don't know. I swear I don't. But it wasn't me."

I felt the pressure ease slightly, relieving the worst of the pain. She sat still for a moment, as if considering my words.

"I would never do anything to hurt you," I added quietly.

After a long minute, she let go of my arm and released me. Once I was on my feet, I put my arms around her and hugged her. Then I punched her in the arm, not too hard, and said, "For crying out loud, why'd you think I'd do a thing like that?"

She hung her head and kicked at the ground, looking chastened. "I didn't really think so."

She ended up coming with me to Flanagan's and we talked late into the night, drinking beer and smoking cigarettes. I noticed how the other girls stayed clear of Nettie. They gave her a nod of recognition, but didn't talk to her. She knew why. We both did. Nobody wanted to bring suspicion on herself by associating with her.

Neither of us had a guess who the snitch is. Though Nettie suspected I'd reported her, she swore she didn't mention my name when they questioned her. She didn't mention any names. That's the Nettie I know, so I'm sure it's true.

"They said they'd get me a general discharge if I gave names," she told me. "No dice! I knew it was a lie. That's just how they get you to sell out your friends. They got nothing from me. Bricker tipped me off weeks ago, told me how it works."

"Bricker?" I asked.

"Yeah, Chief Petty Officer Bricker, our own mother hen. She took me aside and gave me the lowdown. Told me how to answer their Mickey Mouse questions. She must have known they were coming after me."

"I don't understand. Why'd she try to help you?"

Nettie laughed shortly, knocking the ash off her cigarette. "She's one of us. Oh, she didn't say so, but it's obvious, isn't it?"

It hadn't been obvious to me before, but once I considered it, I realized it must be true.

"Couldn't she help you?" I asked.

Nettie shook her head. "Naw. Nothing she could do once they nabbed me. They took my uniform, my tags, everything. Undesirable discharge. That's what I got. Gina too. She's gone back home. Left yesterday." She shrugged. "Back to civilian life for both of us."

"What're you going to do?"

"Not sure. I'm staying with Vera and Pug right now. I'll get a job. Something will come along. I can work in a filling station. Pump gas, fix cars. You know how I like sticking my hands in some old crate's engine."

"I do know! You're a crackerjack mechanic."

"You keep your nose clean," Nettie advised, winking. "You're a good kid. Good sense too."

When Nettie left Flanagan's tonight, I knew I wouldn't see her again.

I wondered if a filling station would hire a woman. I've never seen a woman pumping gas. Maybe during the war they would. There seem to be no rules anymore about what jobs a woman can or can't do. But when the war's over...I'm worried about Nettie. One thing I know for sure is that her dream of being a pilot is over. The undesirable discharge will see to that.

It will follow you all your life like the mark of Cain.

July 8, 1944.

Holy mackerel! That's what I said when Lucy Brewster came walking into Flanagan's tonight. That sweet little girl in coveralls had turned into a knockout in a dress and heels, her dark hair hanging down loose around her shoulders. But I recognized her right away. I'd have recognized those big eyes anywhere.

I offered her a chair at our table and bought her a drink. Two sips on that Manhattan and her cheeks were glowing pink. She was wearing her wedding band tonight. Her lips were painted red and her legs were gorgeous in shimmering stockings. She must have noticed me staring at them because she said, "I was lucky to get these."

"I'll say!" I agreed. "Not many girls have legs like that."

Lucy laughed nervously. Her cheeks got redder yet. "I meant the stockings."

"Oh!" I said, pretending to be embarrassed.

"I haven't had a new pair of stockings for over a year. I heard Bingley's Department Store was getting in a shipment today. A couple of us took a bus over to Oakland and stood in line for an hour to get one pair."

"So you thought you'd take them out on the town tonight? Good idea."

"You're funny." Lucy's eyes laughed at me over the rim of her glass.

"Paper Doll" by the Mills Brothers was playing on the

jukebox and a man and his wife were dancing. When the song finished, I asked Lucy if she wanted to hear something.

"Whatever you like," she said.

I put a nickel in the machine and played "For Me and My Gal," a duet by Gene Kelly and Judy Garland. Then I took hold of her little hand and we danced. We danced all night, fast or slow, whatever was playing. Jitterbug and the lindy and everything else. That Lucy can cut a rug. She likes to dance as much as I do. That's one thing I can do with a girl that nobody cares about. There are never enough boys to dance with, so female couples on the dance floor are common. It works out for me because I prefer it that way.

Tonight I danced only with Lucy. She turned down a man who asked her. She doesn't think it's proper to dance with other men while her husband's away. Her hand seemed so small and delicate in mine. When I twirled her she laughed, a light, giggly laugh, every time she spun around. I laughed too…a lot. I hope she had as good a time as I did. I hope she comes back again.

July 10, 1944.

I'm patting myself on the back for having sense enough to move down to the bottom bunk after Nettie left, so the new girl's up above me. Her name's Bettie. She's from Oakland, a local girl from a poor family. She's tall and gawky with buck teeth and a scary smile that shows her gums. She's not a beauty, but she's eager to please and she's funny, quick to offer help, and good-hearted. She seems very innocent. She taped a photo of her parents to her locker on her first day. Above that she taped a picture of FDR and stuck a little American flag on the corner. Every morning when she gets out of bed, she stands at attention and salutes that photo. It always makes me smile. Especially because she's wearing pajamas with cocker spaniel puppies on them while she's saluting.

She and Maria, as the younger pair, have become fast friends. Maria is much less quiet now that she has Bettie to draw her out. To hear them talking about this or that ginchy sailor who cast an eye their way is fun because it sounds so earnest and childlike.

So many of the women here have become hard-boiled. But these two are still overflowing with sweet innocence.

It's less than a year since I joined the WAVES. I can see in Bettie what I was like back then. It seems so long ago. Bettie looks up to me and Hazel as the wise old-timers, asking our advice and following our lead. Both of us already feel protective of her, like big sisters.

I think a girl can age very fast in the military. I feel like I would like to slow that process down for Maria and Bettie, if I can, to let them keep their dreams and optimism for as long as possible. I sound like a crusty old salt, which is not me at all! But these bright-eyed girls do make me wonder if I've lost a little of the joy of living.

July 17, 1944.

I know I was complaining just a few days ago to Hazel that nothing ever happens around here. There's fighting all over the world and here we sit in our safe homefront cocoon marching up and down the concourse with nowhere to go. Sometimes it's so frustrating. We listen to the radio every day and watch the newsreels and see what's happening in Europe and the Pacific. It's hard sometimes to be so far from the action. So I said to Hazel, "Nothing ever happens here. It's just too darn quiet."

Then, like somebody was sending me a message, this morning the ground shook and windows rattled and we heard an explosion, a big explosion, somewhere off to the northeast. The sirens sounded and everybody ran to their stations. We were all trying to figure out what happened. Did the Japs bomb us? But we hadn't seen any planes. And we would see them here at NAS Alameda. We're watching for them round the clock.

We finally got the report. It wasn't an enemy attack at all. Wasn't an earthquake either, which some people thought. It was a munitions explosion at Port Chicago, the naval magazine on Suisun Bay. Two Navy ships docked there blew up, the E.A. Bryan and the Quinault, both of them built right over there at the Richmond shipyards. Hundreds of men, most of them Navy enlistees, were killed. They were loading munitions there as usual and something went wrong. An accident, not an attack. I heard it blew out the windows of the Fairmont Hotel all the way over in San Francisco. That was thirty miles away!

What a terrible thing to happen, those new ships and all those men. I think I've had enough excitement for a while. I think maybe quiet isn't so bad after all. We all said a prayer for those men tonight, the men killed and injured in that explosion.

July 19, 1944.

This morning the captain said he wanted to go take a look at the Port Chicago explosion and I was all ready to bring the car around when he said, "I'll have Giannelli drive today. They're still pulling bodies out of there. It's no place for a woman. You wouldn't want to see this."

"Sir," I said, standing at attention, "I respectfully disagree. I'm your driver and it's my job to drive you where you want to go."

He came right up to my face, then, his eyes set hard, and said, "Seaman, you ever seen a dead body, burned to a crisp and torn apart, eyeballs melted, full of the stench of rotting flesh?"

"No, sir!" I said, thinking he was trying to scare me, which he was. But I didn't think it was right, protecting women from everything bad that was happening, not when we were supposed to be sailors in the U.S. Navy, the real deal. I knew there were women serving in combat zones, like nurses, who were seeing terrible things. If they could do it, I could do it too. "I'm ready to do my duty, sir," I said and stood my ground.

Then he smiled and said, "Very well, Seaman. Shake a leg."

It turned out I didn't see any dead bodies, for which I thank my stars. I stayed with the car while a group of officers went to look over the devastation. But I did see plenty from where I stood. There were logs the size of telephone poles lying on the dock, blown out of their moorings. There was wood everywhere, all broken up into pieces. Just piles of splinters everywhere. The train cars on the tracks where they unload the munitions were crunched like a giant hand had wadded them up. The railway station itself had only two walls left standing and the roof had collapsed. I'd parked beside a building with a tin roof that was sagging down inside. The sides of the building were leaning in and the windows were gone. The building next to it had been completely demolished. Most of the buildings in sight were in similar shape. The air smelled of sulfur and oil mixed with the metallic smell of burnt machinery. The SS E.A. Bryan liberty ship was gone. Not a scrap of her remained. The SS Quinault Victory was torn apart before she ever sailed a single mission. I could see her propeller half submerged in the bay. It was eerie to see that smoking wreckage and everything so quiet. The only thing moving were a few men walking through the rubble, pushing pieces of wood and metal around. I think they were looking for bodies.

When the captain came back from his tour, he didn't say anything and I drove him back to the base. I've been thinking ever since about those men who were killed. I heard they were colored, most of them, navy men who weren't allowed to serve in combat missions, like us, like the WAVES. But they died serving their country just the same, not in battle, but in a different kind of war zone. I wonder if they're going to get any recognition for that, like a medal.

July 22, 1944.

Three weekends in a row now Lucy Brewster's come to Flanagan's. I think she's lonely a lot in the evenings because her mother-in-law works swing shift. Maybe she misses her husband, although she hasn't mentioned him much. She seems to enjoy herself, especially when she dances with Bettie. Bettie doesn't know how to dance worth salt, but she doesn't hold back from giving it a whirl. She just moves any way the urge takes her. It's fun to watch her swinging Lucy around like a rag doll, Lucy laughing with such abandon. Lucy's a great dancer, but you'd never know it watching her with Bettie.

Lucy has kept to her rule of not dancing with men. She feels safe, I guess, sticking with her usual group of WAVES, and we all benefit from her company. She's a smart, high-spirited girl. I don't think I've ever known a girl like Lucy.

I'd like to think we're becoming friends. Up to now, I haven't known anyone locally. Not having local friends is most noticeable on weekends when the other girls take off and the base is practically deserted. Since Nettie and I broke up, I spend my weekends in the barracks, doing laundry and reading. Sometimes I'm invited to parties, but I've never cared much for parties and there's always a man there who thinks any woman without a steady date is fair game for a night of fun. Men assume women in the military are easy. It gets tiring trying to fight them off.

I may be getting a reputation as standoffish, as I keep to myself more than ever. I have my bowling league and the weekends at Flanagan's and that's about it. Both Hazel and I are considered aloof, though I think people like us well enough. We're more serious than some, here to do a job for America, not to have fun. Hazel would rather read a book than talk to anyone anyway, and I, well, I think I hang back from socializing because of what happened to Nettie. The navy seems to have it in for homosexuals. Last week two more men were drummed out. One woman I know, an E-3, got married yesterday to a boatswain's mate because she's gotten so scared of being found out. She's still got her girlfriend and he's still got his boyfriend. That's how they're escaping suspicion. I don't know if it'll work. It seems like a drastic solution. I don't think I'd go that far.

I realize now how lucky I was I didn't get called in with Nettie and Gina. I escaped a close call.

Here I am with the room to myself again. Bettie spends her weekends with her family. She's taking Maria with her now, so the two of them are in Oakland where her folks live. And Hazel has a married couple she stays with, her cousin or something, so Friday nights like tonight, it's just me. Which doesn't matter, since it's after midnight and I need to hit the hay anyway. I don't feel very sleepy, though.

Sunday I'm taking Lucy bowling. I found out tonight she's never been. Imagine that! We arranged it tonight while I walked her home. Her house is just two blocks from Flanagan's. It was nice to be out in the quiet evening, just the two of us, after the noise and smoke of the bar. We'd only gone a few feet when the blackout signal sounded and everybody turned off their lights. There was no moon, so the night was as black as could be. The bridge across the Bay went dark and you couldn't see San Francisco, not a glimmer of it. Lucy took hold of my arm and we walked the rest of the way like that, arm in arm, discussing our plans for Sunday.

"You've got to promise not to make fun of me," she said. "I won't go with you if you don't promise."

"I promise," I said. "I won't make fun of you. And if anybody else rags on you, I'll roll him up in a ball and toss him down the alley."

She laughed at that. "Well, then, I hope somebody does!"

I said goodbye to her on her front porch. Then I walked back to Flanagan's and caught a ride back to the base with one of the guys.

July 24, 1944.

I picked up Lucy at her house and we walked to the bus station, me in my uniform and she wearing a pink skirt and a short-sleeved blouse. She looked so young in her bobby socks with her hair clipped back on both sides with pink barrettes. I'd never seen her in her regular daytime clothes. She was all smiles with her rosy cheeks and flashing eyes as we rode the bus into Oakland. I suddenly became someone I hadn't seen in a while, a silly, giggly girl on a bright summer Sunday in the company of a good, comfortable friend.

At first, Lucy was terrible at bowling, but she got better. By the time we were done, she was keeping about thirty percent of them out of the gutter, but quite a few were still bouncing down the alleyway. I never laughed so much in all my life. Even though I'd promised not to make fun of her, I don't think she minded my laughing one little bit.

Afterward, we went to the soda fountain at Conn's Drugstore to get an ice cream cone. We twirled on the counter stools until we were dizzy. On the bus ride back to Alameda, Lucy talked about her family and her childhood in Arkansas. She told me about her parents and her brothers and their strawberry farm. I'd never heard her talk so much before. I think she embarrassed herself because when the bus got to our stop, she looked up, startled, and said, "Oh, my! I've been talking your ear off!"

I told her I didn't mind at all. I liked it.

"But now it's your turn," she insisted.

We walked the few blocks from the bus stop to her house while I told her a bit about life in New York, my parents and colorful sea-faring grandfather and my brother Paul, the blisterfoot in the army.

She invited me in, so I met her mother-in-law Arlene and saw a photo of her husband Arnie, an official army photo in which he looked very handsome in his crisp tan uniform. Their house is small but comfortable with a vegetable garden out back and a few chickens running loose. Arlene gave me a cup of tea at the kitchen table and seemed relieved when I said I didn't need sugar. She'd run out of sugar because they'd just baked cookies to send to Arnie. No sugar and no butter until next week. Arlene's a friendly, cheerful woman, thin and bouncy, always in motion, even while sitting.

It felt good to be in a real home for a change. Very relaxing. I didn't want to leave, but did leave before I overstayed my welcome. Lucy invited me to stay for dinner, but I decided not to burden them with an unexpected dinner guest, especially one used to eating like a man.

"You'll stay next time, then," suggested Lucy. "We'll plan for it."

I felt so full of energy, I decided to walk back to the base. It's just two miles.

As I'm lying on my bunk writing about this wonderful day, everybody else is arriving back in from their weekend.

"I went bowling," I told Hazel in answer to her question about my day.

That didn't seem to half cover it, but it would have been hard to put into words how I felt about the rest of my day. At best, anything I had to say about Lucy, her comfortable friendship and her welcoming home would have sounded corny. So that's all I said, then just sat and listened to the excited voices of Bettie and Maria as they told about their trip to the beach and the many men who wished to make love to them. They giggled as they recalled how they'd refused to give any of them the time of day.

August 13, 1944.

In no time, 322 Santa Clara Avenue has become my home away from home. Lucy and her mother-in-law seem happy to have me around. I try to make myself useful. On weekends, we all three go out together. We took the ferry to San Francisco yesterday and had a picnic in Golden Gate Park. On work nights, Lucy and I've been going to movies or out dancing. Sometimes we just stay in and listen to the radio. Arlene gets off work at midnight, and I usually leave before she gets home. They've loaned me a bicycle. It took some work, but I got it in good enough shape to take me back and forth from the base to their house.

My absence has been noticed.

"You got a boyfriend?" Bettie asked me a couple weeks ago.

I saw the look Hazel gave me, waiting to see how I'd answer. She alone among my roommates knows it's unlikely I'd have a boyfriend. Maybe she thinks I have a girlfriend. It's her custom not to pry, so she hasn't asked.

"No," I said. "I've made friends with a family in town. Really nice people."

Hazel gazed at me for a moment, then smiled warmly and returned to her novel.

CHAPTER SIXTEEN

Gwen parked in front of 322 Santa Clara Avenue and stepped out of her car. It was a quiet residential area with old elms growing together into a sparse canopy above. Some of the original houses on this street had been replaced and many had been renovated. This particular one, once the home of Arlene Brewster and her daughter-in-law Lucy, looked not just old-fashioned, but old. It had a wide, covered porch with a couple of blond wicker chairs on it and square columns framing the front door. In the flowerbed fringing the porch, orange and yellow zinnias bloomed cheerfully.

That should make a pretty picture, Gwen thought, removing her camera from its case.

She took some front-on photos, standing on the sidewalk before the open gate. As she composed her shots, the house framed in her view screen seemed to cast a spell on her, calling to her from the past with its strange, alluring story. The house was a fixture in that story, the very stage where the action had taken place behind that forest green front door with its semicircle window and its intriguing brass knocker. She could imagine those three women—Arlene, Lucy and the sailor without a name—like characters on a stage, playing out their roles here day to day. She felt it would almost be possible to enter that scene, to open the door and step through to another reality like Alice through the looking glass.

Gwen was entranced by a story like this, the past coming vividly alive in her mind, allowing her to briefly inhabit the lives of people who had gone before. Certain people, certain stories, captured her this way. For those stories she would go without food and without sleep, driven to complete the missing parts of the tale.

She was inside the fence now, snapping a shot of the door, peering at the camera screen as her feet carried her along the narrow pathway, up the gray wooden steps onto a porch of thick painted planks. She focused on the knocker, a brass ring framed with brass leaves, discolored with age.

As she peered at the screen, she was roused from her concentration by a dog barking inside the house. The front door opened and a frantic little dachshund came running out and jumped excitedly around her feet. She looked up to find herself face to face with Shelby. It took her a moment to register this as they stood staring in surprise at one another. She let the camera drop to dangle from its strap, her heart leaping for joy at her unexpected good luck.

Even as she was trying to understand the situation, she couldn't help noticing how cute Shelby looked, dressed in an old, stained "Hillary for President" T-shirt and shorts cut just above the knee. She had a smudge of dirt across one cheek.

Still distracted by the story she'd been living in her mind, Gwen barely knew what she was doing as she took a step toward Shelby and gathered her in her arms, kissing her as if it were something they did every day. Her mouth tasted sweet and spicy. Shelby was passive at first, but then put her arms around Gwen and returned the kiss, full and eager, for several delicious seconds until she took a step back and broke off their embrace.

Shelby mumbled incoherently before lapsing into a gape of incomprehension. "How did you find me?" she asked at last.

"I, uh, I wasn't looking for you." Gwen was still not entirely sure she wasn't dreaming. "What are you doing here?"

"What am *I* doing here?" Shelby stared. "I live here. What are *you* doing here?"

"This is your house? Wow, this is weird! I had no idea."

"Really?" Shelby stared. "Then who did you come here to kiss?"

Gwen shook her head. "Sorry. I'm a little confused."

Shelby looked semi-serious as she said, "You're nuts, aren't you."

"No. I mean…maybe." Gwen tried to imagine the last few minutes from Shelby's point of view: Gwen showing up uninvited, sneaking around outside the house with a camera, and then grabbing her and kissing her without warning. "Cinnamon!" she announced triumphantly. "That's what it is. You taste like cinnamon."

Shelby sighed. "I was drinking a cup of herbal tea before you turned up, taking a break from cleaning house. If you're mostly sure you're not nuts, why don't you come in and I'll make you a cup." She moved aside to let Gwen pass.

"Thanks," Gwen said, stepping inside. The little dog ran in ahead of her, then turned and sat at her feet, looking up at her with his tail wagging. Gwen knelt to pet him. "Hi there, fella."

"His name's Oscar," Shelby said, shutting the door.

When Gwen straightened up and observed the room, she was startled to see a jumble of furniture all packed tightly together, sofa against sofa, chairs stacked on one another, three mismatched lamps lined up on a coffee table. It looked more like a storeroom than a living room. There was even a disassembled bed among the assortment.

"Uh, who's nuts now?" she asked, jerking her head toward the furnishings.

"Organizing this place is going to take some time," Shelby said breezily.

Suddenly, Gwen understood everything. "Oh, right! You're house-sitting. This is your grandmother's house. And that's her dog."

"And your name is Gwen," Shelby said very slowly and deliberately, pointing at Gwen's face.

Gwen laughed. "No, no, I just forgot. I mean, seeing you here was such a surprise. It's all starting to make sense now." She followed Shelby into the kitchen, her mind working at full speed. "But the coincidence is uncanny, that you're living in the same house as the one in the journal."

"What journal?" Shelby took a cup out of a cupboard as Gwen sat at the table.

"That's why I'm here. The address in the journal. It was this house."

Shelby looked up from pouring tea into the cup, her forehead furrowed in frustration.

"I found an old World War Two journal at the museum," Gwen explained. "The woman who wrote it was friends with Lucy Brew—" She was suddenly struck with a thought. "Oh, my God! Is your grandmother Lucy Brewster?"

Shelby placed the teacup in front of Gwen. "Yep." She sat in the opposite chair.

Gwen let out a high-pitched whistle. "And your great-grandmother was Arlene and your grandfather was Arnie?"

"You found a journal about my family?"

"Sort of. They were friends of the woman who wrote it."

"Who was she?" Shelby asked.

"A woman in the Navy. I don't know her name." Gwen took a sip of tea, then swallowed so fast she burnt her throat. "But your grandmother would know her name!" She put the cup down. "Oh, oh! I definitely have to do that interview now."

"I did ask her about it. She says okay."

"Awesome!" Gwen took a more cautious sip of tea, tasting it this time, cinnamon and oranges.

"Tell me more," Shelby asked. "What's the journal about?"

Gwen summarized the story for Shelby. As she did so, she thought about how the journal's author had sat here in the same room so long ago, feeling a sense of belonging.

"It's a fascinating journal," Gwen said. "I can't stop reading it."

"It's anonymous? Not even a first name?"

"No. She wanted to hide her identity in case the journal was found. Realistically, though, that wouldn't have been enough to protect her."

"From what?"

"She'd have been kicked out of the navy if anybody read it. She was a lesbian."

Shelby's eyes widened. "No kidding!"

"She's surprisingly frank about it. This is quite a find, really. You know how we were talking about stories the other day? Well, this is a rare one. I wish I had more time to read it. I've got a city council meeting to go to tonight, so I've been busy preparing some material for that."

"To persuade them to let the museum stay?"

"Yes. I haven't had much spare time this week. Also, I tend to get distracted. Like today. I suddenly had this address so I felt compelled to come look."

"I don't blame you. And look how well that turned out for you."

Gwen nodded, thinking how darling Shelby looked, even in her work clothes. She reached over and rubbed away the smudge from her face. They stared silently at one another for a moment before Shelby glanced at a black-and-white photo on the refrigerator, then removed it and placed it on the table facing Gwen. She pointed to the taller of two women. "Do you think this could be her? The other woman is my grandmother."

Gwen studied the picture, focusing on the taller woman's features, trying to put the journal voice to her. She had dark wavy hair and broad shoulders. Her suit was cut to accentuate her waist. She wore gloves and a little hat with netting on it. Lucy wore a dress and both of them looked as if they were dressed for a special occasion. Gwen recalled the description of Lucy as a "knockout" from the journal. It was true. She was a beautiful young woman and there was definitely a family resemblance between her and Shelby. She turned her attention back to the other woman with her sharper features, hard jawline and straight nose. There was an intelligent slope to her forehead and a general look of distinction about her.

"I don't know," Gwen said. "Why do you think it might be her?"

Shelby shook her head. "Nana was a little vague about who she was when I asked. Just a friend from the war, she said. They lost touch after that. It's the right time frame, the right place. That's all."

"Is that all you know about her?"

"I know her name's Marjorie."

"Marjorie," Gwen repeated, enjoying the idea that she might have a name for her mysterious diarist. She took another sip of tea, trying to decide if her young sailor seemed like a Marjorie.

Shelby looked thoughtful. "I wonder if Nana knew her friend was gay."

"Why? Wouldn't she have been friends with her if she knew?"

"I don't know what anybody, including Nana, would have thought about it back then."

"She probably never gave it a thought," Gwen speculated.

Shelby looked into Gwen's eyes. "Now, though, she'd be fine with it."

"She would?"

"Sure. She told me so just the other day, that she had no problem with me and Lori."

"Lori?" Gwen stiffened.

"My girlfriend. My ex-girlfriend, I mean."

Gwen realized with alarm that she hadn't even thought to ask Shelby if she was involved with anyone. The idea of an ex-girlfriend brought her up short. For all Gwen knew, she was dating someone else. What a doofus! Gwen silently scolded herself. That question should definitely come before a kiss.

"You're single now?" Gwen asked.

"Oh, yeah. There's been nobody since Lori and we broke up a long time ago. She's old news, believe me. She's about to get married, actually...to a guy."

"Oh! That's tough."

Shelby nodded. "It was. But I'm totally over it. And Nana's cool with me being gay."

"That's great! The support of family is so valuable. I'm really anxious to talk to her. Do you think we could set that up for today?"

"I'll call her and find out."

Shelby went to make the phone call and Gwen took one more look at the photo before wandering into the front room. She felt a little giddy with the anticipation of hearing Lucy Brewster's story. For a while, she'd worried that she would never know the identity of the journal writer. Among the thousands of WAVES stationed at Alameda in the 1940s, nothing had yet turned up in the journal to distinguish her, nothing she could investigate anyway, except maybe her assignment as the CO's driver. That had been the best bet up until today. But now she knew she would have a name in hand before the day was out and she couldn't wait.

"Okay, all set," Shelby said, striding into the room, Oscar on her heels. "Her physical therapy is over for the day, so she's all yours. Or, as she put it, 'Where the hell else would I be?'"

"Oh, she's a feisty one!"

"She's cranky. The place is wearing on her. Talking to you will get her mind off the rest of it. It'll be good for her."

"I'll run by the office and get the recorder, then I'll go right over there. Do you want to come?"

"I've got a guy coming over in a while to give me an estimate for building a wheelchair ramp on the porch. But I'd like to see the story when it's ready."

"Sure. I'll send it to you after I get it transcribed." Gwen hesitated. "Um, that little incident earlier..."

Shelby raised her eyebrows inquiringly.

Gwen felt awkward. "I don't know why I did that. I wasn't thinking. I hope I didn't offend you or anything."

"No, you didn't offend me."

"No?" Gwen felt herself grinning.

Shelby smiled with her entire face. "Just the opposite."

Accepting that as encouragement, Gwen reached an arm around Shelby's waist and pulled her close. Shelby tilted her head, her face an open invitation. Gwen kissed her. She felt Shelby yield to her, her lips parting. They kissed passionately, the sort of kiss that takes over your whole body in a falling, melting sensation.

Shelby moved closer and slipped her arms around Gwen's waist, drawing their hips together and sending a fire coursing through Gwen. She cradled the back of Shelby's head in her hand, exploring her mouth more deeply. After a few moments, she reluctantly pulled away.

"I should get over there," she murmured. "Unless you want me to stay here awhile."

Shelby smiled warmly. "I think you should go. That guy'll be here any minute. But I'll see you soon, I hope."

Shelby gave her one more kiss before opening the door. Gwen tripped at the top of the stairs, sending her camera into an acute swing across her chest. Recovering, she walked backward to the street so she could keep Shelby in sight. Her giddiness, she realized, wasn't all about interviewing Lucy Brewster.

"Good luck with the city council tonight," Shelby called.

CHAPTER SEVENTEEN

"Good afternoon, Lucy!" Gwen said cheerfully, holding out her hand to the small elderly woman sitting up in bed with a diminutive television inches from her face. "I'm Gwen Lawford, here to interview you."

Though she couldn't see the TV screen, Gwen could hear the distinctive sounds of a baseball game.

Lucy wore a long nightgown and a Giants baseball cap. Gwen could see something of Shelby in the old woman's face and something of the young woman in the photograph Shelby had shown her.

Lucy took her hand briefly, then pressed the button on the side of her bed to switch off the TV. "You're a friend of my granddaughter?"

"Yes," Gwen confirmed. "Do you want to go somewhere private for this?"

"Is she over there?" Lucy asked, nodding toward the other half of the room.

"Your roommate? No. The bed's empty."

"Then let's just stay here. I haven't got much energy today."

"Would you prefer I come back some other day?" Gwen offered, privately hoping the answer would be no.

"No, no. I'm okay."

Gwen pulled the visitor chair closer as Lucy raised the head of her bed to sit upright. Then she put her tape recorder on the bed stand and positioned the microphone close to Lucy. It was all Gwen could do to keep herself from blurting out her burning questions. But she knew she had to conduct this interview like all the others, methodically and objectively.

"Do you have any questions before we start?" Gwen asked. "Do you know what this is for?"

"Something to do with the shipyards."

"Yes. We're collecting stories from everyone who worked there during the war. For a historical record. It will be posted on the Rosie the Riveter website. Is that all right?"

Lucy nodded. "Can you get my sweater over there on the peg?" She pointed to the far wall.

Gwen jumped up and lifted the sweater off a hook. She noticed the photos arranged on the closet door and stopped to look them over.

"Oh, here's one of Shelby," she said, pointing to one of the photos. Shelby had an arm slung around another girl about her age, dark-haired and dark-eyed, both of them looking like teenagers. They were wearing sweatshirts that read "Alameda High School."

"Yes, that's her. That's her girlfriend Lori in that picture."

Gwen nodded, reminded of what Shelby had said about her grandmother being cool with her lesbianism. Gwen had been overjoyed to learn Shelby was out with her family and had their support. She paused over a professionally photographed family grouping—mother, father, Shelby, brother towering over everyone. It looked to be four or five years old. A nice-looking family, Gwen thought. Too bad her parents split up.

"Are we ready, then?" she asked, draping the sweater over Lucy's shoulders.

Lucy nodded. "Ready as I'm gonna be."

Gwen pressed a button to start the recording. "This is Gwen Lawford and I'm here with Lucy Brewster at Piedmont Gardens Health Care Center in Alameda, California. Ms. Brewster is a resident of Alameda, a retired pharmacist, and a former employee of the Kaiser Shipyards in Richmond, California. Lucy, can you start us off by telling us where and when you were born?"

Lucy pulled herself up higher on her pillows, then turned toward the machine and leaned into it, speaking loud and clear. "I was born in Sparta, Tennessee, in nineteen twenty-four."

"You don't need to get that close," Gwen advised. "Just relax and speak normally. It will pick you up."

Lucy leaned back into her pillows. "The day I was born the dogwoods were in full bloom down in the hollow. They said 'holler' back there in the hills."

The interview proceeded better than many, as Lucy Brewster wasn't suffering from senility or serious dementia, at least in her long-term memories. She did seem weak, though, and Gwen noticed that as she slid bit by bit during their conversation further down into the angle of the bed, she made no attempt to right herself. After an hour, Lucy was crumpled into an awkward looking slump.

Gwen shut off the recorder and stood. "Let me help you sit up," she said.

As she gently lifted Lucy into place and repositioned her pillows, a nurse's aide came into the room with four pills in a little paper cup, all different colors and shapes.

"Your meds," she said loudly, placing the cup on the table beside the tape recorder.

The aide poured a cup of water from a pitcher and then left. Lucy fished out one of the pills and swallowed it with a good gulp of water. Gwen waited patiently while the pills disappeared one by one, hoping that whatever they were for, they wouldn't put Lucy to sleep or muddle her memory. Gwen was anxious to resume. They were just getting to the part where she met Marjorie, the driver for the naval base commander, confirming that the woman in Shelby's photo was the same woman who had written the journal. How extraordinary, Gwen thought, that these two stories had meshed in this way. She tried to remain calm, but she was truly beside herself in anticipation of the facts she was about to discover.

"Are you ready?" Gwen asked.

"Yes. Where were we?"

"You were talking about meeting Marjorie."

"Oh, yes, Marjorie." Lucy smiled wistfully.

Returning from the interview with Lucy, Gwen was so anxious to share it with Shelby she spent the rest of the afternoon transcribing it at the museum computer. She had a name now—Marjorie Banyan, Seaman Second Class. She knew from experience that was plenty of information to flesh out the real person. There would be military records. There would be census records. And who knew what other trails Marjorie Banyan had left behind?

This research was the sort of thing she loved, the unraveling of a mystery. She could hardly wait to get started, to find out what had happened to Marjorie after the war. She had a few more pages of the journal to read and then she would begin the more formal research, the part she craved, the dogged pursuit of information. But she held herself back while she finished transcribing Lucy's interview.

When at last she was done and had e-mailed the document to Shelby, she saw that it was six-thirty, long past closing time and long after the old folks had toddled away. She had to be at the city council meeting in a half hour. She copied her Powerpoint presentation to her thumb drive, hoping it would be convincing enough to sway at least one or two of the council members.

As she shut down her computer, she wondered what Shelby would think of the story of her grandmother's youth. The version she would see was much different than what Gwen had experienced that afternoon. The words themselves were the same, but Lucy's facial expressions and the tone of her voice, the emotion-laden pauses—all of these went undisclosed in the written document. Not to mention the way tears had come to her eyes once as she spoke of Marjorie. Shelby wouldn't see or hear any of that.

But Gwen had seen it and taken note of it. There was no doubt in Gwen's mind that Marjorie had been extremely important to Lucy. The extent of their affection for one another, though, was still uncertain. She was hoping the journal would reveal more. She kept these thoughts to herself. One thing she absolutely didn't want to do was alienate Shelby with unfounded suggestions about her grandmother. Alienating Shelby was the exact opposite of what she wanted. Her mind kept returning to the marvelous kisses from earlier in the day and how hungry they had left her for more.

So let Shelby draw her own conclusions for now, until there was more evidence.

CHAPTER EIGHTEEN

LUCY: I was born in Sparta, Tennessee, in nineteen twenty-four. The day I was born, the dogwoods were in full bloom down in the hollow. They said "holler" back there in the hills. Mama always said she never saw the dogwoods that pretty again, not since the day I was born. That's about the only thing I know about my birth, and I've remembered it all these years. Everybody should know something like that about the day they were born, something nice. That's why I made a point of telling Vivian that the day she was born, a meadowlark was sitting on the fence post outside my bedroom window, singing the prettiest song, singing right through my screams of pain and her angry cries.

There are no dogwoods here, but I remember from when I was a little girl, in the springtime around my birthday, I'd look at those showy white flowers and feel happy. Like they bloomed just for me.

GWEN: That's a nice memory. Tell me about your parents.

LUCY: My father worked on the railroad. My mother was a homemaker, but that was a completely different job then than it is now. She had to make all our food and grow the vegetables and wash the clothes without a machine. I had two brothers. They were ornery boys, both of them, but they were just typical boys. I was the only girl. Boys got the better end of the deal in those days. Maybe still do. In the backwoods of Tennessee it was better to be a boy, no way around that.

GWEN: Your father worked on the railroad. Was that a good job? What was your financial status?

LUCY: We didn't have that much. We didn't get anything new, like clothes and toys unless it was a special occasion. I remember one Christmas my daddy gave me the most beautiful doll. Later, the three of us kids were out in the yard playing with our presents. My older brother Richard grabbed my doll, threw it up in the air, hit it with a baseball bat and busted it all to pieces. I never forgave him for that. Now that he's dead, though, I guess I forgive him for every ornery thing he ever did.

GWEN: Would you say you were poor?

LUCY: We were poor, but we weren't aware of it. Not us kids anyway. We didn't know any different. You had two pairs of shoes, your everyday ones that you held together with twine, and then your Sunday shoes for church. You wouldn't expect more than that. Nobody back there had much. We were all in the same boat.

I remember when Dad's cousin Meryl came for a visit and just went on and on about how Arkansas was such a land of opportunity. It looked like they had money too because Meryl had such nice clothes. She kept telling us we should move there, so we did. When I was eight, we moved to Cherry Creek, Madison County, Arkansas.

GWEN: Life was better in Arkansas?

LUCY: For Meryl it was! Meryl had money all right because she and her husband were in the moonshine business. She had a barrel of sour mash going behind the stove all the time. Mama—

she was a God-fearing woman—threw a fit when she found out, but it was too late to turn around then and go back to Tennessee. Daddy had already planted acres and acres of strawberries in the rich Ozark soil. So we made a go of it.

We sold the strawberries to buy flour and sugar and such. We had our own chickens and pigs. The next spring Daddy planted an orchard, tomatoes and everything, so that's when we really had to start working. It didn't make any difference whether it was the dead of winter or Sunday or whatever, Daddy would get up while it was still dark and come in and yell, "Hit the deck, everybody hit the deck. The mornin' star's away up there." It makes me feel good to think of that even now.

Hard work was all we knew, so we didn't think it was so bad. I don't know if kids today could have lived through it, but everything's changed. We say that sometimes like a complaint, but that's why we were working so hard all those years, wasn't it, to give our kids more than what we had? Well, I guess we did it! I know my grandkids have had no hardship whatsoever. And I don't begrudge them that.

GWEN: Did you go to school or just work on the farm?

LUCY: My brothers and I went to school at the same place, Cherry Creek School. All in the same class. It was just a little one-room schoolhouse. All they cared about was that we learn to read and write and do basic math. A little bit of American history got thrown in there. Nothing fancy, though.

GWEN: Were you happy? Do you remember your childhood as happy?

LUCY: Happy and healthy. As far as I was concerned, it was paradise. I just loved springtime in the Ozarks. In the morning you could look out across the trees and see a hundred different colors of green, from the lightest to the darkest moss color. And the buds of the leaves swelled day by day, all different sizes. All through the mountains, as far as you could see, the green would be dotted with blooming redbuds. It was beautiful. The sun was as hot when it came up in the morning as it was at noon. It was like a big red ball of fire.

We did okay. We got by. Until the thirties when the Depression hit. That's when things got bad. Nobody had any money and there were no jobs. I didn't mind so much for myself. I didn't even mind Hoover gravy, but Daddy was so discouraged during that time. Mama was just plain depressed.

GWEN: What's Hoover gravy?

LUCY: Oh, that's when they mix bacon grease, flour and water together. They couldn't afford milk, so it was made with water instead.

GWEN: And you didn't mind that?

LUCY: No, I didn't mind it too much. It was just the way things were. There was no point in complaining. I knew my parents were doing the best they could.

GWEN: Is that when you moved to California, during the Depression?

LUCY: Yes. Everybody was moving to California, looking for jobs. All the relatives moved out except some of the older folks. My daddy came out in nineteen thirty-five and got a seasonal job at the Hunts cannery. My uncle got a job working on a gold dredge on the Mokelumne River, placer mining. It was a good job and my daddy wanted to get on there too, but he couldn't. They had enough men. He did find a good job, though, the following year, with Standard Oil in the Bay Area. So we moved here, to Alameda, in nineteen thirty-six. I was twelve.

We bought a house as soon as we could. It wasn't a big house, just two bedrooms and one bathroom. It was tight fit, but it was quite a step up for us with indoor plumbing. No outhouse. We thought we'd died and gone to heaven! Things were so different here. Like another world. I don't think Mama ever did like it. She missed the Ozarks and she missed her parents. She only saw them a couple of times before they died. People didn't travel like they do now. Going back to Arkansas for a visit was a big deal.

Mama's way of adapting out here was to live like they did back in the hills. As much as she could. She had a couple of hogs, some chickens and a big vegetable garden. We didn't need to do that here because Daddy had a regular paycheck and we bought everything at the grocery store, but it was her way of life. She still baked bread from scratch even though you could get a loaf of Wonder Bread for a dime. I guess she wouldn't have had anything to do if she gave up all the old ways. The funny thing about that is we used to try to get lunch invitations to our friends' houses because they got sandwiches made with that fluffy white store-bought bread. We thought that was so good, like rich people's bread. Now it's completely opposite. A loaf of bread like Mama made sells for five dollars in the stores now. And that soft, pre-sliced white bread is the cheapest thing you can buy. Funny how things change.

GWEN: Yes, it is. How did you like living here?

LUCY: I liked it fine. I liked school here better because my brothers weren't in the same class anymore. I always loved school and did well. I guess I was lucky we moved here. I think if I'd stayed back in the hills, I wouldn't have had an opportunity to go to high school at all. It would have been too far away. But everybody went to high school here. Not everybody graduated, but I did.

GWEN: What about socializing? Did you go on dates or anything like that when you were in high school?

LUCY: No, I didn't date much. I wasn't allowed to go on dates until I was eighteen. We sometimes went out to a soda fountain, a group of us, boys and girls. Safety, or maybe propriety, in numbers. I was like most girls, innocent and ignorant. Arnie Brewster was one of my classmates, one of a group of kids I went around with. He was the same age as me. After high school, we dated. I got a job as a typist and still lived with my parents. Arnie lived with his mother in the same house I live in now.

I wouldn't say I was ever in love with Arnie. He was just a boy who liked me and he was a nice guy. Like a lot of other boys, he was drafted into the army. We were married in February, forty-four, right before he went off to boot camp. A lot of people did that. A lot of girls thought their boys would never come home and did it as a sort of going-away present. They weren't thinking past the war. I wasn't either. We didn't have a honeymoon, didn't go anywhere.

I moved to Arnie's house. Well, his mother's house. His father had died, so his mother Arlene was a widow, but all her kids were grown by then. Two weeks after we were married, Arnie left for boot camp. So then it was just me and my mother-in-law in the house. Of course, my folks were nearby, but both my brothers were drafted too.

GWEN: So you got married in nineteen forty-four. You were twenty.

LUCY: Just about to be. I was nineteen when we got married and turned twenty that spring.

GWEN: Did you keep your job after you got married?

LUCY: Yes, for just a few weeks after Arnie left. Then I went to work at the shipyards. Everybody was doing that. Even Arnie's mother did it. She was hired as a guard, some kind of security person. I forget what the job was called, but we called them Officer So-and-So. Arnie's mother was Officer Brewster. They had no law enforcement training or anything. But they wore a uniform. Sometimes she patrolled the yards and sometimes she sat in one of the shacks at the gate on Cutting Boulevard where you showed your badge as you came in each day. She worked swing shift and I worked day shift. We thought it was funny if she was at the gate when I left work, just as she started her shift, and I said, "Evenin' Officer Brewster." We both laughed every time at that.

Arlene usually slept in the mornings until noon, which meant she was sleeping when the milkman came around. Our milkman's name was Pete. He was a nice old guy. He didn't leave our milk and butter on the porch like they did in those days. He walked right into the kitchen and put it in the refrigerator, nice and quiet so as not to wake Arlene. Boy, times have changed!

GWEN: When you applied at the shipyards, did you get hired right away?

LUCY: Yes. That same day. I applied in the morning and was working by afternoon. I had to have my picture taken and they put it on a badge, then took me out to the yard. I thought I'd get an office job because of my previous experience, but they said they needed workers in the yard, working on the ships. So I said, okay, just like that. I thought it would be interesting. And it was! Right off the bat, first day on the job, I was way out of my comfort zone, but not in a bad way.

GWEN: So you weren't afraid to do that kind of work?

LUCY: No, not afraid. Well, maybe a little right at first, but they showed me what to do. It was a different world, that's for sure. Some of those women had a mouth on them! Colorful language like I'd never heard before! The first couple of times I heard that, I covered my ears. My mama would have tanned those girls' hides if she'd have heard that. Oh, but I got to used to it and didn't even notice after a while.

The clothes were something different too. I had to wear coveralls and boots and put my hair up in a do-rag. We got our clothes at the National Dollar Store, same as any blue-collar working man, blue jeans or coveralls. They didn't make work clothes like that for women, so we had to get men's, which wasn't easy for me because I was so small. There were a lot of women out there who'd never worn pants before. I think a lot of them found out they liked it. A lot of them also cut their hair short because of safety and convenience on the job. I didn't do that. Now my hair's short, has been for years, but back then I had long, dark brown hair.

The first job I had was as a bucker in Yard Number Two. That's where they broke all the records for speed. We were able to do that because of the new shipbuilding methods developed by Mr. Kaiser, bringing in all the pieces prefabricated. The big whirly cranes would lift up the sections and lower them into place. We'd put them together, riveters and welders. I was a bucker first, later a welder. They called us Winnie the Welder, like Rosie the Riveter, but people don't remember Winnie anymore, just Rosie. Once I became a welder, I had to wear leather pants and gloves. I had to go to a week of school for the welding. They sent us to Richmond High School for that. It paid better. By the time I was done, as a journeyman, I was making a dollar twenty an hour.

GWEN: Did that seem like a lot of money?

LUCY: Yes! It was the only money I'd ever made. I couldn't get over my first paycheck with my name on it and everything. That was quite a thrill.

GWEN: What was everyday life like during the war?

LUCY: Oh, you know. We had air raid drills and blackouts. The siren would go off and you'd turn off all the lights until the all clear. Everybody thought the Japanese were going to bomb the mainland. In California, we thought we were the first line of defense. People always thought they were seeing Zeroes in the sky or submarines in the Bay. There was a lot of paranoia. Nobody expected them to hit Hawaii, though.

GWEN: But everyday life for you, for instance. How was that affected by the war?

LUCY: We had rationing, all these things you had to do without. You couldn't get butter, so we had oleo. That's like margarine, but it was white and they sold it with a little tube of yellow food coloring that you mixed in. Sugar was rationed too. You got one cup a week per person, and as the war went on, everything made with sugar was rationed too, like jam.

Arlene had a car, a thirty-eight Chrysler Royal, but she could only get three gallons of gas a week and you couldn't buy tires, so the car just sat there most of the time. We didn't drive it to work. We took the bus. We had recycling then too. We took our metal in and turned in our used fat to the meat market. Except bacon grease. We always used that for cooking. Every payday we'd buy a war bond. Everybody did. Basically, we just did what everybody else was doing.

But building those ships was the most important thing we did for the war effort. They were so big you could get lost in them. We brought our lunch in lunch pails, those round-top metal ones, you know. Everybody had the same boring lunch pails in those days. No Spiderman or Flintstones. We sat right down in the hull of the ship and ate. Our crew and our leaderwoman all sat down together there and talked and joked through lunch. On days they had a show at lunch time, we took our lunchboxes over to the General Warehouse to watch it. We had the Andrews Sisters one time and Kay Kyser. He came in and recorded a live radio show, *Kay Kyser's College of Musical Knowledge.*

GWEN: That was a tremendous benefit of working there.

LUCY: You're too young to know who the Andrews Sisters were, but you know who Bing Crosby was, don't you? I even got to see him there once. He was my favorite.

GWEN: Oh, I know both. At the museum, we play forties music all the time. The Andrews Sisters are on our regular soundtrack. *Chattanooga Choo Choo*, that's one we play.

LUCY: Yes! That's a good one.

GWEN: What about your job? Can you describe that?

LUCY: Okay. When I started as a bucker, my riveter was a black woman named Patty. We made a great team. We'd race along the seams, her on one side, me on the other holding my buck board against the rivet. Bang, bang, bang, we went along like a machine.

I loved working out there. It wasn't easy, but it was important and it was more interesting than typing all day. All kinds of people worked there, men and women, black, white, Mexican, Chinese. People from everywhere, all over the country, came to work in the shipyards. There were so many people coming in for the war work, there was no place for them all to live. Everybody in Richmond was renting out rooms. People slept in their cars. People even paid to go into a movie and sleep in the theater. Lots of people were setting up bunk beds in their garages, renting out a bed cheap. They rented beds in shifts, to two different people, one for day shift, one for night shift.

The girl I worked with, Patty, she was living with her husband and three kids in somebody's basement. They were on a waiting list for company housing, but that never did come, not as long as she worked with me.

A lot of them came from Arkansas, too, which was fun for me, being from there myself. Even some of our relatives came out. We had quite a few relatives out here. Some went back, after the war.

Yeah, lots of people, all kinds. Everybody was busy working, doing their part. We all got along.

GWEN: So there was no trouble? No racism, no sexism?

LUCY: I wouldn't say there was no trouble. In the shipyards, we women were pioneers in a man's world. I learned mighty fast how to deal with male resentment and out and out sexual propositions. I didn't have much trouble, but I did hear of a couple of cases of men sabotaging women workers. And there was a case of one of the girls being raped on the graveyard shift. I didn't know her, but word got out. We all heard about it. They told us to work in pairs and watch out for one another after that. Most of the men were good fellas and they tried to help you out and keep everything running smoothly. But, like anywhere else, there were a few bad apples. Most of the trouble with the men was just grumbling. The worst I ever got from them was when I needed some help moving something heavy and was told that if I couldn't do my job, I shouldn't be there. Overall, I would say the men were happy to have us there and treated us fairly.

GWEN: Did you do any socializing outside of work?

LUCY: I was too tired most nights after working eight hours, but I did occasionally go to the bar that was close to our house. Flanagan's was only two blocks away. It's gone now. That's where the beauty parlor is. Some of the sailors and WAVES went there, from the base here in Alameda, but it was mainly a neighborhood place. Seaman Second Class Banyan went there pretty regular. That was my friend Marjorie. I didn't meet her there, though. I met her at the shipyards. She was the driver for the base commander and they drove over once in a while.

GWEN: Marjorie Banyan. Can you tell me more about her?

LUCY: Oh, Marjorie was a jewel! She was funny and smart. She was just a joy to be around. She came over most weekends and a lot of evenings too. She had no family here. They were on the East Coast, so she sort of adopted us.

She helped out around the place. She cooked for us on Sundays. I don't think she liked my cooking, to tell you the truth. Marjorie and I had a ball. If not for her, I would have spent all my time home watching the wallpaper yellow. With Arlene working nights, I was alone in the evenings before Marjorie came along. She was good company.

On our days off, we'd go into San Francisco sometimes, take the ferry over to the Ferry Building, you know, same as now, down on the Embarcadero. Then we'd ride a trolley car to Golden Gate Park and listen to a band or just walk. And ball games. Oh, I loved to go to ball games!

Marjorie liked to dance, so we'd go to clubs on weekends. She'd dance with sailors sometimes, sometimes with me. When any of those sailors tried to get a little friendly with her, she'd put them in their place. The zoot-suiters, though, they were even worse, thinking they were such big wheels with their Hollywood haircuts. They didn't bother her because she was in uniform, and they didn't get along with sailors at all, but they would come after me sometimes. It didn't matter where she was or what she was doing, as soon as one of those guys started in on me, Marjorie was there in an instant telling them to get lost. She knew how to handle the fresh guys. She wouldn't tolerate any nonsense from them.

GWEN: It sounds like you and Marjorie became very close.

LUCY: We did. Arlene liked having her around too. Marjorie was very handy around the house. She knew how to fix things. We were moving furniture one day and rammed into the dining room chandelier with a bookcase. Busted it all to pieces. We went downtown and bought a new light fixture and Marjorie wired it up herself. I'd learned all about farming as a kid, but Marjorie had lived in town and her grandpa taught her things like that. Plumbing and electricity. Enough to get by. That light fixture is still there. It still works!

One day she got me on board one of the ships going out for its maiden voyage, one of the big C-4s. Out of all those ships I welded together, that was the only time I sailed on one. Whenever we finished one, the bigwigs all came over and knocked a bottle of champagne against it and took it for a shakedown cruise around the bay. Usually the crews that had worked on it would stand on the docks and wait for it to come back tested good. The way they'd tell us was they'd mount a broom on top, meaning a clean sweep. When we saw that broom, we'd all cheer.

Marjorie had been on these maiden voyages several times. It wasn't a big deal to her. When I told her I wondered what it was like, she got me a pass. I remember walking on board in my Sunday clothes while the shipyard band played, thinking about how careful I was with my welded seams, how they ought to hold up okay, but I couldn't vouch for everybody else's work. There was a fancy buffet on board and all the big shots' wives wearing fur coats and orchids.

The ship launched into the bay and headed out toward the ocean, passing under the Golden Gate Bridge. Once we were clear of the bay, the ship was bobbing all over and making everybody sick because it didn't have any ballast. I threw up on my best dress that day and I was done with sailing. I could put them together, but that was enough for me, and I never got on another of those ships again. Marjorie laughed at me all that day over that.

GWEN: What year are we talking about? Still forty-four?

LUCY: Yeah, nineteen forty-four. This was the summer and fall.

GWEN: By then your husband was out of boot camp and was stationed where?

LUCY: He was overseas. So were both my brothers and Marjorie's brother too. We occasionally got letters from them, and usually they had big black marks added by the censors. We baked cookies and shipped them off to the boys whenever we could. We sent a care package almost every week.

Christmas that year was sad for a lot of families. Husbands and sons were gone. Some had been killed. It wasn't so bad for me, not lonely, mainly because of Marjorie. Arlene, on the other hand, cried all the time in those days. She really missed Arnie. After her husband died, Arnie was the man in her life. I would go so far as to say she missed him more than I did. That wasn't something I thought much about at the time. I didn't know jack about squat back then. Having been married for such a short time, I was completely ignorant about what marriage should feel like, or even what married love should feel like. I didn't know what it was like to be in love. Because of that, I didn't know there was anything missing between me and Arnie.

That's basically how I spent my time during the war. Arnie came home in January, nineteen forty-five. He was injured in the fighting, so he was sent home before the war was over. He recovered, but he had a nerve pain in his leg the rest of his life.

GWEN: What happened to Marjorie?

LUCY: Shortly after Arnie came home, early forty-five, she transferred out and went back where she'd come from, New York.

GWEN: When the war was over, what happened to your job?

LUCY: I got my layoff notice from the shipyards in September like a lot of the women. They didn't need us anymore. I went back to being a housewife. After all the excitement, it was very peaceful. Boring, I would even say, for a while. I didn't get back into the workforce for years after that. We did our part, though, and we did a good job. Must have done something right. We won the war, didn't we?

GWEN: Yes, we did, thanks to people like you.

LUCY: That was quite a time for me. Quite a time. I lived a lot of life in that one year.

GWEN: Did you keep in touch with Marjorie at all?

LUCY: No. I got a letter from her that spring after she left, from New York, but that was the last I heard from her. I know most of the WAVES were discharged after the war. They didn't need women anymore there either. I hope she got to stay in the navy. She loved the navy. She never felt she belonged anywhere more than in the military. She had the snappiest salute you ever saw.

GWEN: What did you do later?

LUCY: I ended up divorcing Arnie in nineteen sixty-two. I got a job in a doctor's office, as a receptionist, an office person, so the old typing skills came in handy again. I raised my girls on my own. In nineteen seventy, I went to college. You may think that was a strange thing to do at that age—I was forty-six—but I just felt like I wanted to do more. It was the spirit in the country at the time, I guess. Everything was changing. Women's lib, that was it, mainly. It gave me some big ideas. Besides, I knew I could do what I put my mind to, didn't I? I learned that a long time ago in the shipyards. Yeah, the shipyards were a real lesson for a farm girl like me. It was an exciting time. Sometimes it feels like yesterday. Where'd those sixty-five years go? I ask myself sometimes.

GWEN: It was a vivid time in your life. You seem to remember it very well.

LUCY: Yeah, it was a remarkable time of my life. A happy, innocent time. I've enjoyed talking about it, remembering all those things. I'm kind of tired now, though. Talking so much kind of wears a person out.

GWEN: Well, thank you for talking to me, Lucy. I've enjoyed it too.

CHAPTER NINETEEN

As Shelby went through Nana's monthly statements from banks, credit union and her financial advisor, she was shocked to learn how much money Nana had accumulated. She wrote the figures down from various savings accounts and investments. Then she added them together and sat staring at her calculator in disbelief. It was true Nana lived very simply and had done so for decades with no house payment, driving an economical older car, rarely traveling. But her pension was modest. Who would have guessed this? Definitely not Shelby, who was still trying to fathom why Nana saved all the plastic tabs from bread wrappers. Maybe that was the same impulse that had led her to manage her money so thriftily.

For today's visit to the nursing home, she decided to take Nana's car, partly just to keep the car running, partly because she was taking Oscar along and wanted him to ride in a familiar car.

When she arrived in Nana's room, she found her lying flat in the bed with a clear plastic tube in her nose. The other end of the tube was connected to a bulky machine beside the bed that hummed loudly. Dinky was asleep on her side of the room.

Shelby squeezed past Dinky's wheelchair, leading Oscar on his leash, and pulled the curtain between the two halves of the room. Nana smiled weakly at her when she came into view.

"What's this?" Shelby asked, pointing at the machine.

"Oxygen. Why don't you turn it off so I can hear you?"

Shelby reached for the on/off switch and then froze momentarily, feeling a sudden fear that she was about to snuff out her grandmother's life. Nana must have noticed the hesitation. "Go on," she urged, "turn it off. It's okay. It's just oxygen."

Just oxygen, Shelby thought, amused. Sort of an essential ingredient for humans.

She flipped the switch and Nana removed the clear plastic tubing from around her ears, pulling it free of her nose, then she spread her hands out on top of her sheet, her mottled, semi-transparent skin showing all the blue veins under it.

"Why the oxygen?" Shelby asked.

"Just having some trouble breathing," Nana replied, as if it were nothing.

Maybe it was nothing.

"I brought you a visitor," Shelby said, just as Oscar decided to bark.

Nana's eyes lit up. She patted both hands on her lap. Shelby deposited Oscar beside her on the side of her uninjured hip and he proceeded to lick her face and hands frantically, his tail moving so fast it was a blur.

"Let me know if he's hurting you," she said. "I can hold him for you and you can just pet him."

"How's my boy?" Nana squeezed Oscar in her arms as he wriggled and continued licking her. "Oh, thank you for bringing him, Shelby!"

"He misses you too."

Shelby sat in the visitor's chair. After a minute of watching

Oscar and Nana give each other some loving, she said, "That was a nice interview you gave Gwen. She sent it to me last night."

"I hope it's what she wanted. It's hard to know what anybody would care about now, about what we did back in the old days."

"I think people are just curious about how different things were. That part about how you were all so surprised with the indoor plumbing, that was funny."

"It's all in what you're used to." Nana ran her hand methodically over Oscar's head and back. "I remember when my Uncle George came to visit us not long after we moved here and he stood in the kitchen for the longest time just flipping the light switch on and off. Just stood there. On, off, on, off. When he got back to the hills, he wired his own house with electricity. I guess he didn't think it was anything worth having before that."

Shelby laughed. "You should've told that story to Gwen."

"Well, you can't tell everything in a couple hours. You have to leave a lot out."

"Yeah, I guess," Shelby said. "I really enjoyed reading about the old days, though."

Though Oscar's tail hadn't slowed down, he was calmer now. Nana held his head between both hands and made a face at him, baring her teeth.

"Gwen's a nice young woman," she said. "I like her."

"I like her too."

Nana looked up to catch Shelby's eye. "Oh? Do you want to elaborate on that?"

Shelby shrugged. "There's nothing to tell...yet."

Nana grinned, then she started wheezing and reached for the water glass. Shelby filled it and handed it to her, waiting until she was breathing more calmly.

"Why are you having trouble breathing?" Shelby asked.

"Who knows," Nana said dismissively. "Who cares?"

Shelby was about to object when Dinky started hollering.

Nana rolled her eyes. "Thar she blows again!"

"Nurse!" Dinky yelled. "Nurse, where are you? I've pressed this goddamned button a dozen times already!"

Just then, Vivian came through the curtain, took one look at

Oscar and said, "Oh, my God! What is that dog doing in here? Shelby, are you responsible for this?"

"They said I could bring him for a visit."

"But this is supposed to be a sterile environment. He's full of germs."

"Oh, he is not," Nana objected. "No more than you are, Viv."

Vivian blinked, looking indignant. "Shelby, I need to talk to you."

Shelby gathered she meant in private, so she got up and followed her mother out of the room to the end of the hallway.

"That's Mom's car in the parking lot, isn't it?" Vivian asked.

"Sure."

"Did you have an accident?"

"No."

"Look, Shelby, if you did, I'm not going to get mad at you, but we need to report it and get the car fixed."

"Are you talking about the front?"

"Yes. I can see something's happened. The hood's bent and the license plate frame is smashed."

"I didn't do it. I mean, it was like that when I went to get it this morning in the garage."

Vivian looked at her for a moment, apparently trying to decide if she was telling the truth. They both returned to Nana's room and the interrogation started again, but this time she asked Nana the questions.

Nana shrugged. "I guess I sort of nudged one of those cement things they plant the light poles in. Some parking lot."

"Nudged? When did this happen?"

"I don't know. A while ago."

"Did you report it?" asked Vivian.

"No. What for? I didn't hit anybody. Just a little ding."

"How did it happen?" pressed Vivian.

Nana frowned. "I went to back out of the parking space and something went wrong. The car went forward instead of backward. Hit the damn thing. Nobody got hurt. No big deal."

Vivian looked worried. "You mean you put the car in drive instead of reverse?"

Nana shrugged and returned her attention to Oscar who was lying with his head on her stomach, happily accepting a head scratching.

"Mom, are you having trouble driving?" Vivian asked.

"Who wants to drive anyway? I think I'll hire a chauffeur and be driven around like Miss Daisy. Or maybe I'll hire a nice young woman to drive me around, like Marjorie." Nana smiled smugly.

"Marjorie?" Vivian wrinkled up her face. "That woman in the photo on the refrigerator? That was back in the forties, Mom. Oh, my God, are you okay? Do you know what year it is?"

Vivian hovered over the bed waiting for her response.

Nana looked indignant. "What the hell are you going on about?" she said. "Of course I know what year it is! It's the year I broke my goddamned hip and had to live in this hellhole."

Vivian backed away, her eyes wide. "There's no need to get upset."

Shelby intervened. "Nana, I think I'll take Oscar home now. He looks like he wants to get down." She gathered him in her arms. "I'll be back tomorrow. Call me if you want me to bring you anything." She glanced warily at her mother as she put Oscar on the floor. Vivian's mouth was pressed into a thin, hard line of discontent.

Shelby hurried out, anxious to escape the tension building between her mother and grandmother. Oscar ran behind her on his stubby legs, barely keeping pace.

CHAPTER TWENTY

August 21, 1944.

I'm spending my weekends and most evenings at the Brewster house these days. After work, I ride the bike over. I keep a few things there so I can change into civvies to work in the garden or tend to the chickens. Weeknights, it's just me and Lucy for supper. We go out to eat sometimes, but stay in mostly. It's comfortable in her house and I like it there. It turns out she isn't much of a cook. She can make a pot of butter beans with ham and cornbread, but that's about it. Pretty much every meal she knows how to make has some form of pork in it, which is a problem with the meat rationing. So I've taken over the kitchen for the most part. I'm not a fancy cook, but I'm not bad at it. I usually cook enough for the three of us and leave Arlene's plate out for her for later.

All the neighbors have a victory garden and we share. If the

Tonerellis have extra carrots, they give us some and we give them a cabbage. We have chickens, so we have eggs, and sometimes we have extra of those too. Over the weekend I built a real chicken coop with raised laying beds, all nice and enclosed so the chickens can get out of the cold and rain. I studied the coop over at the Browns and built it like theirs. Lucy says it's beautiful. I think those chickens thought so too. They were clucking up a storm in there for a while.

We don't eat the chickens, except for a special occasion or if there's a hen that isn't laying much anymore. The chickens, like everybody else, have to pull their weight. We did eat one last Sunday, though. That's another thing Lucy knows how to cook, fried chicken. She's the one who killed the poor thing. I wouldn't have been able to do that. But she's used to it. Back in the Ozarks, it was a run-of-the-mill thing to wring a chicken's neck. And that's exactly what she did too. She swung that chicken around in a circle until its head came off, then she hung it upside-down on the clothesline to let the blood drain out. I think I'd have used a hatchet myself.

Lucy looks like a fragile little thing, but her looks will fool you. She works alongside big men every day welding those ships, eight hours of hard labor. Her strength of mind is powerful too. Not a sentimental girl. That chicken never stood a chance with her.

August 24, 1944.

Lucy doesn't talk much about her husband. I don't think she knows him very well. They were married only two weeks before he shipped out. If she misses him, she doesn't say so. His name is Arnie. I guess that's short for Arnold.

I like taking Lucy out on the town when she's not too tired. Richmond is going full blast around the clock because of the shipyards. People are out at all hours. Restaurants are open all night. You can walk down Cutting Boulevard at three a.m. and it's just as crowded as it is at noon!

We went to a baseball game last Saturday. She loves baseball and goes bonkers watching it. It made me laugh to see her hopping up and down in the stands. We went to Seals Stadium in San Francisco. She told me Joe DiMaggio himself started with the Seals, so they were nothing to sneeze at. It was an exciting game. The Seals won. It's a good thing because Lucy got so worked up when they were down by two runs in the sixth inning she shook her fist and said, "Come on, you so-and-sos! Get on the stick!" I mean, she actually said "so-and-sos." That's the worst cursing I've heard from her so far, so I guess she was downright livid!

At the base, I've been doing less and less driving. I'm more of a personal assistant to Captain Blanchard now. Everything's going great for me. I feel so much more relaxed now that I've got a nice, private place to spend my time. It's more like normal life, like a home. I almost never go to the service club anymore. And I haven't been to Flanagan's for a while either.

Hazel, Maria and Bettie are used to me coming in late now, usually just in time to hit the sack. When I talk about my time away, I always say "the Brewsters" as if there's a whole houseful of them. I don't want Hazel to think there's anything suspicious going on. Because there isn't. It isn't like that.

On the nights I stay on base, I usually spend my time doing chores like laundry and writing letters home. The truth is, when I stay here in the barracks, like tonight, I miss Lucy. I've gotten awfully fond of spending time with her. But I don't want to wear out my welcome. From what I can tell, though, she's still happy to see me when I pedal up to her front gate each evening. A couple times she's been right there in the front yard waiting for me with a big old smile.

August 26, 1944.

Lucy and I went dancing tonight at a place in Oakland called Sweets. They had a swell swing band. We danced every single dance. I bought her a new dress for tonight. It wasn't fancy, but as much as I could afford. She looked like a million bucks in it. Maybe better than a million. She looked so pretty with her hair curled and falling over her shoulders. I know she was surprised to get a gift like that when it's not her birthday or Christmas or anything. I told her I just felt like saying thank you for being such a wonderful friend.

September 1, 1944.

Today I had such a scare. I was alone in the office typing and got a call from the Kaiser hospital in Oakland where they take the injured shipyard workers. "Lucy Brewster's been in an accident," they said. "She asked us to call you to come over."

I panicked. For some reason, I got it in my head Lucy was dying, so there was no time to waste. The captain was out making the rounds and I didn't want to take the time to track him down. The staff car was sitting out front. I didn't think twice about taking it.

I raced to the hospital and ran inside, hollering, "Where's Lucy, where's Lucy?" like a lunatic. I found her in an examining room, sitting on a table with her coverall leg cut off and a bandage on her thigh.

"Oh, hi," she says as calmly as a cow chewing her cud.

I lunged at her and caught her up in my arms, holding her tight, closing my eyes and just feeling her solid, warm, living body against mine. I was still frantic, and so relieved she was okay I was practically in tears. As I calmed down and finally let her go, I realized how crazy it had made me to think of her hurt, to think of losing her.

I drove her home in the staff car. She sat in back with her leg up on the seat. She said she felt like the queen riding in that car with her personal chauffeur. On the way, she told me what had happened. She'd fallen in the ship's hull and ripped open her leg. The sight of all that blood made her think she was going to die and she got scared. Arlene wasn't home, so she had them call me.

I carried her from the car into the house and put her in bed with a *Life* magazine, promising to be back as soon as I got off duty. But I had to get myself and the car back to the base, pronto. I got back just at quitting time. Before I reached the door to the office, Captain Blanchard came out, looking me over solemnly. I stood at attention, saluted and got ready for a dressing down.

"You've been gone awhile, Seaman," he said.

"Yes, sir! Sorry, sir!"

Then he just looked at me for a minute. I was so nervous. I was still flustered over Lucy's accident and I'd never done anything like this before, taken off without leave and stolen the staff car to boot.

"Took the car out to get washed and waxed, did you?" he asked.

I know my mouth must have fallen open as I turned around to look at that dusty car. I turned back and said, "Sir?"

"Keeping things squared away, as usual." He approached the car. I opened the back door for him. He stood right beside me and spoke quietly. "Everything all right?"

"Yes, sir." I swallowed hard and nodded.

Then he patted me on the shoulder, which is not something he normally does. "Check with me next time, will you?" He ducked into the backseat. "Now, how about taking me home?"

That's all there was to it. He never even asked me why. He's a good guy. A lot of the officers don't care for women in the service, but he isn't one of them. By now I guess he figures if I pulled a lulu like this, I must have had a good reason.

I made Lucy eggs and toast for dinner and we sat on her bed and talked until after eleven. Her leg's pretty sore and she's got a nice row of stitches, but she'll heal up just fine. People have died over there in the shipyards, though. It's a dangerous place.

I remember how I felt driving to the hospital today. I kept thinking, what if Lucy dies? What would I do without her? When I ran into the emergency room, half crazy, I was thinking, *hang on, Lucy! I love you! I love you!*

It just came to me like that. I never even thought it before. But suddenly it was there in my mind like a bright, blinking sign. By the time I got her home, I'd figured out I can't tell her that. She'd hate me if she knew that. That's always got to be my secret. So I didn't tell her. Now that I know, I'm wondering how hard it will be to keep it to myself.

September 18, 1944.

Lucy's the most beautiful, sweet, sensational gal in the world! I'm head over heels in love, really in love for the first time in my life. Now I know I was never in love with Nettie. I was fond of her, but it was nothing like this. Lucy's on my mind day and night. I can't wait to get off work so I can see her. She's got one heck of a smile. It can knock your legs right out from under you. She can't guess, I'm sure, what I'm feeling, and that's okay. Just so I can look at her and hear her say my name. That's all I need.

Lucy's usually too tired to go out during the week. I don't mind that at all because our life together at the house is wonderful. After supper, we usually listen to the radio. Saturday nights it's the *Hit Parade* if we're home. We sit at the kitchen table singing along with the radio. Neither one of us can sing worth a toot, but we have a ball. Our favorite show is *The Aldrich Family* on Friday nights. We sit there listening with big grins on our faces. "Henry! Henry Aldrich!" Oh, we laugh and laugh at that show. I've never been so happy in all my life!

September 24, 1944.

Today we went to Fisherman's Wharf. We stuffed ourselves with Dungeness crab we got from an Italian fisherman who threw them into a boiling pot right off his boat. Then we walked out on the pier past the Chinese men and women throwing crab pots into the Bay. At the end of the pier, Lucy leaned against me as we watched a cargo ship gliding through the water on its way into Oakland Harbor. From there, we could see the Golden Gate Bridge on our left and the Bay Bridge on our right. The day was clear and warm, but there was a harsh wind blasting through.

For a while, I forgot about the war and the navy. We seemed so far from anything to do with any of that, even though I knew my base was nearly visible on the southern skyline.

Lucy wrapped her arms around mine and I looked down into her face. I felt like jelly inside looking at her red, red lips and the light in her shining eyes. Her cheeks were blushing pink from the wind. She smiled at me and it was all I could do to keep from kissing her. Instead, I took a cigarette out of my pack and tried to light it. The wind was too fierce. I gave up after three tries. By then, Lucy was watching the gulls instead of me and I'd gotten control of myself.

"I wish you'd give those up," she said, looking at the cigarettes.

"You do?"

She nodded matter-of-factly.

"Then I will," I said decisively. As we walked back along the pier, I handed my pack of Pall Malls to a Chinese man wearing a paddy hat. He grinned and nodded enthusiastically.

Lucy laughed and hugged my arm tighter.

When we got back to the wharf, we stopped at a street vendor's stall. Lucy was fascinated with a musical ballerina in a pink tutu. When you wound it, the ballerina balanced on one foot and put her hands above her head and spun around, as if she were turning through a pirouette. The guy selling it said the tune was from *Swan Lake*, a ballet by Tchaikovsky. Of course I had to buy this toy for Lucy, though she insisted she could buy it for herself if she had to have it, and I know she could. She makes more money than I do, but it made me feel good to do it.

As we came away with the package, Lucy gave me a little kiss on the cheek and I was floating on air the rest of the day.

September 26, 1944.

Your brother has been killed in France.

That was the first line of the telegram I got today from my father. It went on to say Paul was hit by a German land mine, something they call "Bouncing Betty" because it hops into the air before it explodes. What a strange detail to include, I thought, staring at the unbelievable words on that telegram.

I feel numb. I feel so bad for my mother. I know she'll be ripped apart inside. And Daddy too.

I spent the evening in tears. Hazel, Maria and Bettie have been very kind and considerate, fussing over me. Lucy begged me to come over tonight, but I didn't want her to see me like this. As it was, I could barely speak to her on the phone. I could tell she was crying too.

It's after midnight now. I can't sleep. The others have been asleep for a while. I can hear Maria snoring, a regular sound that seems genuinely comforting tonight. I still can't believe it. It's times like these I wish they would let women fight. I could fight. I'd mow the Krauts down like wheat in a field. I'd get a few of them, as many as I could, before they got me, for Paul. He was never cut out to be a soldier anyway. I was always so much tougher than he was. He was small and skinny. In school, the other boys called him a sissy. So tender-hearted. Sometimes I've even wondered if we got all mixed up somehow with me being such a rough girl and he being such a gentle boy. If I'd been there to protect him...Poor boy. He was only twenty-three.

October 1, 1944.

I'm leaving tonight for New York. They're going to bury Paul on Tuesday with full military honors. Closed casket.

October 11, 1944.

This happened two days ago, Monday, but I didn't feel like writing then. It sort of scares me to write it now. I never meant for this to happen. I didn't even want it to happen.

I've been back from New York since Friday. Lucy made fried chicken for my return, like it was a special occasion. She said she missed me a lot. I know I missed her too. Friday night we sat up and talked until after midnight. I told her all about the funeral and how lifeless my father had been. It was scary to see him like that. Lucy's a very good listener. She listened to me for hours, holding my hand across the table. I didn't even realize how late it was until we heard the front door open and Arlene came in, surprised to see me still there. She was wearing her guard's uniform with its gold badge. She gave me a hug before heading off to bed.

"It's so late, you should stay here tonight," Lucy suggested. "You can sleep on the couch."

I was so tired, I decided to stay. She brought me a pillow and blanket, then gave me one of her husband's shirts to sleep in because her clothes are too small. Before she left, she stroked my cheek, her eyes full of sincere feeling, and kissed me on the lips very lightly. Then she went to her bedroom. I sat in the dark for a while, wondering if she could begin to imagine how profoundly that tiny kiss went through me.

All weekend, she was as sweet as could be, more affectionate than she'd ever been. I thought she was just feeling sorry for me because of Paul. All three of us were more subdued than usual. I spent my time reading, sitting on the back porch of Arlene's house, listening to the clucking of chickens. It's a soothing sound. I was glad to be back in California. I didn't realize how much it felt like home until I was gone for a while. Besides, it had been hard being in my parents' house under the circumstances. The weekend on Arlene's porch was a healing time for me. By Sunday night when I rode the bicycle back to the base, I was feeling much better, ready to get back to work and back to my routine.

Monday night, Lucy suggested we stay in and listen to Glenn Miller records. I didn't want her to feel bad for me anymore, so when she asked me to dance, I said sure. We spun around the living room, practicing our swing moves. As usual, she was such a wonderful dancer, her little hand in mine, her body so free and graceful as she twirled and dipped.

But after a while, she seemed different. She wasn't herself. She was weak and flushed. Once I had to clasp her against me to keep her from falling. She had me worried then because she was always so full of energy.

"I have to sit down," she said.

So I took her to the couch and sat beside her, holding her hand. Her face looked so troubled, I thought she was sick.

"What's wrong?" I asked.

"Hold me," she said, breathless. "Just hold me."

I didn't know what to do. I'd been fighting my feelings for her for a long time, keeping them down, trying not to let her see how I felt about her. The way she was being so tender toward me the last few days, it'd been getting harder and harder. I told myself I had to get away, but she was looking at me with such a pleading look. I put my arms around her and pulled her close. It

CHAPTER TWENTY-ONE

Gwen phoned early to ask if she could stop by for just a minute on her way to work. Could it be that Gwen couldn't stop thinking about that marvelous few minutes from yesterday and wanted more? Shelby brushed her teeth and gargled with mouthwash on the chance there was another kiss in store for her. Even if Gwen wasn't coming over just for a kiss, she reasoned, she might offer one anyway.

Floating on that thought, Shelby dashed to the door when the bell rang, greeting Gwen with an eager hello.

"Hi," said Gwen, thrusting a leather-bound book at her. "I want you to read this."

Shelby took it, confused. "What is it?"

felt so good to hold her like that, wrapping myself around her small body. She put her head on my shoulder and I froze, afraid to move.

Then she lifted her head and looked into my eyes and I had no choice but to kiss her. I wanted her so much I thought the top of my head was going to blow off. She wanted me to kiss her. I could see it in her face. So I did. She kept kissing me and I kept kissing her and I lost track of where my body ended and hers began.

I didn't think it was possible, but Lucy loves me the same way I love her, with all her heart and all her body. That's what she told me Monday night before she took me to her bed. I'm so happy and so scared all at the same time. I keep wondering if this is really happening.

"It's Marjorie's journal." Gwen's demeanor was serious and brusque. She didn't look the least bit like she'd stopped by for a kiss. "I finished it last night."

"Okay," agreed Shelby, hesitantly.

"I think you should read it sooner rather than later." Gwen stood on the porch looking as if she had no intention of coming in.

"Why?" Shelby asked, becoming concerned.

"Just read it. You'll understand."

"Okay. I'll read it this morning."

Gwen nodded and seemed to relax slightly.

"Do you want to come in?" Shelby asked.

"No, thanks. I need to get to work. There's a busload of kids coming in this morning."

Shelby nodded, disheartened. Gwen was obviously not happy this morning. Then Shelby remembered what she'd had to face last night and asked, "How'd your meeting with the city go?"

"Not that well." Gwen looked dejected. "I'm beginning to think it's a losing battle. It's always about money, you know. They all talk around it, because nobody wants to admit they put money before everything else. The museum doesn't make money, which would be okay if it wasn't sitting on that valuable piece of real estate."

"So they don't care what happens to the museum?"

Gwen smiled, not the wide smile of delight that had taken up residence in Shelby's mind, but a small indulgent smile. "They say we can move the collection anywhere. Which we can, theoretically, but there's no money for a high-priced space. You know how expensive this town is. Renting that spot from the city is practically free. Besides, I don't think Skipper has it in her to move and start over somewhere else. So I tried the argument that the museum should remain in the same location as the history it housed. Context, you know?"

"That seems like a good argument."

"Not good enough, apparently. They haven't given a final decision, but it's looking bad."

"Sorry." Shelby couldn't think of anything else to say.

Gwen glanced at her watch. "I'd better go. Call me later if you want."

She looked concerned, as if she expected Shelby would need someone to talk to. After a quick hug, she was gone.

Not the most romantic rendezvous she could imagine, Shelby thought, watching Gwen's car drive off. Yesterday Gwen had been irrepressibly, impulsively amorous. After overcoming her initial daze, Shelby had been delighted. Gwen had a lot on her mind today. Maybe it had nothing to do with Shelby. Today she was all business. She turned the journal over in her hand as she shut the door, wondering why it was so urgent that she read it, wondering if Gwen was just being melodramatic.

She was curious anyway what Marjorie had to say about her family, so she poured herself a large mug of coffee and sat in Nana's recliner with the journal, Oscar squeezed in beside her with his head resting on her leg.

CHAPTER TWENTY-TWO

November 9, 1944.

Today I drove Captain Blanchard to the shipyards for a meeting. It was a good day to be there because they were launching a ship, the SS Red Oak Victory. The shipyard band was playing and they had a magician performing. So many ships come out of those yards now that a launch isn't such a special occasion, not enough to bring out the bigwigs, but they still have a ceremony. They hold a lottery among the employees to see who'll get to christen the ship. Arlene has had her heart set on that for a while now, but so far no dice. An electrician, a girl with flaming red hair, won the honor today. She walked up there in her Sunday dress and gloves and banged the champagne bottle on the hull so softly it didn't break. Everybody laughed. She got it the second time, though.

Then that brilliant new vessel slid out of the shipway and into the water as the band played a Sousa march.

November 10, 1944.

Lucy and I usually have a few hours together before Arlene is due to come home. That time is so special, like magic, the hours before midnight, the hours before the spell is broken and I have to leave her for the night.

Last night we were both asleep when Arlene came home. The sound of her key in the front door lock woke me up. I sprang out of Lucy's bed, her warm sleeping breath still on my cheek, then waited for Arlene to go to her own room before I could put on my clothes and slip out the back door. My heart was thumping like crazy as I pedaled back to the base.

This is a very dangerous thing we're doing. Even if Lucy wasn't married to Arlene's son, we would have to hide our love from the world. Nobody would forgive us for this. But I can't help myself. All I want out of life is to be in Lucy's arms.

November 12, 1944.

It's been a year now since I enlisted in the WAVES. Lucy surprised me today with a cake she baked herself after canvassing the neighborhood all week for extra sugar and butter rations. In return, she invited all the neighbors over to share it. It was a yellow cake with white frosting and it was out of this world. "Happy Anniversary!" it said in shaky red lettering. I didn't expect a fuss. I think Lucy wanted to celebrate something and she didn't care what we called it. She was celebrating the two of us, four months since we met, one month since we became lovers. Though we don't talk about it, the feeling that our time is limited causes us to think of our days together as more precious than we would otherwise. It's strange, but the same war that killed Paul and so many other young men has become our refuge from the conventional world. But we both know the conventional world will return.

Everybody seemed to really enjoy the cake. The others were

free to celebrate whatever they wanted to: FDR's reelection, the liberation of Belgium, any number of Allied successes in Europe, each one bringing more certainty of victory and...the end.

December 1, 1944.

What will happen next? Not to the world. That's not for me to decide. That's up to Mr. Roosevelt and Mr. Churchill. But what will happen to me and Lucy? I know this is on her mind too. She told me something terrible the other day. She confessed a secret wish that had crept into her thoughts more than once, that with so many boys being killed in the war, what if Arnie never came home. She felt bad about that. It made her cry when she told me. I have to admit I've thought the same thing, but I didn't tell her that. Of course, I don't really want Arnie to be killed. Nor does she. But you can't help thinking such things, under the circumstances.

The other night she was lying with her head under my chin, talking softly. She said, "I want to go to an uninhabited tropical island, just the two of us, and live on coconuts and bananas. We can make clothes out of grass and palm leaves."

"Why would we need clothes?" I asked.

"You're right. We wouldn't." She laughed. "What should we take with us?"

"I think we should take a couple of good knives and a hammer," I suggested.

"You're so practical. I was thinking of completely different kinds of things. Like books. And the mechanical ballerina you gave me."

I stroked her hair, imagining this tropical island, our private paradise where we would escape the long arm of the law, the disapproval of our families...and reality.

"What would we do all day?" I asked.

"Swim and make love."

I kissed the back of her neck gently and let my hand run down to the deep curve of her waist. I couldn't see her in the dark, but I know so well what she looks like and my hand knows every inch of her skin. A moment passed silently between us, then I heard the deep breathing that told me she'd fallen asleep. I smiled to myself. She fell asleep with the sweet, impossible dream of our island in her head.

December 20, 1944.

The holiday season is less joyous than usual this year, despite the general optimism about the war. So many families are torn apart. Some are in mourning, like mine. I didn't ask for leave to go home for Christmas. The Captain thanked me for staying here and manning my post. Loyal and patriotic, that's what he called me. But patriotism doesn't have anything to do with it. I don't want to leave Lucy, even for a week. I told my folks my leave request was turned down. Yes, I lied to them and it felt lousy.

Lucy isn't the only reason I don't want to go. Remembering Mama and Daddy from October makes me not want to be there. Too sad. There's nothing I can do to cheer them up. Trying to celebrate Christmas without Paul would just make things worse.

Lucy's going to her parents' house for Christmas Day. Bettie's family has invited me and Hazel to join them and we've both accepted. It should be fun. Bettie has a pack of relatives. It'll be noisy and full of drunken uncles. That'll be nice. Something to take a person's mind off things. I'll be stopping by to see Lucy and Arlene Christmas Eve. That's when she'll open my gift, a stack of records topped off with Bing Crosby's "White Christmas." Of course that's her favorite Christmas song, hands down. I also got her "For Me and My Gal." I always think of that as our song. The first song we ever danced to.

Despite how careful I've been about mentioning Lucy, I know Hazel has figured out what's going on. Last week she asked me if she could see a picture of Lucy. I only have one, the one Arlene took of both of us in our Sunday clothes on the front porch of their house. That day we were all three going to San Francisco to the theater. Lucy has a picture just like it. I showed it to Hazel. When she handed it back, she looked me in the eyes and smiled a tiny, sad smile. She didn't say a word.

January 4, 1945.

Lucy received a telegram today from the army. Her husband was injured by a Jerry grenade and was taken to a hospital. The injuries aren't life-threatening. He's expected to recover. As soon as he's well enough to travel, about three weeks, he'll be flown back to the States.

The news hit us both like a bulldozer. Flattened us. Lucy's been crying all day. Arlene thinks it's because she's upset about Arnie. I've been trying not to cry, but it really hurts me to see Lucy so torn up. Of course we knew this would happen, but we didn't expect it until the war was over and we've both been secretly wishing that the war would never be over. I know that's a lousy thing to wish, a selfish thing, but it's so hard not to wish for your own happiness. Our happiness just seems to depend on everybody else's misery.

I can't move. I feel like a big ball of lead is sitting in my gut. I don't know what I'm going to do without her.

January 11, 1945.

We've been talking. It started like our other imaginary stories, impossible plans of escaping the world together. But this time it's different. Lucy's desperate for me to take her away, for the two of us to run away somewhere together. I asked her if she was afraid of Arnie, if she was in danger. She said no. Arnie's a nice guy. But she doesn't love him. She loves me. She wants us to be together forever. I do too. I want nothing more than that. She's saved a lot of money, she told me. It isn't an impossible dream. She's saved a big chunk of what she's made at the shipyards. It will support us for a while, until one of us can get a job.

Canada. That's where we're going. We're taking a Greyhound bus. Even if we could get a car, we couldn't get very far with the gas rationing. We've set our date for Saturday, January 20. Two days after we leave Alameda, we'll disappear into the great open spaces of Canada with new names, posing as sisters. Sisters can live openly together. Lucy's already come up with our new names: Lily and Twila Sandhurst. I hope I get to be Lily because

I can't imagine myself answering to Twila. I told her that and we had a good laugh over it. We're giddy and scared at the same time.

As I sat at my desk today, listening to Captain Blanchard's steady voice on the phone in the next room, I pictured it in my mind. The Monday after we leave, he'll come into the office and I won't be here. He'll wait for me, maybe an hour. Then he'll have someone check the barracks. The others will say they haven't seen me since Friday. By the time they realize we're gone, we'll already be over the border or near it. All they'll find is my uniforms. I don't need those where I'm going. A few days later, Lucy's husband will come home to his mother. They'll figure out that both of us disappeared at the same time. They'll put two and two together. There will be no turning back.

But we won't know about any of that. We'll be free, together and happy. Nobody will ever know what happened to us. Not our friends or our families. No one. We'll be brand-new people with no past. But we'll have each other.

Lucy's getting more excited by the hour. She feels like a heroine in a romance novel, being swept away from her ordinary life into a grand adventure. She's so courageous. I asked her if she would mind never seeing her parents again. No, she said, not if it meant being with me. Nothing else matters, she said. She seems absolutely certain of that and I'm trying to believe it too. Again I have the feeling of being much older than she is. Or maybe just weaker. Because I do have doubts. Not about Lucy. I love her more than my life. But about the wisdom of this course we're taking.

I felt like a bank robber today when I went to my bank and withdrew my money. I'm so scared and so excited. My hands shook and I could barely speak. I haven't managed to save much, not like Lucy. She knows how to manage things, that girl. We'll be okay. We'll be swell. Our life together will be wonderful. What a daring thing we're about to do!

January 17, 1945.

I got a letter from Daddy today. I know he's still suffering terribly from my brother's death. He didn't have much to say, but what he did say made me so sad.

I'm so proud of you, my girl. I never thought my daughter would be able to do the things you've done for your country. Now that your brother's gone, I'm sure you know you're everything to both of us. It was hard that you weren't able to be here for Christmas, but we know what you're doing is important. You're a good girl. I hope that darn navy will let you off for a couple of weeks soon to come visit your old folks. I know it would do your mother a world of good to see your bright, smiling face. She misses you more than ever now. Me too. We love you, sweetheart.

After I got that letter, I sat on my bunk for a half hour just staring at it. Then I rode the bike over to Lucy's house. She came running and hung on my neck and kissed me and kissed me. She's so excited about our escape. She spent the evening packing and chattering like a child at Christmas. What should she bring? What kind of house would we live in? Could we have a dog? Would we see moose? She swung between these thoughts and her guilt over "poor Arlene" and "poor Arnie" and how they would feel betrayed and confused. She was certain, though, they would both recover quickly, forget about her and go on with their lives.

I put my own things, the clothes and sundries I keep at her house, in a small bag. As the night wore on, I felt my plans changing, almost against my will. I tied my bag to the bike to take back to the base. When I left Lucy for the night, her eyes were shining with love and happiness. I wanted nothing more than to disappear into that vision forever, to live there and not to live in the real world.

My father's letter is staring at me from the wall where I pinned it. I have a heavy, sick feeling in my chest. I'm afraid to tell Lucy what's on my mind. I'll let her sleep tonight still dreaming of our new life. But tomorrow—

I feel like a heel. I love her so much. But I also love my parents and the navy. Honestly, I'm afraid of the life I would have with her, the secrecy and isolation. I'd never see my parents again. It would destroy them. They would've lost both their children. And their daughter would have disgraced and dishonored them.

I've changed my mind a hundred times tonight. But I can tell which way it will end up. My heart is breaking.

January 30, 1945.

I've requested a new assignment. I'm transferring to the East Coast. I told Captain Blanchard my parents haven't been able to overcome their grief over my brother's death and, as their only living child, I thought it would mean so much to them to have me near. He put in for a family hardship transfer and delivered my papers to me yesterday. Today I'm packing. I'll be on a plane tomorrow morning.

Mama's ecstatic. She's already planning on making all my favorite foods. She thinks I'm going to run home every night for supper. It was so good to hear her happy!

This is the right decision. I keep telling myself that, despite how much it hurt to tell Lucy we weren't going to run away together after all. I don't think we would have had such a good life if we'd done it. I think it would have been hard. She thinks you can live on love. But I'm not so sure. Walking away from her was the hardest thing I've ever done. I love her so much. But what chance did we have? It seems sometimes like the whole world is against our kind of love. Why that should be, I don't know. I don't know why I am the way I am.

When I said goodbye to her, she broke down and wouldn't stop crying. She clung to me and I thought she'd never let me go. My skin was punctured by her fingernails. I didn't mind the pain on my skin, but the pain in my heart was almost deadly.

Oh, Lucy, I hope you'll forgive me! I'm a coward. I wasn't the hero you thought I was. But I did love you. I do love you. I will always love you.

CHAPTER TWENTY-THREE

With tears in her eyes, Shelby turned the page. The next page of the journal was blank. She flipped through the remainder of the book to see that all of the remaining pages were blank. That was the last entry: January 30, 1945. She closed Marjorie's journal and sat in Nana's recliner listening to the clock tick, letting the story sink in.

No wonder Gwen had been so odd this morning. Shelby felt disoriented. She could barely comprehend her grandmother's story, the secret life of her heart that had gone unspoken for over sixty-five years. It was hard to believe this had really happened, not only had happened, but had happened to Nana.

How strange it must have been for her to feel herself falling in love with a woman, this farmer's daughter from Arkansas who got married just because that's what people did, who had retained her virginal heart until she met Marjorie. She had probably never even heard the word "lesbian" when she found herself falling in love with one.

Shelby's eyes finally began to focus on the clock. It was a little after noon. She hadn't had breakfast. At some point in Marjorie's story, finishing the journal had become her only thought. Now that she'd finished it, her stomach was growling impatiently.

She went to the kitchen where she was momentarily distracted by the photo on the refrigerator. She tried to imagine those two young women as lovers. She was still in the grip of the story, she realized, as she felt suddenly, overwhelmingly forlorn. She tore her gaze from the refrigerator and rapidly ate a bowl of cereal. She then dressed and took her bike out of the garage, aware that Marjorie too had often ridden a bicycle from here to the navy base.

She stood outside the little gate in front of the house, gazing at the porch, holding the image from the photograph in her mind. Marjorie had stood with one arm around the post and the other around Nana's shoulders, looking down at her. Nana had stood looking at the camera, one arm around Marjorie's waist. Shelby had memorized that image. As she stared at the porch, it suddenly came to life like a scene in a movie. She watched as her grandmother turned toward Marjorie and looked up at her, smiling affectionately. Marjorie bent her head down to give Lucy a kiss. The two of them then turned and walked into the house, hand in hand.

Shelby threw her leg over the bike and pushed away from the house.

Gwen was sitting at her desk, peering at her computer screen. She looked up as Shelby flung open the door. Then she leapt up and came rapidly across the room to enfold Shelby in her arms. They stood holding one another wordlessly for a minute or more. When Gwen released her, Shelby slipped the journal from her pocket and handed it over.

"How do you feel?" Gwen asked, searching her face. "Come sit down and let's talk."

"It's so hard to believe." Shelby sat beside the desk. "It's like it's about someone else. I can't picture it as Nana."

"It was so long ago. I suppose she was a different person then."

"Yes, obviously. That whole running away to live on love scheme doesn't sound anything like her." Shelby shook her head. "Where exactly did you find this?"

"One of the boxes in storage. I've been through it again to see if there was anything else of Marjorie's, but didn't find anything. If the rest of her stuff is here, it's in another box."

"What do you mean 'the rest of her stuff'?"

Gwen looked apologetic. "Normally, how we end up with things like this is after someone dies and their heirs donate their belongings to the museum. Usually, there's more to it. Things like uniforms, medals, papers. Letters, often. I was hoping to find some letters or even another journal. One written later."

"So she's dead?" Shelby asked.

"I assume so. But I don't actually know that. I've been doing some research this morning and I found some even more fascinating information on Marjorie Banyan."

"More fascinating than that?" Shelby pointed to the journal.

Gwen smiled. "Well, maybe not. That's hard to top, isn't it? But let me show you what I found."

Gwen opened a manila folder and turned it around for Shelby to see. There were some printed pages inside, including some articles from the Internet and a color photograph. Shelby lifted out the photo of an attractive woman in a navy uniform, ribbons on her chest beside a bronze medal, her dark hair curling around the edges of her cap.

"Is this her?" Shelby asked.

"Yes. That was in nineteen seventy-three."

"She was something! What was her rank?"

"Lieutenant commander."

"Really? So she *did* stay in the navy."

"Not exactly. When the war was over, she was discharged like most of the WAVES. She went to college, then reenlisted in the navy as an officer. She was stationed at various bases around the world—Japan, Germany, and then spent some time in Vietnam in nineteen sixty-eight and sixty-nine. The Bronze Star was for her service there."

"So how high did she go?"

"That was it. That's the real story. When she got back from Vietnam, she was investigated for homosexual activities. These articles I found are about her discharge and the suit she brought against the navy. This was one of the early cases where the military ban on gays and lesbians was challenged. There was a whole spate of them around nineteen seventy-five, all branches of the military. Coincided with the rise of gay activism in general."

"No kidding?" Shelby stared at Gwen, then back at the photo of the poised, confident looking naval officer. The look on her face was sober, no hint of a smile. As she examined the image further, she began to recognize the features of that earlier Marjorie, Nana's Marjorie.

"In the early seventies," Gwen said, "homosexuals were fighting back against the military ban for the first time. Emerging gay rights groups and the ACLU took up the cause. Marjorie was just the sort of client they were looking for, a highly decorated officer with an exemplary record, someone who could inspire public compassion."

"What happened?"

"The first thing that happened was she was asked to resign. She refused. The navy wanted to keep it quiet because the news media was running with these stories and drumming up all kinds of sympathy for these people. This wasn't just a nobody they were dealing with. This was a woman with a spotless career, a veteran of three wars. So they asked her to retire with full benefits, a much better offer than she could have expected. As long as she left, they'd sweep the whole thing under the rug."

"But that didn't happen?"

"No." Gwen's eyes were sparkling with the joy of her discoveries. "She decided to fight. I'm sure the navy was sorry it ever started this investigation, but once it was started, the ball just kept rolling. At her administrative hearing, several very important officers testified to her fitness for duty, including two admirals. Even so, she was found guilty and given an undesirable discharge, which was typical."

"Guilty of what exactly?"

"Being a homosexual, which Marjorie freely admitted. The charge was hard to fight because they weren't normally accused of not doing their job. After her discharge hearing, she hired a civilian lawyer to take the case to court, to sue the Navy to reinstate her. At the time, it was an incredibly bold thing to do."

"Did she win?" Shelby asked.

Gwen shook her head. "No. There was almost no chance she could've won. The harder people were pressuring the military to relax the ban on gays, the more hard-nosed they were getting. I'm sure she must have known how unlikely a win was."

"Then why'd she do it?"

"She did it for us, of course, for the principle, for the future, for what eventually happened in two thousand ten."

"The repeal of Don't Ask, Don't Tell," Shelby said quietly, thinking about how long that battle had been waged.

"Sometimes it's more important to fight than to win. She said that. It's in the articles." Gwen pointed to a line on one of the printouts. "She did it to make a small dent. Thousands of small dents later, the wall's come down. But you've gotta start somewhere. Courageous people like Marjorie sacrificed themselves for the cause."

Shelby nodded. "What was the end result?"

"After she lost her case, her lawyer appealed and a couple years later, tried to take the case to the Supreme Court. They refused to hear it. In the end, she was unemployed, had no pension, and had to walk away with an undesirable discharge."

"Wow! So she lost everything?"

"She didn't lose her principles. She didn't lose her dignity. She was a real hero."

Shelby glanced again at the imposing woman in the photo, then let her thoughts wander further back in time. "But not such a hero for my grandmother."

"No. I thought of that. In her own view at the time, she let your grandmother down. Ran out on her. But, realistically, what choice did she have? It's hard for us to imagine what it was like back then. And she was very young. Hard to defy the whole world at that age. But twenty-some years later, apparently she was able to."

"What happened to her after that, after she left the navy?"

"I don't know. I haven't had time to do any more research. But I will. I should be able to get a date of death from the Social Security index, as well as her last known residences. Just a matter of time and we'll have the whole story. At least the facts of the story. If we're lucky, there'll be surviving family members to talk to. Maybe a partner."

"If we're lucky?" Shelby asked.

"Sorry. I tend to think of these things as a challenge, a mystery to solve. I just meant I might have luck finding out more information. From your point of view, it's a whole different thing, isn't it?"

Shelby nodded.

"More personal, of course," Gwen said, laying her hand over Shelby's. "I wasn't sure how you would take this."

"It's sort of a shock. But I'm glad you let me in on it. I'm glad to know."

"Are you going to talk to your grandmother about it?"

"I'm not sure. After hearing the story, I'm sort of thinking, what's the point, especially if Marjorie's dead? It might just dredge up a lot of pain she managed to get past. There's nothing to be gained by forcing her to relive that."

"You're probably right." Gwen smiled sympathetically. "Sorry, but I've got to go. Business with the city. I've got a meeting in a half hour." Gwen picked up her leather satchel, then asked, "Are you okay?"

Shelby smiled to reassure her.

Gwen put her arm around Shelby's shoulders and walked her to the door. They emerged into the parking lot and the afternoon heat, cut by a light breeze coming off the Bay. San Francisco stood out in sharp relief on the other side.

"What's your meeting about?" Shelby asked.

"It's a follow-up to my presentation to the council. They want to see the numbers, which won't impress anybody. But it does give me another chance to talk about the museum and try to shift someone's opinion." Gwen sighed. "It's been a hard fight. I doubt if Skipper realizes how dire this is."

Standing by her car, Gwen turned to look at the museum. "No great surprise people don't want this ugly old building sitting in the midst of this gorgeous view, is it?"

"It's not that ugly," Shelby said. "Not to me. It's got some interesting architectural elements. It's an awesome example of the Arts and Crafts movement. A lot more appealing anyway than the other buildings on this base, like the Quonset huts and utility buildings."

"That's because it wasn't built by the military. A private residence once, I think. About a hundred years old now. It's no wonder the place is falling apart. Rusty's usually pretty good, though, at cobbling it back together."

"What was this building used for?" Shelby asked, "when the navy was here?"

"It was the CO's house. His living quarters. His office was up in the main building, but his family lived here. As you can see, it was a big house. Remember the photos in the stairwell? All those guys lived here during their commands, including Marjorie's Captain Blanchard."

"Do you think she drove the car right up here where we're standing to pick him up?"

"Maybe. Probably."

Shelby gazed at the front of the building, trying to imagine Marjorie driving up in a sleek black car, wearing her smart blue uniform. When she turned back, Gwen leaned down and kissed her. Her lips were cool, soft, lingering just long enough to hint at desire.

"If I didn't have this meeting," Gwen said, frowning, "I wouldn't run off like this. Maybe we can get together tomorrow night?"

"I'd like that."

"Reading Marjorie's story, doesn't it make you glad we don't have to hide like that?"

Shelby thought of her mother, but nodded and said, "Sure does!"

CHAPTER TWENTY-FOUR

Pam Elliot at the Alameda Historical Society was both interested and eager to help Shelby in her quest to find some historically significant reason to preserve the museum building. She brought out everything she had on the history of the navy base, but what Shelby had hoped to find just wasn't there. It had been a long shot, she knew. As the personal residence of the base commander, the house must have had its share of visiting dignitaries and that was Shelby's angle, to find a reason to put the building on the state or national register. If she could do that, she knew it couldn't be torn down.

"Somebody famous must have slept there," she insisted.

What she was hoping for was Eisenhower or Roosevelt visiting the navy base during World War II. It would take something like that, at least, and even more than that, like the signing of some important document during their stay. So far the only celebrity Pam had to offer was Phyllis Diller, a one-time resident of Alameda, whose husband had worked on the base in the 1950s. That Phyllis Diller had entertained her husband's co-workers with her jokes before she went into show business was interesting, but it had no bearing on the museum.

Pam and Shelby sat at a long work table covered with papers, books, and drawers of microfiche film. Shelby had never used a microfiche reader and was alarmed to find the historical society's records were not all digitized. The process had taken longer than expected. But Pam, a thin fiftyish woman who flitted like a butterfly through the room, knew her way around the material. Without her, progress would have been impossible. She also knew a lot about Alameda history. Maybe Shelby should have taken her word for it when, shortly after her arrival, Pam had said, "No, I don't think FDR ever came to Alameda."

"This Admiral Pruitt isn't good enough, I guess," Pam said.

"No, not really." Shelby sighed and leaned back in her chair. "No history was ever made there, apparently."

It was worth trying, Shelby told herself. It would have been so cool if she could have done something to help save the museum. Gwen seemed to have lost hope.

"Do you want to look further back?" Pam asked. "Before World War Two? The building is older, right?"

"It's at least a hundred years old." Shelby remembered the photo in the stairwell, with its 1911 date. "But I have to get going."

Shelby wanted to get in her daily visit to Nana before the nursing home served dinner. She hadn't forgotten for a moment that Gwen had asked to see her tonight. She wanted to be back home in plenty of time to get ready for their date.

"If I find anything else," Pam said, "I'll call you."

Shelby thanked her for all her help, then left for the nursing home.

When she arrived in Nana's room, she found the bed empty. In fact, both beds were empty, but the television over Dinky's bed was blasting so loudly she paused there to turn the volume down. She heard someone from inside the bathroom. It sounded like a wheelchair hitting the walls, so she sat in the visitor's chair to wait.

But it wasn't Nana who came out of the bathroom a few minutes later. It was Dinky. Seeing Shelby, she said, "She's gone."

"Gone? Is she in physical therapy?"

"No. They took her to the hospital about an hour ago. Your mother was here."

Shelby stood, feeling suddenly panicky. "What happened?"

Dinky shrugged. "Nobody said a word to me. Just a bunch of people running around, then the ambulance drivers came in and took her. They do that here. They don't want anybody to die in this place. Gives them a bad name, so whenever somebody takes poorly and they think they might kick the bucket, they ship 'em off to the hospital."

Alarmed, Shelby was about to ask another question when her phone rang. Dinky was now back in bed and turning the volume on her TV back up, so Shelby walked into the hall to hear her mother say, "We had to take Mom to the hospital. She has pneumonia. You can come over if you want. Call your Aunt Vickie for me, will you? But tell her everything's under control. I don't want her taking off work to come over here."

"Okay, I'll call her. Is this serious?"

"Pneumonia is serious, Shelby, especially in the elderly, especially when there are other health issues."

Shelby called Aunt Vickie. Although the message she left was calm and reassuring, she couldn't help thinking about that recurrent phrase, "complications due to a broken hip," one of which, she remembered, was pneumonia.

She found her mother at the nurse's station, filling out paperwork. Vivian looked strained and worried. She took a deep breath. As she let it out, her shoulders slumped noticeably. "At least they didn't have to put her on a respirator. Maybe we got it in time. Although she's done nothing at all to help herself this whole time. Sometimes I think she doesn't care one way or another if she lives or not."

"Why do you say that?" Shelby asked, startled.

"It's what the social worker's been telling me all along. She's not fighting to recover."

"Well, it's got to be really hard at her age. Things take a lot longer to heal."

"It's not the physical aspect they're talking about. It's the state of mind. It's a proven fact that people with the right attitude recover quicker and more completely from this sort of traumatic injury, regardless of age."

"You think she doesn't want to live?"

Vivian sighed. "She doesn't want it badly enough. That's what the social worker says and I think she's right. Mom spends far too much time lying in bed. Some days they can't even coax her to get dressed until after lunch. She should be walking up and down the halls as much as she can take. With the walker, I mean. Obviously, she shouldn't be running relay races."

"Why didn't you tell me this before, what the social worker was saying?"

"I didn't want to upset you. I know how close you are to her."

"I would just as soon know the truth, Mom. I can take the truth." How ironic that her mother thought she was the one who needed protecting.

Vivian cast a sad, affectionate smile toward Shelby.

"Have you talked to her about this?" Shelby asked. "Have you told her she needs to work harder?"

"Yes, of course I have. She says she's too tired. Or she's in too much pain. Which is the same as saying that it's just too much trouble. And one day—" Vivian paused to steel herself. "One day she said to me, very calmly, that she'd lived a long life and wasn't afraid to die. She said if her time was up, she was okay with that."

"Maybe that's how she felt that particular day." Shelby felt distressed, wondering if her mother was exaggerating. "Maybe she was just feeling lousy that day."

"It wasn't just that day. This morning she told me there was nothing left for her to do. She was too old to do anything interesting and she had no spaces left on her dance card. That's exactly what she said. No spaces on her dance card. What the hell does that mean?"

Vivian started sobbing. Shelby moved over to hug her and

they stood together in a close embrace until Vivian patted Shelby's arm and pulled away.

"You've been a big help," she said. "You've been such a comfort to me through all of this. I don't think I could take it without you. I know I snap at you sometimes, but I want you to know how much I appreciate you being here and shouldering so much responsibility."

Shelby smiled and gave her mother's hand a squeeze. "Thanks."

"I'm going in to see if she's awake."

Shelby followed her mother into Nana's room where they found her asleep, breathing noisily into an oxygen mask. She lay on her back in a featureless gown with both arms out straight beside her. In her right arm was a needle taped down over a purple bruise, delivering a clear liquid through a plastic tube.

Shelby dropped into the visitor's chair, feeling exhausted. Vivian stood at the window, looking out, until a young nurse's aide came in with a tray containing a small glass jar and a hypodermic needle.

"Stop!" Vivian commanded.

Shelby came to attention, wondering what the problem was. The CNA looked similarly perplexed.

"What is that?" Vivian asked.

"An antibiotic," the aide answered calmly.

Vivian looked irritated. "Yes, but *what* antibiotic?"

"Erythromycin."

"Okay. Go ahead, but don't you touch her without gloves. I know you've got patients with staph on this floor. That woman's life is in your hands and they'd better be sterile."

"Yes, absolutely." The aide took a pair of gloves from a box by the door and pulled them on, looking unruffled by Vivian's aggression.

Satisfied, Vivian sat down and said to Shelby, "She's allergic to amoxicillin. Just wanted to be sure."

Shelby gazed silently at her mother who only moments ago had been crying in helpless despair and was now resolutely in charge and completely controlled. She had seen this before, though not recently. In a crisis, Vivian was usually a mess. It had always been that way as far back as Shelby could remember. When Shelby was eight, on a family camping trip, she'd been bitten by a snake. She couldn't tell her parents what kind of snake it was, so Vivian immediately assumed it was a rattler, which they later knew it was not. It was a harmless snake trying to defend itself against the taunting of a child.

While her mother fell into hysterics, her father ripped his shirt apart and tied off her leg above the bite, then put her in the backseat of the car and told her to lie still with her leg elevated. He had remained calm and kept smiling at her the whole time. She did remember, though, how he had taken her mother away from the car for a moment and when they came back, she was no longer screaming about her baby dying. As they drove out of the mountains to the hospital, Vivian had sobbed quietly and muttered to herself. Based on scenes in movies, Shelby had assumed her father had slapped her to bring her to her senses, but as she got older, she decided he had more likely just told her to shut up.

Incidents like that had led Shelby to wonder how Nana could put Vivian in charge in a seriously life-threatening situation like this. This scene with the nurse's aide reminded Shelby of another occasion a couple years later when her family had gone fishing at one of the swift-moving mountain streams in the Sierra foothills. Shelby and Charlie had gone exploring in the woods and Gary had gone downstream to find a better fishing hole, so Vivian was standing by herself on the riverbank, fly fishing for rainbow trout. It was Vivian who told the story to them later, but it was fully corroborated by another witness, a teenager named Kevin.

Kevin and his little sister Mandy were playing at the river's edge, leaping from rock to rock, when Mandy, who was six years old and not wearing a life jacket, slipped off one of the rocks and got dragged into the current. Kevin started hollering and Vivian, who was downstream, heard him. Then she saw the girl's bright red shirt coming toward her as the girl thrashed about, grabbing unsuccessfully at rocks in her path. Vivian immediately dropped her pole and ran into the frigid stream, grabbing the girl, whereupon she herself got swept off her feet. But she kept hold of Mandy and managed to drag herself to shore further downstream, a feat requiring more composure than Shelby had thought her mother capable of.

As the aide left the room, Shelby thought about those two days and wondered at the mystifying difference. Why was Vivian completely helpless in one instance and completely competent in the other?

"I'm going to stay here night and day if I have to," Vivian vowed, her face full of determination. "All we need is for Mom to get a staph infection on top of everything else."

CHAPTER TWENTY-FIVE

"Wow, you look terrific!" Gwen said to Skipper as she walked in the front door of the museum. She was wearing her dress blues and all her ribbons on the breast of her jacket. She stood up straighter than usual. She looked sharp and proud, her lips pressed together in a self-satisfied smile.

"Thank you," she said.

"What's the occasion?"

"Oh, it's a big party over on the Red Oak. All hands on deck tonight. Birthday for Captain What's-his-name. He's a hundred years old. Tough old salt. God, Junior Grade, that's what we called him back in the day. Now he's just one of us, one of the old-timers still kickin'. He doesn't kick so high now, though." She laughed. "Grady's picking me up in a few minutes."

The *SS Red Oak Victory* was a WWII-era ship built at the

Richmond shipyards, undergoing restoration and open to the public as a tourist attraction. It was permanently docked at the site of the shipyards and was a beloved relic of the past for the old-timers. The WWII vets, though there weren't so many of them around anymore, were fiercely loyal to one another and all came together to celebrate their significant rites of passage. These days, Gwen had noted, that usually meant a funeral. It seemed their service during the war was the most important time of their lives, as if nothing else had affected them as much during the over sixty-five years of living since. They kept in touch and treated one another like family members.

Skipper edged over to the desk chair and slowly lowered herself into it. Gwen noticed that her navy blue pants hung loose on her legs. The belt holding them up wasn't just for looks anymore. Over time, she had shrunk, not just in height.

"What've you been up to all day?" Skipper asked when she was settled in the chair. "You've been sitting in here glued to this machine every time I came down."

"Oh," Gwen sighed. "I've been trying to track somebody down. Lots of tedious research into military records and genealogical databases."

"That's just your cup of tea, isn't it? No wonder you've been lost to the world."

Gwen nodded, acknowledging to herself that it was indeed her "cup of tea." It was slow going, like panning for gold. Mostly you came up with worthless trivia, but every once in a while you'd get a tiny grain of something that glimmered with relevance. And once in a great while, you'd get a nugget of information that would tie everything together or open up an entirely new area of exploration. The research calmed and nourished her. She could spend a whole day poring over details that would drive another sort of person nuts—names, dates, places—and remain interested. She had spent the day doing just that, looking for clues to reconstruct Marjorie Banyan's life.

The day hadn't been wasted. She'd found some things. There was an interview with Marjorie in the 1990s about her pivotal 1970s suit against the navy. By then about seventy years old, she had spoken humbly about her doomed fight. "I loved the navy," she had said. "I had a hard time believing they would make me go. After they did, I floundered around for a while. I came back here, back to the Bay Area. I always did love it here. You know the song, 'I Left my Heart in San Francisco.' I did that. Alameda, actually, in my case."

Gwen had realized with a start that Marjorie was referring to Lucy, some fifty years afterward. That was some grand passion, apparently. At the time of the interview, Marjorie was living with a woman named Ann Fraser. Armed with that bit of information, Gwen had discovered they'd lived in Marin County and Ann Fraser had died in 2004. Gwen wondered if that was when Marjorie's journal had been donated to the museum. But she'd still found no death date for Marjorie herself. The house they'd lived in was sold in 2007. That was where she was now, after a day of research. Not bad.

"I do love it," Gwen acknowledged to Skipper. "It's so interesting to unearth these pieces of a person's life, to gradually assemble them and get a sense of who she was as a unique individual."

"Some old-timer?" Skipper brushed some lint off her pants.

"Yes. A contemporary of yours, as it happens." Gwen was suddenly struck with the idea that Skipper could have known Marjorie. They could have been stationed here on the base at the same time. In fact, they *must* have been here at the same time.

Gwen came to attention and stared hard at Skipper. "Her name was Marjorie Banyan. She was Captain Blanchard's driver."

"Marjorie!" blurted Skipper. "You're researching Marjorie?"

Gwen practically leapt out of her chair, thinking she was such an idiot for not questioning Skipper earlier. Of course they'd known one another! They all knew each other.

"Yes!" she confirmed. "So you did know her. You were both right here in nineteen forty-four."

"Oh, sure." Skipper nodded matter-of-factly. "Marjorie showed up here after I did. She came from somewhere back East, I think. She had a sort of East Coast accent. She was in Barracks D, I remember. With that Cora Dell Who's-it. Cora Dell was from the South. She wasn't very sharp, but she was sweet as candy. A precious little doll. Boys fell all over themselves when she marched by. I remember her plain as day. She wasn't here long, though. I don't know whatever happened to her." Skipper chuckled softly. "Whenever she was on galley duty, she'd always give me extra gravy and say—"

Gwen clamped her hand on Skipper's forearm to focus her attention. "Let's talk about Marjorie," she urged. "She transferred out early in forty-five, before the war was over."

"That's right. She went back East to be near her family. I remember her brother was killed. Very sad."

"Did you keep up with her? Did you know she was kicked out of the navy in seventy-three?"

Skipper nodded emphatically. "I know all about that. She made a stink, didn't she? Ran them up the flagpole for the whole country to see. Oh, they should never have tangled with that one. That Marjorie had 'em all lined up with their drawers down."

"So you were there? You saw all of that?"

"No, no." Skipper shook her head. "I followed the story in the papers. Marjorie was stationed in, uh, whatchamacallit... Norfolk! I was here. But, you know, I kept tabs on my old mates. All of them. Followed their careers, went to their weddings and their funerals."

Skipper looked wistful. Excited now, Gwen opened her notebook in anticipation of new information. She heard a car pull up out front as she took up her pen.

"Did you know her partner, Ann Fraser?" she asked.

"I met her a couple times. She died a few years ago, I think."

"That's right. I was able to find out that much. Do you know if Marjorie has any living relatives? Like cousins or something? She had no other siblings and, of course, her parents would no longer be living. But maybe she was close to some other family member I could track down."

"Cousins, huh?" Skipper screwed up her face as she considered the question. "Not that I know of. We weren't that close back in the old days, not real close friends. Marjorie kind of kept to herself anyway. She was friendly, but not part of the gang I ran with." Skipper nodded thoughtfully to herself, then trained her pale blue eyes on Gwen. "But I can ask her tonight if you want."

Gwen stared, wordless, as time seemed to come to a full stop until the door opened and Grady stepped in. He was also in full military dress, looking formal and handsome.

"Ahoy, girls!" he bellowed, removing his hat and tucking it in the crook of his arm.

Skipper waved at him and made a move to get up. Gwen seized her arm to get her attention back.

"You're seeing her tonight?" Gwen asked. "But I thought she was dead."

"Who?" Skipper asked, looking alarmed.

"Marjorie Banyan."

Skipper struggled to her feet with the aid of Grady's arm.

"Marjorie's dead!" Skipper looked up at Grady in disbelief.

His mouth fell open. "When did that happen? I just saw her last month and she looked healthy as a cow. Wasn't she supposed to be at the party tonight?" He shook his head sadly. "They'll probably say a few words about her. That's going to sink Turnbull's ship, isn't it?"

"He's not even going to notice," Skipper said dismissively, "as long as he gets a piece of cake. Poor Marjorie. She was one of the good old gals."

"What'd she die of?" Grady asked.

Skipper turned to look inquiringly at Gwen and Grady followed suit.

Gwen sighed deeply. "I didn't say Marjorie died," she said.

"You didn't?" Skipper looked confused.

"No, I didn't. Based on what I've just heard, I think she's probably very much alive."

"Oh, I'm so glad to hear that!" Skipper turned to Grady, nodding and smiling.

"Then who died?" Grady asked.

"Maybe it was that other one," Skipper suggested. "You know, that Lieutenant What's-it. Maybe it was her. She must be ninety by now."

"I know who you mean," Grady said, tapping his face with his index finger. "The one that had the stroke last year. Side of her face is all frozen now. She can only smile halfway like this."

He pulled up one side of his mouth in a grotesque expression that might have made Gwen laugh if she wasn't so focused on the thought that Marjorie was not only still alive but well within reach this very evening.

"Maybe she had another stroke," Grady said. "If it was on the other side, maybe she's not lopsided now."

Skipper nodded, then slapped him playfully. "No, you dope! It must have killed her. The second stroke killed her. Remember what we're talking about? Who died."

"Oh, right." He laughed self-deprecatingly. "I forgot. Well, that's a shame. Wish I could remember her name. She was nice."

"Nobody died," Gwen said firmly.

They both turned their full attention to her.

"Is Marjorie Banyan going to be at this party or not?" she asked.

"She'll probably be there," Skipper said, "since she's not dead."

"Can I go with you? When does it start?"

"Eighteen hundred," Skipper glanced at the wall clock. "Just twenty minutes. We should get going. We don't want to miss happy hour."

"You can't go like that," Grady said to Gwen, puffing out his chest to highlight the need for ceremonial dress.

Gwen looked down at her jeans and sneakers, then back at their uniforms. The two of them stood facing her as a solid front of resolve, making it clear she would have no chance getting into this party as she was. She wasn't about to let this opportunity pass by and she didn't trust either of these two to pass along a message to Marjorie that would guarantee further contact. Getting home and back to change would take far too long.

"We have a few contemporary uniforms in the collection," she remembered. "I could wear one of those."

They both gave her stern looks.

"Just for an hour or so?" she suggested tentatively.

The stern looks were compounded by shaking heads.

"No, of course not," Gwen relented. "An appalling affront."

"You could go as our mascot," suggested Grady, brightening. "Everybody loves it when he shows up. The costume's upstairs."

"Mascot?" Gwen was apprehensive, imagining some cartoon animal.

Grady turned a questioning glance at Skipper, who nodded emphatically.

"Oh, yes!" she agreed, her eyes twinkling with roguish delight.

CHAPTER TWENTY-SIX

Gwen felt ridiculous. Both Skipper and Grady were giggling under their breath as the three of them climbed the ramp onto the deck of the *SS Red Oak Victory*, a hulking metal cargo ship, its dull gray paint streaked with rust, its window glass cloudy. A plaque above the door gave its launch date as November 9, 1944. Gwen had been aboard before. She'd taken the standard tour and knew this ship had served in WWII, Korea and Vietnam before being mothballed in 1969. It had been rescued later to become a floating museum, back in the very spot where its life of service had begun. As she observed the rusted rivets and welded seams, she wondered if Lucy Brewster had had a hand in building this ship.

If this had been a Fourth of July party, Gwen wouldn't have felt so conspicuous. It seemed counterintuitive to sneak into a private party making this big a spectacle of yourself, but as the veteran at the top of the ramp heartily shook her white-gloved hand, she realized there would be no obstacle to her entry.

"Look who's here!" Grady shouted as they descended into the interior of the ship and dozens of gray heads turned their way.

Why did I agree to this? Gwen wondered, forcing a smile as several uniformed officers saluted her.

She might have guessed their mascot was Uncle Sam. Who else? The uniform, which consisted of a blue tailcoat, white vest, red and white bowtie, red striped pants, white shoes and a top hat, was garish and too large for her. They had cinched up the pants with a belt, but the trouser cuffs were still dangerously close to the floor. She'd drawn the line at the facial hair, a monstrous white mustache and long goatee, refusing to wear it, to Skipper's immense disappointment.

In response to the joyful greeting of the guests, Gwen extended her right arm, pointing with her index finger in the classic "I want you" pose and began to think maybe this wasn't so bad after all. The important thing was that she was here.

The party was being held in the mess hall where a bar had been set up on one end and red, white and blue paper streamers were strung along the ceiling. Tables were covered with white butcher paper and music was playing low, a soundtrack very similar to the one played in the museum.

"Is Marjorie here?" Gwen whispered to Skipper as they entered the room.

Skipper tried to look serious as she gazed over Gwen's costume. "When I see her, I'll let you know."

Gwen stuck close as Skipper made a direct line to the bar where she ordered a martini. "What'll you have, Sam?" she asked, eyes twinkling.

"Nothing for me, thanks," Gwen said, smiling at the other guests as casually as she could. Most of them were decades older than she was.

Skipper took a long, thin sip of her martini, then smacked her lips. "There she is," she said abruptly, nodding toward the other side of the room where a table held a four foot long sheet cake.

"Which one?" Gwen asked, scanning the old folks around the cake.

"The one in the green suit."

A willowy woman stood leaning over the cake. She wore a tasteful two-piece suit and print blouse. Gwen was reminded that Marjorie was unable to wear a uniform, branded as she was with the less than honorable discharge. Standing there, an old woman in ordinary clothes, she presented a stark contrast to the photos Gwen had recently become familiar with, the uniformed officer from the seventies at the height of her career, or the girl of twenty-one on the porch of Lucy's house. Those images from the past left Gwen feeling stunned and tenderly moved. She felt she'd known that woman in her youth, known her well enough to have shared her secret loves and heartaches. She reminded herself she'd never been invited into Marjorie's heart, but had accidentally stumbled in. The closeness Gwen felt toward that young woman was entirely one-sided. Marjorie didn't even know she'd shared herself.

"You should say happy birthday to What's-his-face first," Skipper suggested, pointing to an ancient man in a wheelchair. His head hung down on his chest as if holding it up was too much effort, but he seemed alert, taking in the scene, accepting his congratulatory greetings one by one.

Gwen made her way through the crowd, shaking hands, keeping an eye on Marjorie, until she was standing before the old man's wheelchair.

"Happy birthday!" she shouted, assuming he was hard of hearing. She shook his hand.

He acknowledged her with his eyes, sunken orbs under half-closed lids, but there was plenty of expression in them. His mouth turned into a crooked smile as he recognized the costume.

A couple of the guests insisted on taking a photo of Gwen and the birthday boy, so she posed beside him for a few minutes. When she was free, Gwen saw Marjorie still standing by the cake. She was conversing with a distinguished looking man in a highly decorated uniform with a bank of several gold stripes on the sleeves of his jacket, one wide one topped by three narrower ones. An admiral, surely, she decided.

She hesitated, not wanting to intrude on their conversation, and spent a moment examining the cake. It depicted a scene of small islands fringed with battleships. The lettering read, "Full steam ahead, Captain Turnbull."

As soon as the admiral moved on, Gwen dashed over to Marjorie, who smiled at the costume. Gwen knew immediately it really was her. Her brown eyes were the same. They were intelligent and thoughtful, full of confidence. Her bearing was graceful, her posture perfect. Her hair was surprisingly thick for her age, more of a true gray than white.

"Ah," she said, chuckling, "a female Uncle Sam. Isn't that refreshing!"

"You're Marjorie Banyan, aren't you?" Gwen asked.

She nodded, then wrinkled her mouth into a look of concentration, as if she were trying to place Gwen.

"You don't know me," Gwen added. "My name's Gwen Lawford."

"How do you do," Marjorie said in a clear, steady voice, shaking Gwen's hand.

Gwen felt flustered, her throat a little fluttery. "I'm really glad to meet you. I was hoping to have a few minutes to talk to you. There's still a half hour before the ceremony starts. Do you think we could go somewhere quiet?"

Marjorie looked curious, then nodded. "Let's go to the officer's mess. It's just down the corridor, past the kitchen."

Marjorie led the way to a room containing four tables covered with plastic red and white checked tablecloths. Each table contained a round black ashtray. Not for use, Gwen assumed, but for historical accuracy. A single long green naugahyde bench was built against one wall. On the other side of the tables were straight-backed wooden chairs. Two porthole windows were open to the outside and each was flanked by straight panels of forest green curtains.

When they were settled across one another at one of the tables, the Uncle Sam hat between them, Gwen produced the journal, handing it over silently. Marjorie held it gingerly in both hands, staring at it for several seconds before raising her gaze, startling Gwen with eyes awash with tears. Her face was pained and full of questions.

"It turned up at the base museum in Alameda," Gwen explained. "That's where I work."

"I never knew what happened to this," Marjorie said, her voice quavering. "I guess it got left behind when I shipped out. I probably left it in my usual hiding place in the barracks."

"The building was torn down a couple years ago. Maybe that's when it turned up."

"So you read it?" she asked. "All of it?"

"Sorry. I didn't know you were still alive. I thought it was part of a donated estate."

Marjorie attempted a small laugh. "Then I guess you know all my secrets."

"It was quite a story."

Marjorie opened the front cover and ran her finger along the torn edge of the first page. "How'd you know it belonged to me?"

"Oh, that was a stroke of luck. I interviewed Lucy for the Rosie the Riveter project and her story was the other half of yours. She put the name to the story for me."

Marjorie's eyes widened. "Lucy? Is Lucy...?"

Gwen nodded. "She's recovering from a broken hip. Otherwise, she's fine."

Marjorie's face revealed her struggle with her emotions. Finally, she said, "I've often wondered what happened to her after the war, if she had a happy life."

"But you never tried to reconnect?"

Marjorie shook her head. "When my father died several years ago, I went into a very sad period of my life. Ann, who knew about Lucy, tried to get me to look her up at that time."

"Ann Fraser, your partner."

"Yes. She passed a few years ago. We were together over twenty years. I still miss her every day. Back then, when my father died, she thought my sense of loss was all bound up with what happened with Lucy during the war. She thought I might feel better if I saw Lucy again. I don't know if it would have helped or not, but I couldn't bring myself to do it. I never knew what had become of her."

"Well, I can tell you a little about that. She had a couple of daughters, divorced her husband, went to college and became a pharmacist. She's retired now, of course, and has four...yeah, I think four grandchildren."

Marjorie smiled, amused. "Really? How interesting. Did she ever remarry?"

"No. But she did stay in Alameda. She still lives in the same house."

Marjorie raised her eyebrows. "I drove by there once with Ann. I was showing her all my old haunts, you know. Took her out to the base, then we went to Santa Clara Avenue and sat in the car outside Lucy's house." Marjorie shook her head. "That's something, to think she might have been in there at the time. Gives me a chill."

"Would you like to see her?" Gwen asked.

Marjorie stared, as though this thought had never entered her mind, as if it were an impossible thing Gwen was proposing.

"Oh, I don't know." Marjorie sighed and looked at the table, then she raised her eyes to Gwen's. "Does she want to see me?"

"She doesn't know anything about this. Up until an hour ago, I didn't even know you were alive."

"It's been such a long time. But I don't know if it's been long enough for her to forgive me for being such a coward."

"You're hardly a coward," Gwen objected. "You're a hero! What you did in the seventies was an incredibly courageous act."

Marjorie smiled ironically. "Maybe it was. Maybe it was just my way of making up a little bit for what I did to Lucy. I hated myself after I left her. I could hardly face myself. It was a long time before I felt human again. It was very hard to be a lesbian back then. You had to lead a double life, a life full of lies and hypocrisy. After Lucy, I devoted myself to my education and career and let my heart go dormant. It seemed easier. There was so much secrecy and shame too. I know we're all proud now, but you can't really be proud in a climate like that. I mean, you kept it to yourself. You had to. I saw a lot of good people drummed out during my career. I always felt so utterly helpless."

"Everyone had to face the battle alone in those days," Gwen commented.

"Yes. You're right. And that's no way to win a war." Marjorie placed her journal on the table between them. "You might think this is funny, but I never even knew the word 'lesbian' until I was about your age, late twenties. I mean, I was one, but I didn't know what I was. I didn't know what to call it. We knew the word 'homosexual.' And 'queer.' But the men weren't called 'gay' either. The thing is, if you don't have a label, you can't form a united front. Some people think labels are destructive, but there are a lot of instances where a label gives you a community, and a community gives you strength. If you don't even have a name for what you are, you don't identify with others like you. We lived very private and lonely lives. That was the worst thing. We lived in shadows. And we had no idea how many of us there were."

Gwen listened, interested and sympathetic. She was well educated in gay history, but hearing about it from someone who had lived it was ultimately more satisfying than anything she had read.

"Gradually, though," Marjorie continued, "we began to find each other. I don't mean as sexual partners. I mean as sisters, the sisterhood." Marjorie laughed lightly. "After the war, we called ourselves 'members of the church.' That's sort of funny, isn't it?"

Gwen nodded, thinking it both funny and ironic.

"What we learned, eventually, was that keeping our secret was a form of self-oppression. It allowed the rest of society to deny our existence. It seems obvious now, but that wasn't the way we thought then. It took a lot of societal unrest to show us what was possible. Women were rising up. Minorities were rising up. We started doing the same. We started coming out and speaking out, demanding rights. After Stonewall, everything changed. I changed too." Marjorie's voice had gotten stronger and more insistent. "By the time I finally did love someone again, I wasn't about to let anybody make me feel ashamed of it."

"You could have retired with no penalty," Gwen pointed out.

"Yes, that was the deal. But I just couldn't slink away again. I just couldn't. And I knew it was a major opportunity. Changes were happening. I thought I could do something. I knew they had to take me seriously, because of my rank and record. I knew there was a chance I could make a difference. So, no, I couldn't just walk away, not with my head held high." Marjorie clasped her hands together on the table.

"Well, you didn't," Gwen said. "And we're all grateful to you for that, for being an intrepid pioneer."

"I was very proud for standing up to them. It wasn't easy. You learn to live with a perpetual fear of discovery. It's hard to break through all that fear, decades of fear, and stand there, revealed. It was one of the hardest things I ever did. It was years of hearings and appeals. And so humiliating. The things they ask, the things they talk about in court...They read your letters. There's no discretion. Some days I didn't think I had it in me. I remember telling my lawyer more than once I wanted to quit." Marjorie sighed. "I hope it did some good, ultimately."

"I'm sure it did. It's part of the tapestry." Gwen found it easy to imagine the dignified presence Marjorie must have assumed during her many court appearances. That dignity was still very much a part of her bearing.

"The larger cause was important to me," Marjorie said, "but in my heart what I really wanted was to be allowed to stay. From the day I enlisted at the age of twenty, I dreamed about someday serving on a ship. That's what being a sailor is all about, isn't it? That's what I was waiting for. Why should it matter that I was female? Why should it matter that I was a lesbian? I was a damn fine sailor."

"When were women finally allowed to serve on ships at sea?"

"Nineteen seventy-eight, just a year after my final appeal was lost at the federal court level. The Supreme Court wouldn't hear my case, so it was over." Marjorie smiled sadly.

"I'd like to talk to you more about that," Gwen said, "when you have some time, about what it was like being a lesbian in the military in the early days. Your journal was completely fascinating. We don't have anything like that in the museum."

Marjorie glanced down at the slim book. "Would it be of use, do you think?"

"Oh, absolutely! I mean, if you felt okay about it. It's very personal, I realize."

"Let me keep it for a while and think about it. This old book and I've been separated for a long time. If I can work up the nerve, I may just read it again."

Gwen nodded, then put her gloved hand over both of Marjorie's. "I can ask Lucy if she'd like to see you. If she wants to, what would you say to that?"

Marjorie looked up from her hands. "I'd say…" Gwen noted new tears forming in Marjorie's eyes. "That would be swell," she finished quietly.

CHAPTER TWENTY-SEVEN

Shelby had been home from the hospital only a few minutes when the doorbell rang and Oscar ran to the front door barking. She followed him and peeked through the peephole to see a colorful figure on the porch, a woman dressed in a red, white and blue Uncle Sam costume. Astonished, she kept peering until she realized it was Gwen, recognizing her reddish mop of hair. She pulled the door open. Gwen definitely looked strange, but she also looked arresting—tall and brilliant. The smile on her face was so wide and so goofy Shelby could easily believe she'd totally flipped out and was running amok.

"Thank God you're home!" Gwen said, sweeping past her into the house. "I've got wonderful news! You won't believe it."

"Why are you dressed like that?" Shelby shut the door and followed Gwen to the kitchen.

"I crashed a party." Gwen was so excited, she was clearly having trouble containing herself. She grabbed Shelby by the shoulders. "I met Marjorie!"

"Oh, my God! No way! The real Marjorie?"

"The real *live* Marjorie." Gwen released Shelby and pointed at the photo on the refrigerator. "She's lovely and smart and she wants to see Lucy."

"I thought you said she was dead."

"Why does everybody keep saying that?" Gwen shook her head. "Can I get a glass of water?"

Shelby handed her a glass from the dish drainer. "How'd you find her so fast?"

Gwen filled the glass with tap water and gulped some down before answering. "I should have thought of it sooner. All those war vets know each other. They've got a tight network, so, of course, Skipper knew her."

Gwen finished the water. She was gradually calming down.

"Where does she live?" Shelby asked.

"In a swanky retirement village in Mill Valley called Cypress Villas. Turns out she went to work for a military contractor after she left the navy and did okay."

"You told her you read her journal?"

Gwen nodded. "I returned it to her. The expression in her eyes when I mentioned Lucy—I mean, it's enough to make you believe in true love, you know? The kind that endures through endless time and space. The kind that lasts forever. I don't think that woman ever got over Lucy. We've got to get them together!"

"I don't think that's a good idea. I don't think it's safe."

"Safe?" Gwen set her hat on the table. "Do you think they're going to explode or something if they come into contact?"

"No, no." Shelby shook her head. "Emotionally safe. I mean, you can tell there's still a lot of pain. Nana still hasn't said a word to me about it. I don't really know how she'd feel about seeing Marjorie."

Gwen frowned. "I see what you mean. I guess we can't decide that for them. It's only fair to let your grandmother decide for herself. Let's ask her tomorrow, okay?"

"This isn't really a good time."

"Why not?"

"Sorry. I forgot you didn't know. Nana's in the hospital. She's got pneumonia."

"Oh." Gwen's face clouded. "Is it serious?"

"I don't know. She kept saying something like this was going to happen. Some complication. You know, it's not just a matter of tissue healing for someone her age. Inactivity is really bad for her. Not to mention the very real risk of giving up, of recovery seeming too difficult because life in the future doesn't look like a barrel of laughs." Shelby could see she'd let all the wind out of Gwen's sails. She felt badly about that. "I'll ask her, though," she said. "As soon as she's better. I just don't want to upset her right now."

Gwen looked anxious, then nodded slightly. Was it possible she was thinking the same thing? That after sixty-five years, Marjorie and Lucy could be on the verge of finding one another only to lose one another again?

"Are you hungry?" Shelby asked. "Do you want to get a pizza?"

"I'm famished. I was so anxious to tell you about Marjorie, I ran out of that party without even getting a piece of cake."

Shelby stared at Gwen for a moment, taking in the effect of the patriotic stripes on her tall, thin frame. She let out an involuntary laugh. "You look ridiculous!"

Gwen nodded, then pulled off the white gloves and tucked them in her back pocket. "Ridiculously hot?" she asked, then grinned suggestively and raised her eyebrows, handing over her empty water glass.

Shelby smiled, feeling the thrill of anticipation and knowing the evening was about to get much hotter. She went to the sink. As she set the glass down, she felt Gwen behind her, slipping her arms around her waist and locking her hands over her stomach. Gwen pressed herself against Shelby's back, trapping her against the kitchen counter and sending a shock wave of excitement through her body. Then she kissed the back of her neck, sensuously. Shelby closed her eyes and tilted her head to allow Gwen easier access to her neck, leaning back against her.

As Gwen continued to kiss her, Shelby reached back and put a hand on Gwen's hip, urging her closer. She complied, pressing her hips firmly against Shelby's thin cotton shorts. Shelby felt her pulse racing.

Gwen spun her around, gripping her tightly and kissing her mouth, one hand at the back of her head like before. It was already a familiar gesture, Gwen's gesture, commanding, lustful, electrifying. Shelby liked the feeling of being held that way, possessively, her head in Gwen's hand. She felt herself tumbling into a freefall of desire as Gwen's other hand slid under her shirt and over the bare skin of her back, then around to the front, teasing and fondling her through her bra.

Gwen was clearly as excited as she was, breathing hard, gripping Shelby anxiously. Shelby reached for the big white buttons on the outlandish blue topcoat and rapidly undid them. She was about to push the coat off Gwen's shoulders when she heard a nearby scream, loud and high-pitched and shocking.

Gwen jerked away and both of them turned toward the noise, seeing Vivian peering in at the kitchen window, her face contorted in alarm.

"Oh, my God!" Shelby exclaimed, leaping for the back door. "Mom!" she called, flinging it open. "Mom, this isn't what you think! It's nothing. We're just joking around."

Vivian was nearly running from Shelby, rounding the corner of the house. Shelby leapt off the back porch and ran after her. "Mom, please stop! Come inside and we can talk."

But she didn't stop. She was heading toward the street. Shelby caught up to her and tried to take her arm, but Vivian shook her violently off. Shelby could see she was in tears. A few moments later, she was driving rapidly away.

Shelby kicked the fence post of the open gateway, then sat on the porch step, her face in her hands, feeling defeated. She heard the door open behind her and turned to see Gwen looking angry and resolute. She'd nearly forgotten Gwen in her panic over Vivian, but now she remembered what she'd said and how it must have sounded to Gwen.

"Oh, God, Gwen, I'm sorry," she said, standing to face her.

Gwen stood stiffly, looking even more absurd in the Uncle

Sam costume with such a dire expression on her face. "That hurt," she said simply, then walked past Shelby and out to the street to her car.

"I'm sorry!" Shelby called after her. "I didn't mean it!"

She sank back to the steps as Gwen drove away, dejected and empty, not sure which of these disasters was worse, her mother's horror or Gwen's anger. But it didn't really matter which was worse. They were both bad.

CHAPTER TWENTY-EIGHT

Shelby was grateful Charlie's car wasn't in the driveway when she arrived at her mother's house. He didn't need to be a participant in this catastrophe.

She found her mother in her bedroom, face down on the bed, still fully clothed, sobbing.

"Mom, I—" she began, feeling helpless. She stood in the middle of the room while her mother remained where she was, unresponsive, her face hidden in a pillow.

Shelby still wasn't used to the year-old décor in this room with its floral prints and heavy, old-fashioned cherry-stained furniture. In her mind, she called it "retro divorcee defiance" because it was Vivian's attempt to expunge her husband from her bedroom. The therapist's idea. "Make it your private, personal space with all your favorite things," the therapist had advised.

"Let it reflect your personality and only your personality." So Vivian had gotten rid of everything, including the carpet on the floor, which was now covered in hardwood slats. Shelby wondered how much this redecorating project had actually helped.

"Can we talk?" she asked, sitting on the edge of the bed.

Vivian sniffled and slowly sat up, facing Shelby with an accusing and pained expression. "Fine, Shelby Ann. What improbable story do you want me to swallow?"

"I'm not going to tell you a story, Mom. I'm not going to protect you from this anymore."

Vivian wiped at her eyes with the back of her hand. "What do you mean?"

"It's time for the truth." Shelby braced herself and looked her mother in the eye. "I'm a lesbian."

Vivian pressed her lips firmly together, her stare unrelenting. "No, you're not!"

"Yes, I am." Shelby spoke calmly, though her heart was beating wildly.

"Since when?"

"Since always. Lori and I weren't just friends."

"Oh, please, Shelby! Now you're just being ridiculous. Lori's completely blameless in this. As you well know, she's about to marry Stephen, so she's obviously not gay."

"Mom," Shelby said as gently as she could, "Lori and I were a couple the entire time we lived together and even before that. We met my first year in college. We fell in love. Maybe she's gay and maybe she isn't. I don't know. But I do know I am."

Vivian still stared and said nothing, but Shelby could see the hurt in her eyes.

"I didn't mean for you to find out like this," Shelby said. "I wanted to tell you, but it just never seemed like the right time. I'm sorry. I mean, I'm not sorry I'm gay. I'm sorry to upset you."

Vivian was no longer crying. "Who was that woman?"

"That was Gwen."

"Uncle Sam? What the hell was that about?"

Shelby understood the need to be angry at everything, that Vivian needed to vent. "She went to a costume party. That must have looked really strange to you."

Vivian stared, then shook her head. "You have no idea."

Shelby sat with her hands in her lap, trying to think of something to say.

"Why are you doing this to me?" Vivian asked quietly.

Shelby balked. "I'm not doing anything to you. I'm just living my life."

Vivian burst into tears again, holding her face in her hands. Shelby tried to comfort her, patting her on the back.

"All I ever wanted was a healthy, normal family," Vivian sobbed. "Then your father runs off with that bimbo. And Charlie gets a girl pregnant and throws away his education, not to mention his child. Signs her away like a piece of furniture! And now...now you're telling me you're gay."

Shelby thought briefly about how Vivian would react when she found out Nana had once had an affair with a woman. She didn't have to find out about that, though. She had enough to deal with already. No, she didn't ever need to know that.

"Why, Shelby, why are you gay? What happened?"

"It's just who I am, Mom. Nothing happened."

Her mother looked in her eyes, her own eyes clearly tortured, then put a hand gently to her cheek. "I just don't want you to suffer."

"I'm not suffering. It's okay. Why do you think they call it gay?" Shelby chuckled nervously. "Everything's going to be fine. Really. You'll see."

Vivian gradually relaxed as Shelby rubbed her back soothingly.

"Sorry, Mom," Shelby said. "I really didn't do it to upset you."

"No, I know." Vivian looked up, her eyes red. "Do you have to be gay?"

Shelby shrugged, wishing she weren't such a disappointment. "I think so, yeah."

Vivian's voice was uncertain. "So that boy, Todd, he's not—"

"Just a friend."

Shelby gave her a Kleenex and waited while she blew her nose. She seemed to be over her initial shock. She even managed a tiny smile as she wiped her nose.

"What were you doing over there in the backyard anyway?" Shelby asked.

Vivian took a deep breath. "I've been talking to a real estate agent about selling the house. He asked me about dry rot, so I was just looking around all the windows, seeing what condition they were in."

"Nana's selling the house?"

"I don't think we have much choice. You yourself said she's not able to keep everything up."

"Did she say she wanted to sell it?"

"I mentioned it to her. She didn't say one way or the other. It's like she doesn't care."

"Where will she go?"

"We haven't gotten that far. I'm just making inquiries. Investigating all the options." Vivian was obviously still flustered. Her voice trembled and Shelby could tell she was trying hard not to lose control. "Shelby, could you please go now? I want to be alone."

"Are you sure?"

Vivian nodded vigorously. Shelby knew she wasn't done crying.

"Okay." Shelby stood. "I'll call you tomorrow. And please try not to think of this as a tragedy. It doesn't have to be."

As she left, she felt tremendously relieved she'd finally come out to her mother and hoped they'd be able to work through it without too much damage. Then her thoughts turned to Gwen and that deadly serious look on her face. In its way, it was much more damning than anything her mother had expressed.

CHAPTER TWENTY-NINE

"I'm really nervous," Marjorie admitted as Gwen led her along a corridor in the hospital, giving her arm for support.

Gwen, too, was nervous, but didn't want to say so. Because it was Sunday morning, Gwen knew that Shelby's mother would be in church. Shelby was not an early riser and normally didn't visit her grandmother until afternoon. Gwen was counting on Marjorie having Lucy to herself this morning.

Going behind Shelby's back was eating on Gwen's conscience, but ever since she'd found Marjorie, she'd been driven to get these two together. When Shelby said she wanted to wait until Lucy was better, Gwen had initially agreed, but the more she thought about it, the more she thought that was both a bad and risky idea. What if Lucy didn't recover from the pneumonia?

Gwen had convinced herself that being reunited with

Marjorie was the only thing that would give Lucy the will to live.

All of this rationalization was separate from Gwen's feelings about Shelby, which were now clouded by the knowledge that she was closeted. She'd been frantic when her mother had seen them. Gwen wasn't available to women who weren't comfortable with their lesbianism. That was one of her hard rules. She had no intention of living in shadows, as Marjorie had put it. She wouldn't do that for anyone, ever again. The idea brought back painful memories of life with Melissa.

Shelby's words to her mother— "It's nothing. We're just joking around"—had been hard to take. She kept hearing those words and along with them the trivializing of any relationship she might have had with Shelby. That's what it meant to be closeted, to deny your love and deny its legitimacy. So she hadn't returned Shelby's brief but emphatic voice mail messages. "Can't we at least talk about this?" "Won't you give me a chance to explain?"

As sweet as Shelby was, as incredible as kissing her had been, this was a clear-cut deal breaker. Gwen needed some distance. She shook herself and forced herself back to the moment.

Marjorie didn't know they were on a secret mission. Gwen had told her Lucy wanted to see her, the sooner the better, and as far as Gwen was concerned, that was the truth. Though no one had said it, she felt in her heart that these two wanted nothing more than to be reunited, to bring some resolution to their old hurt. Gwen had looked them both in the eyes as they spoke of and remembered the other. She trusted her gut instinct, that being reunited was more good than bad for them both. Painful, yes, but resolutions in life were often longed for and often denied. Here was a rare opportunity, if not to right a wrong, then at least to bring some peace of mind to the injured parties.

"Are you sure she wants to see me?" Marjorie asked, leaning heavily on Gwen's arm.

"Positive."

"What will I say?"

Gwen stopped and patted her hand, engaging her eyes. "Don't worry. It'll be fine."

"It's just been so long." Marjorie looked distressed.

"But you do want to see her, don't you?" Gwen asked.

"Yes, yes, I do. But I'm hardly the girl I was back in nineteen forty-four."

"I'm sure she knows that. And neither is she." Gwen smiled encouragingly and they continued along the hallway.

When they arrived in Lucy's room, they found her sleeping with an oxygen tube in her nose, her breath raspy. Transfixed by the woman before her, Marjorie stared for a moment before releasing Gwen's arm and moving closer to the bed. She leaned in to examine Lucy's face. Gwen heard her catch her breath. She turned to look at Gwen, her expression one of wonder.

"It *is* her," Marjorie whispered. "Holy mackerel! She's old!"

Then Marjorie laughed lightly and touched a hand tentatively to Lucy's cheek. "Still beautiful, though."

Gwen swallowed hard to knock down an upwelling of emotion.

Lucy opened her eyes, then blinked deliberately and stared.

"Hello, Lou," Marjorie said gently, her voice quavering with emotion.

Lucy stared for a moment, obviously confused. "Marjorie?" she said at last, her voice clear and calm.

"Yes, it's me."

Gwen felt tears forming in her eyes. She quickly wiped them away.

"Am I dead?" Lucy asked, her voice perfectly serious.

Marjorie chuckled. "No. You're still among the living."

Lucy glanced around the room to verify her location. "You're real?"

"I'm real. If we were in heaven, do you think I'd be all old and wrinkled like this?"

Marjorie moved her hand from Lucy's cheek and took hold of her hand, smiling down at her.

With tears running down her cheeks, Gwen stepped out of the room. In the hallway, she took a deep breath and leaned against the wall. It was obvious that the intervening decades had done nothing to diminish the poignancy of this love affair.

Even Marjorie, who had gone on to love again, had remained powerfully under its spell. Gwen felt an overwhelming sense of joyful accomplishment at having brought them together again at last.

CHAPTER THIRTY

Shelby carried a plastic bag of Nana's possessions into the nursing home. The hospital stay had been short, only three days. Dinky sat in her bed watching them parade in. For once she did not have her television on. A nurse pushed the wheelchair in, bringing Nana back to her hellhole.

"I'm back," Nana called loudly.

Dinky grinned and waved. "I knew you'd be back. I'm leaving tomorrow. Going home."

"Well, good for you!" Nana turned to Shelby and said, more quietly, "Thank God!"

Shelby was relieved to see Nana so lively. Feisty, even. She got into bed on her own, slowly and deliberately, maneuvering herself from the wheelchair to the edge of the bed with small, pained steps.

"Mom," Vivian said, sitting in the visitor's chair, "we need to talk about what we're going to do when you get out of here."

"Do we have to talk about that now?" Shelby asked.

"Yes, we do. Arrangements have to be made. Your social worker and Vickie and I all agree you shouldn't be living alone anymore. For a while, you won't be able to do everything on your own anyway. You need some kind of assisted living, at least as an interim step. As I see it, we have several options. You can move in with one of us or we can find you a nice retirement home."

"Live with you?" Nana asked, putting on her baseball cap. "I'd rather die."

"Well, joking aside, that may be the best option. Either me or Vickie."

"I'm not joking. I would rather be dead than live with either one of you. It would be like going to hell. Besides, Vickie's allergic to Oscar."

"Okay." Vivian took a deep breath, clearly trying to remain calm. "Retirement homes, nice ones, are extremely expensive. With your income, I don't know if you'll be able to afford much, but I'll look into it."

"She has some savings," Shelby interjected, remembering she hadn't shown her mother the state of Nana's finances.

"That's good," Vivian said. "And with the sale of the house, you'll have a nice lump sum to invest. It's lucky you kept that house. Do you have any idea how much a house in Alameda is worth? The ballpark figure the real estate guy gave me was very encouraging."

"Do we have to sell the house?" Shelby asked. "It's been in the family for so long. It's a nice house."

"What's nice about it?" Vivian asked. "It's small, old, and all the windows are warped."

"It's got charm. Character. It's a classic Craftsman bungalow."

Vivian threw up her hands. "Oh, you mean architecturally? Please! Let's just drop it."

Shelby realized she'd hit a nerve. Anything to do with architecture reminded her mother of her father. Besides, she'd been impatient with Shelby ever since Friday when Shelby had come out to her. She hadn't mentioned that or the incident that precipitated it, but her manner was consistently brusque and cold. Shelby tried not to take it too personally. She knew Vivian was just hurt and needed time to adapt.

"Sorry," Shelby said, then realized she was saying that too often and should quit. "What if I stayed there. Nana could come home and I could take care of her until she was fully recovered."

Nana's face brightened and she nodded.

Vivian considered this momentarily, then said, "After what I saw the other day, I don't think that's such a great idea."

"What'd you see?" Nana asked, sitting up straighter.

"Never mind." Vivian's voice was tense.

"She saw me and Gwen kissing in the kitchen," Shelby offered.

Vivian's mouth fell open and she stared at Shelby disapprovingly.

"How sweet," Nana said. "I don't know why you think that would bother me, Viv. Gwen's a lovely girl. Why shouldn't Shelby kiss her?"

Vivian jerked her attention back to her mother. "Mom, you're so naïve sometimes. They wouldn't just be kissing. Since Shelby seems determined to bring this out in the open, you may as well know. She says she's gay." Shelby noticed her mother's voice was getting higher as she became more agitated. "That's right! Your granddaughter thinks she's a lesbian."

Nana smiled at Shelby, her eyes twinkling mischievously. "Oh, I already know that."

"You do?"

Nana nodded. "And now Dinky does too."

They all turned to see Dinky propped up on her elbow, listening intently. Vivian stood, huffing, and pulled the curtain between the two halves of the room.

"Damn!" they heard from Dinky's side.

Shelby tried to suppress a grin as she made eye contact with Nana. She was overjoyed to see her so spirited. She was obviously feeling much better.

"And that doesn't bother you?" Vivian asked more quietly.

"Why should it bother me? What's your problem, Viv? Your daughter's in love. Be happy for her. Quit being such an uptight, self-righteous jerk."

Vivian looked stunned. She stared for a moment before recovering.

"Mom, I do want Shelby to be happy," she said with measured calmness. "But surely you're not okay with them having lesbian sex right under your nose."

Nana hooted. "Right under my nose?"

Vivian looked exasperated. "You know what I mean. Even *you* must know what lesbians do."

"Oh, yes, I know what lesbians do. I know better than you do, Viv, what lesbians do because I've done it myself."

Shelby stiffened, watching her mother warily. From the other side of the curtain, she heard "Damn!" again.

Vivian stammered and took a lurching step backward. Shelby put an arm around her shoulders and Vivian shook her off, unwilling to be consoled. Shelby shot a warning look at Nana, trying to urge her to back off this subject. But her face was full of determination. Nana wasn't in a mood to handle anybody gently.

"What are you talking about?" Vivian asked through her teeth. "Is this some kind of joke?"

Nana, serious now, shook her head. "It's time we got it all out in the open."

"Nana," cautioned Shelby.

"It's okay," she assured Shelby, then turned back to Vivian. "Before you were born, Viv, I fell in love with a woman. It was the happiest time of my life. You need to get off your high horse and figure out what matters in life. Love is what matters. That's all that's ever mattered and all that ever will matter. People always try to tell you why loving this person or that person is wrong." Nana reached her hand toward Shelby, who took hold of it. "If it's honest, it isn't wrong. Shelby, don't ever be afraid to love someone, no matter who doesn't like it, and that includes your mother."

Nana shot a pointedly disapproving glance at Vivian, who seemed to wither, looking dazed. Shelby felt sorry for her.

"You may not have anything to worry about, Mom," she said. "Gwen and I may not be getting together after all."

"Oh." Nana asked, "why? What happened?"

"When Mom showed up, I panicked and said some things that hurt Gwen's feelings. She's pretty upset with me. She won't even return my calls."

Nana frowned. "Now look what you've done, Viv. You've torn these two girls apart."

"What?" Vivian said indignantly.

"No," Shelby said, "it's not her fault. I handled things badly. I've been handling things badly for a long time. I was afraid—" Shelby turned to her mother. "I hurt Gwen because I was trying not to hurt you. But I ended up hurting everybody."

Vivian's expression softened into sympathy for just a second before her attention was drawn to Dinky's side of the room where a woman's voice said, "Hello, is this Lucy Brewster's room?"

Shelby pulled back the curtain to see an elderly woman carrying a vase of daisies and daylilies, moving slowly. She was a handsome woman, graceful and tall, wearing tan pants, a print blouse and putty-colored orthopedic shoes. Shelby took the vase from her. Then she looked into her eyes and recognized her.

"Oh!" Shelby exclaimed.

"You must be Shelby," Marjorie said, holding out her hand. "I'm—"

Shelby took her hand, stunned. "I know who you are."

Shelby turned to Nana, who didn't seem surprised. Marjorie moved to the side of Nana's bed and leaned over to kiss her cheek. Clearly, this was not the first time she'd seen Nana in over sixty-five years. What's going on? Shelby wondered, marveling that Marjorie was standing beside her.

"They told me at the hospital you'd been discharged," Marjorie said.

"I didn't know you were coming for another visit," Nana said, "or I would've had somebody call and let you know where to find me."

"You must be feeling better. You look much better. Lots of color in your cheeks today."

Vivian coughed to get Nana's attention.

"Marjorie," Nana said, "this is my daughter Vivian."

"Nice to meet you," Vivian said, shaking Marjorie's hand. "Marjorie? I've heard that name before, somewhere recently."

As Shelby caught Nana's eye, she knew she was about to drop another bombshell. Mischievous resolve was all over her face. There was just no stopping her today.

"Marjorie is my lesbian lover," Nana said matter-of-factly.

Vivian collapsed into a chair. Shelby's hand went to her mouth, suppressing a gasp. Marjorie's eyebrows raised in amused surprise. And from behind them, Shelby heard, "Damn!"

CHAPTER THIRTY-ONE

Shelby pushed open the museum door. She was nervous, but determined. She hadn't been able to get through to Gwen by phone, so she'd decided on an in-person visit to explain and apologize again, certain that she could set things right if given a chance.

Afternoon sunlight poured in at an angle through the high south-facing windows, lighting up the patchwork linoleum. Her shoes clicked across it as she walked through to the uniform room where a scratchy version of "Auf Wiedersch'n, Sweetheart" was playing. The room was deserted except for the dozen or so mannequins modeling suits of white and blue.

She heard a noise in the next room and followed it to see Gwen on a ladder, adding photos to a display board.

"Oh, it's you," she said, looking over her shoulder. "I heard footsteps. I thought it was Grady saying goodnight." Gwen descended the ladder. Her expression was neutral.

The cool reception felt lousy. Seeing that familiar face again, Shelby wanted to take Gwen in her arms and kiss her, but her body language was stiff and off-putting.

"Is this a new exhibit?" Shelby asked as casually as she could manage.

"Yes. Inspired by Marjorie."

Shelby noted the heading on the photo board: "U.S. Navy: Refuge and Oppressor." She stepped closer, reading the quotation under that heading. "Ever since women were allowed to serve, lesbians have always been a strong presence in the military." There was an article and photo of Marjorie Banyan in her forties posted beside the 1955 photo of Skipper and Florence, moved from its previous location to this new storyboard. The photos were arranged to ornament a timeline running from 1777, the year of the first homosexual dismissal from the United States military, to the present. The label, "Homosexuals Unfit to Fight" appeared next to the year 1942. "Homosexual Acts Grounds for Dismissal" tagged the year 1972. A "Don't Ask, Don't Tell" bumper sticker angled away from the year 1993. And a newspaper headline reading "DADT Repealed!" adorned 2010.

"It's all about gays in the military," Shelby observed.

"Yeah. Well, specifically gays in the navy, since this is a navy museum. Skipper's sent the word out on her network to see who wants to donate material to it. We should be able to get some interesting stuff."

Shelby recognized Marjorie's journal on the counter beneath the photo board. "Marjorie donated her journal?"

"Yes. That's what started this whole thing. Don't worry, I'm not putting the journal on display, just a few photocopies of selected pages. There won't be anything about your grandmother here, though Marjorie did say Lucy has no objection. Not *everyone* is ashamed of who they are."

I should have expected that, Shelby thought. Obviously, Gwen was still hurt.

"I'm not ashamed," Shelby insisted. "You haven't even given me a chance to explain."

"Because you don't need to explain. I understand living in the closet. I understand how hard it is to stand up to the world, especially when your own family doesn't support you. You do what you have to do to keep their love and respect. Family is important. I'm not angry at you. I just don't want to be with someone who lives like that, even if you think you have very good reasons for it."

"But it's not really about that," Shelby objected. "I don't care what people think. I'm out with people at school and work."

"You're out with people who won't reject you or who don't matter, but not where it really counts." The look on Gwen's face was serious and raw. "I'm not going to change my mind. I've been through this before. Melissa's closeted. The entire time I was with her, I felt negated. It was horrible living like that. I felt sad and fearful all the time. I felt she was ashamed of me, of loving me, and it hurt every time she introduced me to someone as her friend."

"I didn't know," Shelby said quietly, remembering that she and Lori had introduced one another the same way.

"The other day when you told your mother we were nothing, it reminded me so much of how that felt. And it felt like crap."

Shelby felt frustrated. "I'm so sorry about that. I wasn't thinking."

Gwen stared steadily at Shelby with her calm brown eyes. "I know. That's what came out when you weren't thinking. That's what came out of your heart. Denial."

Shelby realized she had tripped one of Gwen's major switches. Making everything okay again wasn't going to be as easy as an apology. What would it take, she wondered? While she was trying to figure that out, Gwen changed the subject.

"I hear Lucy's out of the hospital," she said. "That's good news."

"How'd you know that?"

"Marjorie told me. She came by this morning." Gwen turned back to the ladder and moved it a few feet to the right. "To bring in the journal."

"You took Marjorie to see her, didn't you, despite what we agreed?"

"I decided it would help."

"You couldn't know that. It might have really upset her." Shelby saw Gwen's shoulders stiffen and realized she didn't really want to have this argument. "You shouldn't have done it behind my back, that's all."

"No, I shouldn't have. Sorry. But I wanted Lucy to have something to live for. And I wanted her to know what part she played in history." Gwen gestured toward her display board.

"Nana didn't play any part in that. All she did was fall in love. Neither did Marjorie back then. They were both just victims of circumstance."

Gwen shrugged. "It happens that way sometimes. Most people who influence history didn't set out with that intention."

"But they didn't influence history. Nothing good came of their affair."

"I disagree. I think it's precisely because of their affair that Marjorie did what she did later. She most definitely played a role in history then."

Shelby looked at the photo of Marjorie in her uniform, heavily decorated, striking and serious, an impressive looking woman.

"That's something that's always intrigued me," Gwen said, smiling for the first time since Shelby arrived. "What goes into making a hero? Why does one person take a courageous stand and another shrink back? Or why does someone behave heroically at one time in her life and not another? You can't answer by saying that some people are cowards and some are brave. That's a misleading oversimplification. Some of the most celebrated acts of heroism in battle, for instance, have been the result of a death wish. Is that bravery?"

Shelby enjoyed listening to Gwen talk like this. It was one of the things that had appealed to her from the beginning.

Gwen's hard expression had softened. "I don't agree with Marjorie, that she was a coward in nineteen forty-four. It was an act of self-sacrifice. She did it mainly for her parents. By the time she sued the navy, her father had passed away."

Gwen was clearly full of respect for Marjorie for protecting her parents. Then why was she being so harsh with Shelby for wanting to do the same thing? Shelby was about to pitch that argument when their attention was drawn by a clunking sound from the staircase. Skipper appeared, lumbering slowly down, one hand gripping the railing, one hand waving a framed picture.

"I found it!" she called triumphantly. "I knew it was up there."

Gwen ran to the stairs and took the picture from her. "What are you doing using the stairs!"

Skipper managed to take the rest of the stairs, slowly and painfully, while Gwen stood ready to catch her should she fall forward. She didn't speak until she had reached ground level, and then she did so breathlessly. "Damned thingamabob broke."

"The elevator? Oh, great!"

"Hey, there," Skipper called, waving in Shelby's direction.

"Hi, Skipper," Shelby said. "Good to see you again."

Gwen turned the photo so Shelby could see it—Skipper standing at attention in dress whites while another officer attached something to her collar. "This is Skipper the day she became a lieutenant."

"That fella giving me my pin was the base commander right here," Skipper said. "That's Captain Whatchamacallim. He was only here a couple years. I've seen a whole fleet of them come and go."

"You outlasted them all," Gwen said with admiration. "I'm going to put this inside the case if that's okay with you. Leave it in its frame."

Gwen walked over to the new display case and lifted the glass top, positioning the photo inside.

Skipper clucked at the newly assembled exhibit. "I never thought I'd be part of something like that!"

"How does it feel?" Gwen asked.

"It feels great. Strange too. But it's too late for them to boot me out now. I'm retired."

"Right," Gwen agreed. "It's too late and it's no longer illegal." She gestured toward her timeline and its 2010 repeal of the gay ban.

Skipper grinned with satisfaction. "About damned time!"

She pointed at the new photo. "That one there knew about me and Florence. He was no dummy. A lot of them did know. But they turned a blind eye, you know. They liked me. I did my job. I didn't give them any grief." Skipper scrunched up her face looking at Marjorie's photo on the wall. "That didn't always work. Poor Marjorie didn't make waves either. She was a lifer like me. She gave the navy everything. Never out of line. Not till they tried to get rid of her. Then she let 'em have it! Torpedoes away!" Skipper threw up her hands and laughed gleefully.

Gwen smiled and laid a hand on her shoulder. "She did, didn't she?"

As Gwen's eyes caught Shelby's, her smile gradually faded. She'd said she wasn't angry and Shelby could see that was true. She was sad and sorry, as if fate itself had decided they had no future together.

"All right, Skipper," Gwen said, "let's get out of here. Time to head home."

Skipper nodded as Gwen went to fold the ladder.

"Gwen," Shelby ventured, "how about grabbing a burger at Ollie's?"

Gwen glanced at Skipper, then answered breezily. "No, thanks. I'm busy tonight." She leaned the ladder against the wall, then patted Skipper on the shoulder. "Ready?"

"Yep." Skipper tilted her head sideways to look up at Gwen. "What about Grady?"

"What about him? Isn't he gone already?"

"No! He's stuck in the deelybob between the first and second floor."

Just then they heard the sound of metal clanging against metal, echoing through the walls of the building—clang, clang, clang, purposefully and impatiently.

Gwen's eyes widened and she bounded around the corner toward the elevator.

"I thought I mentioned that," Skipper mumbled, grimacing at Shelby.

CHAPTER THIRTY-TWO

A handful of people gathered around a trim, sixtyish woman in a park ranger uniform near a metallic structure of arching beams. She was speaking about the monument, a tribute to the Rosie the Riveter shipyard workers from World War II. Shelby had never been to this park before. It occupied the former site of Kaiser Shipyard Number Two, the very spot where Nana had worked as a bucker and welder. There was nothing left here from that era. To the west was San Francisco Bay. To the east were rows of modern condos. Between was this patch of trampled grass. A typical Brownfield project. The docks, the cranes and the shipyard buildings were all gone.

Holding Oscar's leash in one hand, Shelby pushed the wheelchair closer to the ranger so she and Nana could hear her speech. The stainless steel sculpture beside her was adorned with black-and-white photos of women. Their words, inscribed in metal, were peppered throughout the structure.

"Without these women," the ranger said, "that war could not have been won. We simply wouldn't have had the labor force required."

She gestured to the structure behind her and said, "The design for this memorial was inspired by the ships that were built here. This piece represents the ship's skeletal hull as it appeared while under construction. Following the walkway toward the bay, you're walking the length of such a ship. The platform out at the water represents the stern. So I invite you to read the information here, take that walk, and reflect on the invaluable debt we owe these women for their dedication and their sacrifices. Thank you."

As the visitors filed off to look at the memorial more closely, the ranger came over to Nana and said, "Hello. Let me guess. You're a Rosie."

"Yep," Nana confirmed. "Shipyard number two. Welder."

"Oh, right here in Richmond. That's wonderful."

"We came in late and missed most of your speech," Shelby said.

"Well, some other time."

"Did you work here too?" Nana asked.

"No. But my mother did. She was a riveter. Her photo is right here. Let me show you."

Shelby pushed the wheelchair over to the spot where the docent pointed to a picture of a young woman in coveralls flashing a wide grin. As the docent was drawn away by a visitor with a question, Nana pushed up the bill of her Giants cap to get a better look at the photos while Shelby read one of the many quotations.

Let me tell you this. I was 23. I never had a job. My husband was an electrician. I told him, "I'm going to work, too." He said, "No you're not." That same afternoon I went to the hiring hall.

Shelby smiled down at Nana, then pushed the wheelchair leisurely around the memorial while they read the inscriptions and looked at the photos.

One of the pavers they walked over held another quotation that reminded Shelby of Gwen's comment about how revolutionary the factory work was for women.

When I got my first paycheck, it was $16.30 a week. I was so happy. I stuck it on my wall in the bedroom, then in the kitchen. I didn't want to cash it. I thought I was so rich.

The faces in these photos were all similar in some ways, despite the fact that the women varied in age and ethnicity. They were all joyful, eager, determined. Most of them had never done anything like this. It was a personal revolution for each individual. None of them had any idea where it would lead to for women, collectively. They didn't know they were making history. Like Gwen had said, people who influenced history didn't always set out to do so. These women just wanted to help win the war. They didn't know how it would change them. They didn't even know, in most cases, that it would change them. But it did, profoundly.

Moved to tears, Shelby glanced at Nana. She was dry-eyed, but solemn. They gradually made their way along the length of the walkway to the overlook platform at the edge of the bay.

A plaque contained an anonymous quotation: *You must tell your children, putting modesty aside, that without us, without women, there would have been no Spring in 1945.*

Shelby locked the wheels of the wheelchair and sat on a bench beside it. Oscar curled up against the front wheel. It was a warm day and the sailboats were out in force. Gray and white gulls dipped near them in their continual search for a handout.

"This is a nice tribute," Nana said. "Tasteful and dignified."

"Yes, it is. I'm glad we came."

"It must be hard for you to imagine what it was like then. There was so much going on here. The shipways, plate shop, machine shop, pre-fab yard, cranes. It was huge. There were twelve shipways in this one yard. We could build twelve ships at one time. The whirley cranes rode on a set of tracks on the sides of each shipway. They could move alongside the ship, bow to stern that way. There were all these other buildings all around where people were putting things together. Tens of thousands of workers every day." Nana gazed around at the calm waterfront. "All gone now." She turned her gaze out to the bay. "The view, though, is almost the same. The San Francisco skyline's changed a bit, but not so you wouldn't know where you are."

Shelby looked across the bay to the city, trying to see it with her grandmother's memory.

"Right over yonder," Nana said, looking behind them, "was where I first saw Marjorie, in front of the General Warehouse."

Shelby looked in the direction Nana pointed, even though there was nothing to see, except in their imagination.

"She was standing beside the staff car, holding her hat in her hand, smoking a cigarette. I was just getting off work, walking out to the gate wearing my coveralls and do-rag. Marjorie had on her white uniform for summer, stockings and lipstick, her shoes shined up like mirrors. She was very striking. That's why I remember so well. She looked up when I passed and I smiled at her. Just a friendly smile, you know, one working woman to another. She gave me a wink and blew a puff of smoke."

Nana stared into the distance, seeming to be lost in thought.

"This place was such an important part of your life," Shelby remarked. "I never realized that until lately."

"It was exciting working here. Gave me a taste of freedom. I learned I could make it on my own. I don't think I got that right away. I think it only sunk in later, years later when I realized I could dump Arnie and do just fine."

"He wasn't much of a husband, was he?"

"He was okay in the beginning. He was a simple man with a limited imagination. He gave me a couple of kids and I'm grateful for that. In those days, the only way you had kids was the old-fashioned way. But he got sad and disillusioned about life and took to drinking. He never could pull himself out of that."

"Why did that happen?"

"I don't know. His life was no harder or more depressing than anybody else's. I think just about anybody could succumb to that sort of disillusionment if they let themselves. It boils down to strength of character or lack of it. That's what I think."

Shelby watched the gulls for a moment. "Do you ever think about what would have happened if you'd run away with Marjorie?"

"Haven't thought about it much, no. Not in a long time, anyway."

"She feels guilty for not doing it."

"Well, she shouldn't. It was just a fantasy we clung to in a desperate moment. There never was much chance it would actually happen. I think she made the right choice for herself. It would have damaged her too much to run away from her career and her family. It would have been a hard life. We had so many strikes against us. We were out before we stepped into the batter's box." Nana sat up straighter in the wheelchair. "No, it was never really an option for us."

"That must have been so painful, though, to say goodbye, to give up that dream."

"It was. It was hard to keep it to myself too. Of course, there was nobody to tell. Nobody would have sympathized. I felt so guilty and so lonely. I often wanted to die during the summer that followed. But life went on, I toughened up and gradually recovered."

Shelby smiled sympathetically and held Nana's hand briefly. "I still can't believe what you said to Mom the other day. You really shocked me when you told her about Marjorie."

Nana grinned. "I didn't know I was going to do that. It was probably the pain medicine. They gave me a shot of something before I left the hospital."

"It wasn't the pain medicine!"

"No, it wasn't." Nana chuckled. "It was because of the way she was talking about you. Ticked me off. Besides, it was time to give up that secret. If we don't want the rest of the world to treat it like a big deal, then we shouldn't either. I don't mind anymore if everybody in the whole world knows about me and Marjorie."

Looking into Nana's face, Shelby believed her. "Mom said you might be getting released in a week or two."

"So they say. I can't wait to get out of that place. Ever since Dinky left, it's driving me stir-crazy."

"You hated Dinky."

"Oh, I didn't hate Dinky. She was okay."

Shelby stared.

"This new one is worse. She lies in her bed all day sleeping.

Never says a word. You wouldn't know she was there at all if she didn't fart once in a while."

Shelby shook her head. "Marjorie's been to visit you quite a few times, hasn't she?"

"Yes. We're getting to be a regular item in that hellhole. You know, that place she lives in doesn't sound half bad. They do all your chores for you and drive you around to things like plays and concerts. It sounds like a resort. They've even got entertainment on the premises. Marjorie said that old man Lippincott went skinny-dipping in the fountain yesterday and attracted quite an audience."

Shelby laughed.

"I'd sort of like to take a look at it," Nana announced.

"I think that can be arranged."

Nana unwrapped one of her mints and popped it in her mouth. "How's it going with Gwen?"

Shelby sighed. "We're finished, apparently. She thinks I'm not comfortable with being gay. She thinks that's why I kept it from my family."

Sucking gently on her mint, Nana said, "And you disagree?"

"Right. I didn't come out because Lori wanted it that way. She insisted."

"Is that the only reason?"

"That's the main reason. And I was worried about upsetting Mom. You know how she is. She just has all these ideas about how things should be. I was afraid she'd have another nervous breakdown. And Dad too. He's always been so proud of me, had such dreams for me."

"You think he wouldn't be proud if he knew you were gay?"

Shelby lowered her head. "I really don't know."

"It sounds like a lot of excuses to me. Very convenient for you that your girlfriend wanted to keep it secret."

Shelby looked up. "What do you mean?"

"Maybe Gwen's right. Maybe you're afraid of losing the love and respect of your family."

"Not without cause," Shelby countered. "Mom's practically quit speaking to me since I told her. When she does speak to me, she can't look me in the eye. I know she's really upset about it. If she ends up back on tranquilizers because of me—"

"Try not to encourage that." Nana rolled her eyes. "I love Vivian, but she has her faults, like trying to make you feel guilty for being honest. You have nothing to feel guilty about. Don't let her do that to you. That's why I turned the tables on her the other day."

"You mean when you told her it was her fault Gwen and I broke up?"

"That's right." Nana smiled fondly. "You think you need to protect her, but your mother has a resiliency you don't give her credit for. When she was a child, she was always having panic attacks, anxiety attacks, hyperventilating. What I called hissy fits in those days. I learned that the best way to deal with a hissy fit was to ignore it. If it didn't accomplish anything, like getting her sympathy, attention or her way, then she stopped." Nana pressed her lips together and shook her head. "It may sometimes look like I'm indifferent to her pain, but I'm not really. I just don't believe in indulging it. A lot of that fuss when your father left was her attempt to manipulate him into coming back. What you need to understand about your mother is that she'll live up or down to whatever you expect of her. You've been expecting too little. Challenge her once in a while and you might be surprised."

Shelby was both puzzled and intrigued by this summation of her mother.

"As for your father," Nana said, "I'd think he'd be able to sympathize with you. He was smart to get out while he still had some life left in him. I have to admire him for waiting until you kids were grown, but now he's living for himself. There comes a time in everyone's life when you have to live for yourself and quit worrying about what the world thinks." Nana stared hard at Shelby. "The world will just keep on spinning regardless."

CHAPTER THIRTY-THREE

As Shelby slid into a red booth opposite her father at Ollie's diner, she thought about all the ways in which a child could disappoint a parent and imagined she was about to hit on a good percentage of those.

"I haven't been here in years," Gary said, his eyes twinkling with amusement. "Still the same, isn't it?"

"Hasn't changed a bit. They still have that steak and onions you used to like so much. With the baked potato and all the fixin's."

"Oh, that's a little rich for me now. I think I'll be nice to my body today and go for something lighter." He looked through the menu and settled on a chicken salad sandwich. Shelby ordered the turkey club.

"This place is on the California register, you know?" Shelby said, searching for a way to introduce her subject.

"Is it? That's great. I like to see that, a historic business that's still a successful business. Doesn't happen too often. A lot of these old places are just an eyesore. This one's been taken care of, marketed brilliantly." He squinted up at the ceiling. "Still, if they popped the ceiling up on this side, they could put in a row of skylights and draw in some morning light."

Shelby let out an involuntary laugh, which she realized sounded derisive. Her father lowered his gaze to give her a questioning look.

"Well, they couldn't do something like that, of course," she explained. "That would destroy the architectural integrity."

"I know that, Shelby. I was just saying—"

The waitress swung by with their sodas. Shelby wondered what it was like to look at a charming building like this and only see room for improvement. Again she worried that her father would have no appreciation for her new plan. But she had to tell him anyway.

"Dad," she said, plucking the paper off the top of her straw, "I asked you to meet me here because I want to talk about the job."

"Sure, Angel, what do you want to know? You're not asking for a raise already, I hope." He laughed good-naturedly. "Even though you're my daughter, you still have to start at the bottom. I'm a firm believer in fair play and honest work."

"It's nothing like that. I've been rethinking the direction I want to take. I've never really had the same feeling for design you have."

"Oh, you don't need to worry about that. It'll come. You have to start somewhere. We'll teach you everything. Once you get into it, you'll find your own style. That takes time. Nobody has that in the beginning. But you have a natural artistic eye that'll be invaluable in this business."

The waitress returned with their plates. Shelby was frustrated. How was she going to do this other than by just coming right out with it? When they were alone again, she steeled herself and announced, "I'm not coming to work at Pratt and Rutherford after all, Dad."

He looked up, his fork poised over his plate. "What? Why not? Is this because of Lucille? Do you need more time with her?"

"No. It's just me. I'm not cut out for this work. It doesn't interest me."

"Shelby, what are you saying?" He put down his fork, his expression incredulous. "After seven years of college as an architecture major, you've decided you have no interest in architecture?"

"Not exactly. I am interested in architecture. I'd say I have a real sense of wonder and appreciation for buildings. Like this one. I love it. I love its sleek lines and its chrome and shiny Formica. I love everything about it and I wouldn't change a thing. But most of all, I love that it's old. It's older than me and older than you. And here it sits in the same spot it's always been, looking the same as it did when Nana first saw it. That really makes me feel good. Safe and happy."

Gary sighed and picked up his sandwich. "That's a very sentimental point of view," he said before taking a bite. He continued talking as he chewed. "It's just a building. It's a functional piece of construction. Serves a purpose and does it well. If it didn't, it would be worthless."

"But that's the difference between us. I don't think it would be worthless, even if it wasn't being admirably functional. It would still have the value of its history, of the part it played in people's lives." Shelby was thinking of Gwen and her museum building, of the similar argument she was making for it. "I mean, don't you suppose a lot of people remember this place and cherish their memories of it?"

"I suppose they do," Gary conceded, "but that isn't enough of a reason to have it here. A good chicken salad sandwich, now that's enough of a reason." He put his sandwich down. "But I still don't understand what you're getting at. Appreciating old buildings doesn't prevent you from designing new ones. If you don't want to do that, what do you want to do?"

"I want to work in restoration and preservation," Shelby said, excited to be voicing her new aspirations. "I want to help safeguard the country's cultural heritage."

Gary narrowed his eyes at her. "Tell me you don't want to be one of those porch huggers, Shelby."

"Some old buildings should be preserved."

"I agree. There are a lot of buildings I'd like to see preserved. I just think people go too far, let sentimentality cloud their judgment."

"Yes, I know. Like that Victorian in the Tenderloin those people were up in arms about. The one you had all that trouble with."

He nodded. "Yeah, like that. Total piece of junk. It was impossible to save that building. It would have taken millions of dollars. Those are the people I'm talking about, the porch huggers. Sentimental, short-sighted and uninformed."

"Yeah, but see, Dad, that's what's so perfect about this. I have the knowledge to advise those people, to be on their side and help them know what's worth fighting for."

He bit the end off his dill pickle while eying her thoughtfully. "Okay, so you want to help preserve historic buildings. You can do that in your spare time. There's no need to give up your career for that."

"Except I want that to be my career, not just a weekend hobby. I already signed up with the California Preservation Foundation, as a volunteer. They were thrilled to get an architect."

Gary frowned and stopped eating. "I'll bet. You do realize, don't you, that the whole point of being a volunteer is that you work for free?"

"Sure. But it's a way to learn things, meet people and find out how everything works. It'll evolve into a real job. I know it will."

"Shelby, you have a real job at Pratt and Rutherford. Let's just stick to the plan, okay? You can work with the foundation in your spare time. Meanwhile, you'll get some solid experience, which will be valuable whatever you decide to do with it later. You're being idealistic. I don't understand what's got these ideas in your head. You've wanted to be an architect since you were a little girl." He held up a hand, seeing she was about to argue. "Okay, so that hardly counts, but you've just spent seven years as an adult working toward this goal and now that you've made it, you suddenly want to throw it away? Doesn't make sense. It's just cold feet. Don't worry. You'll do fine." There was a pleading look in his eyes. "Angel, you're on the verge of holding your dream in your hands." He held his hands between them, palms up. "To design buildings and watch them grow from the dust of the ground into the sky where they'll stand for generations." He looked up at his imagined building.

Shelby waited until he was facing her again, then she said, "Dad, the thing is—" He waited patiently, passively while she gathered her courage. "The thing is, that dream was never really mine."

He looked confused. "What're you saying?"

"Remember when Charlie said he wasn't interested in architecture or engineering at all and if you were going to force him to go to college, he was going to major in baseball?"

"Yeah, sure."

"Do you remember how disappointed you were? One time I heard you say he must not think much of his old man's accomplishments. You said it like a joke, but I don't think you were joking. And then you asked me if I thought architecture was a worthy occupation."

"And you did. You said you couldn't think of anything you'd rather be."

Shelby bit her bottom lip and looked at her plate.

"You're not saying you said that just to make me feel better?" he asked. "You're not going to tell me you studied architecture for the last seven years just to boost my ego, that you never liked it and wish I'd been a photographer or something."

"No." She looked up. "I like architecture. I just want to do something different with it than you did."

"And you just discovered this?"

"Uh-huh. Sort of. I mean, I knew it wasn't my dream to work at Pratt and Rutherford, but I never thought much about what else I might do. I didn't exactly have a dream and it always seemed like a good plan."

"It *is* a good plan," Gary insisted.

"It was a good plan before I had a plan of my own. It was your plan."

He took a deep breath. "I see."

One of the things Shelby had always appreciated about her father was his even keel. Even when he was angry, he never lost his temper. And when he was disappointed, the only way you could tell it was in his eyes. Like now. She hated to see that, but she'd made up her mind to go her own direction.

"Why not just try it for a while," he suggested. "You can always do the other later."

"Why start off on a course you know isn't the one you want to pursue?"

"You seem very sure of yourself."

"It just feels right."

He looked at her soberly. "How are you going to pay the rent?"

"I won't have any rent for the next few months. Nana's coming home soon. I'm going to stay at her house and help her recuperate. But I'll get a job. I can always go back to waitressing, temporarily." Shelby stuck out her bottom lip in an exaggerated expression of misery.

Gary smiled slightly. "You've obviously thought this through. I spoke to your mother yesterday. She told me the plan for Lucille. It sounds like that will be mutually beneficial."

Shelby realized with relief that he was coming around to her side, if not enthusiastically, at least without further protest. She knew she could win him over completely when she had something to show for her work.

"Your mother had a lot of news, actually," he said. "She also told me you'd gotten involved with a woman named Gwen."

Shelby tried to gauge his thoughts by his expression, but he wasn't looking at her. He was focused on his cole slaw, stabbing his fork into it absent-mindedly.

"Yes," she said quietly, "that was the other thing I wanted to talk to you about."

"Is it serious?"

"Well, no. I'm not actually with Gwen. I'm not with anyone right now. I mean, I'd like to be with her. She's funny and smart and cute. But I don't think it's going to work out." She stopped, waiting for him to pay attention, but now he was pushing the cole slaw around as if he were looking for a prize, so she decided to go on. "If I were going to be with somebody, I'd want it to be her...because I...I wouldn't want to be with a guy, is what I mean."

He looked up at her, his expression calm and sympathetic. "I know what you're trying to say, Angel. It's okay. I'm fine with it. Too bad it didn't work out, if you really like her. Maybe love will find a way, eh?"

Thrown by his complacency over her second big revelation, Shelby turned her attention to her own sandwich, which she had barely touched. But before she had taken a second bite, she put it down again and asked, "You're not upset?"

Gary brushed his hands together, then wiped them on a napkin. "I won't pretend I'm not disappointed, Angel. I've spent a long time dreaming of how things would be when my little girl grew up and went out into the world."

Shelby lowered her gaze. She had, just for a moment, thought maybe her father would be okay with her being gay. It was a naïve hope, she realized.

"I always had this picture in my mind," he continued, "of how some day we'd be partners. We'd have a brass plate on the door that said Pratt and Pratt. I've often thought how much I'd like that, working side by side with you, and then retiring and leaving the company in your capable hands. But I wouldn't want you to do something you don't like." He gave her an affectionate smile. "To tell you the truth, Shelby, I'm proud of you for making this decision, as much as I wish you wanted to work with me. It shows conviction. Not to mention guts. You're turning your back on a sure thing to pursue your passion. How can I not admire that?"

Shelby smiled back, feeling suddenly hopeful.

The waitress came by to collect their plates. "Any dessert for you two?" she asked.

"I think I'd like a big slice of boysenberry pie," Shelby announced, feeling her appetite returning.

"Me too!" Gary slapped a hand on the edge of the table. "Make that two slices of boysenberry pie. A la mode?"

Shelby nodded enthusiastically, remembering berry pie a la mode here at Ollie's from many years before.

"Two B-berry a la modes," the waitress announced, then left.

"If your plan doesn't work out," Gary said, "if you ever change your mind, there will always be a drafting table with your name on it in my company."

"Thanks, Dad. I really appreciate that."

He reached across the table and patted her hand.

"But about Gwen," she said, still not sure if he had understood and determined that everything should be out in the open, "you wouldn't have a problem with her if I was able to patch things up?"

He knit his forehead in puzzlement. "Why? Is there something about her you think I won't like?"

"No, no. I meant, you know, because I'm not into guys."

He shrugged. "I didn't have a problem with it when you were with Lori. Why would I now?"

Shelby stared. "You knew I was gay?"

"Sure. I've known for years."

"But Mom didn't know. How could you know and not her?"

"She didn't want to know," he said matter-of-factly.

Shelby was about to comment further when their pie arrived, two thick purple slices of warm comfort with a scoop of vanilla ice cream melting on top. They both happily picked up their forks and dug in, laughing at one another across the table.

CHAPTER THIRTY-FOUR

"That girl, What's-er-name," Skipper said, shaking her index finger at the desk, "left you something."

"You mean Shelby?" Gwen asked.

"Yeah, Shelby. She was in here while you were out."

Gwen noticed a manila folder on the desk. A yellow note was stuck to the outside. "It's a shoo-in!" it read.

"She said it was important," Skipper added.

Gwen opened the folder to reveal a form inside. *National Register of Historic Places*, she read, *Inventory Nomination Form. Daniel Hebberd House*.

It was an application form for the national register. Confused, Gwen scanned the form further until she noted the address of the Daniel Hebberd House. It was the same address as the museum. It was this very building. Gwen read through the text explaining the historical significance of the property, gradually understanding what she was reading.

"What is it?" Skipper asked.

Gwen let herself sink into her desk chair, staring unbelievingly at the paper in front of her.

Skipper persisted. "Is it bad news?"

Gwen shook her head. "No. It's good news." She looked up to meet Skipper's eyes. "It's freaking fantastic news!"

Skipper hobbled as rapidly as possible over to the chair next to Gwen and sat down. "Tell me."

"Shelby has saved the museum!"

A big smile spread across Skipper's face. Gwen knew she wore one to match it.

"How'd she do that?" Skipper asked. "Blackmail? Extortion? That little girl's a sneaky one, isn't she?"

Gwen laughed. "It's all legal. Apparently that guy in the nineteen-eleven photo, Daniel Hebberd, was the architect who designed and built this building. He went on to become famous. He designed a lot of houses in Alameda, as well as the original courthouse, which is already a state historical landmark. There's a bunch of stuff here about the unique features of this building, but what it boils down to is that Shelby has applied for national landmark status for us."

"National landmark status?"

"Yes. Because of the building's architectural significance, because it was the first house designed by Daniel Hebberd. He lived here, apparently, for six years when he was a young man."

"So it can't be torn down?"

Gwen held up a hand of caution, as much for herself as for Skipper. "If it's approved. It sounds like she thinks it's a good candidate. And if it can't be torn down, the city will have no reason not to renew your lease. What better use for a national landmark than as a museum?"

"I'll be damned!" Skipper jumped up and swung her cane wildly, barely missing the desk lamp, as Gwen cringed in anticipation of flying glass.

"I can't believe it," Gwen said. "I was so focused on the collection. I never thought about the building."

"It's the oldest thing on this base," Skipper said firmly, as if that had always been her mantra. "It should be protected."

Gwen looked askance at Skipper. "Why didn't you say that a year ago?"

Skipper shrugged. "I can't wait to tell the boys. I'm gonna call them when I get home. See you tomorrow. Give What's-er-name a kiss for me."

Skipper smiled crookedly, then made her way out while Gwen read more carefully through the application form. It was a copy, signed and dated the previous day by Shelby. Gwen assumed the original had already been filed. What a wonderfully thoughtful thing for her to have done, to go to the trouble to do all this research.

Gwen sat back in her chair and sighed, thinking of Shelby. Maintaining her resolution not to see her had been hard. It was a battle of mind over heart. At any given moment on any day, either one was winning, but so far she'd resisted when the memory of that sweet face threatened to wear her down. Whenever she thought she might cave in, she dredged up some painful memory of life with Melissa, like gritting her teeth while Melissa's mother asked if she was seeing anyone and Melissa breezily answering, "No, Mom, nobody special." That phrase, "nobody special," never failed to stab at Gwen's heart, even now. It was an effective reminder of why she had to stand firm against her desire for Shelby.

When the door opened, Gwen looked up, assuming Skipper had forgotten something. But it wasn't Skipper. It was a woman of about sixty wearing a strand of pearls and a long-sleeved, knee-length pastel patterned dress, carrying a white patent leather purse. A second passed before Gwen recognized Shelby's mother.

She'd seen her only once before and hadn't gotten a good look at her, but she was certain that's who was standing in the doorway smiling self-consciously. *Does she always dress like that?* Gwen wondered, trying to shake the image of Donna Reed from her mind.

"You're Gwen?" she asked.

Gwen nodded. "And you're Shelby's mother."

"Vivian," she said, nodding.

Gwen stood, wondering what this was all about and hoping Vivian wasn't going to go nuts on her.

"You look so different in regular clothes," Vivian said amid a nervous laugh.

"So do you."

Vivian laughed again, looking down at her dress. "I've just been to a wedding. Shelby's friend Lori. It was very nice. Classic. The groom and bride both wore white. You can't go wrong with white. Shelby decided not to go. Too upsetting for her, I guess."

"Could be hard to take," Gwen agreed. "Your ex marrying a guy."

Vivian's smile seemed forced. *No*, Gwen thought, *not Donna Reed, after all. Stepford Wife.*

"Can we chat?" Vivian asked.

An image flashed through Gwen's mind: Vivian pulling a revolver out of her purse and pumping her chest full of bullets, smiling that Stepford Wife smile the whole time. *I read too many mysteries*, she scolded herself.

Gwen indicated the chair next to her desk and Vivian sat down, crossing her legs and folding her hands primly over the purse in her lap.

"I hope I'm not keeping you from something," she said.

"No. I was just getting ready to go home. We close at four thirty."

"Oh. Well, this won't take long. I came because of you and Shelby, because the two of you are—you know—dating."

"We're not. Not anymore."

"Right. That's why I'm here." She gripped the edge of her purse emphatically. "This is all my fault, the split between you two. I feel so bad about it."

Gwen was shocked. "Did Shelby ask you to come?"

"She has no idea I'm here. Believe me, she'd never ask such a thing. She'd be sure I'd make a bigger disaster of things than they are already. I hope I don't. I really do want her to be happy. It's just hard for me to imagine such a different kind of happiness from the one I've wanted for her. You know, a devoted husband, beautiful children, a comfortable home." Vivian laughed. "That's my version of happily ever after, I know. Not hers."

"Do you think hers is really so different from that?" Gwen asked gently.

"Maybe not. But it might be harder to get if you're living outside the mainstream."

"I think happily ever after is hard to get no matter who you are. But the very first ingredient has to be being true to yourself."

Vivian gazed at her for a moment before saying, "You seem like a nice young woman. My mother thinks you're wonderful."

"I like her too."

"Shelby was just trying to protect me," Vivian said, avoiding direct eye contact. "But on some level, I think I already knew about her. She never had any boyfriends, for one thing. I mean, a cute girl like that with no boyfriends. That was a clue. And her friendship with Lori did always seem…unusual." Vivian looked up with a small smile. "When Lori got engaged to Stephen, I thought maybe I'd misunderstood. I hoped I had. Frankly, if she'd come to me after I saw you two together that day and told me you were rehearsing a play or something, I'd have put everything I had into believing that. Well, especially considering how you were dressed."

Gwen pictured herself in the Uncle Sam costume. That must have looked totally bizarre.

"But she didn't lie about it," Vivian continued. "She told me the truth. In terms I couldn't misunderstand. She's gay. I know that. She's not confused or embarrassed by it. She just didn't want me to fall apart. That's why she kept it secret. It wasn't out of fear of the consequences to herself. It was because she was afraid I couldn't handle it. I feel terrible about that now. I put so much unfair pressure on her." Vivian met Gwen's eyes. "She's really a good girl."

"So you're here to ask me to give her another chance?"

Vivian nodded. "If you have feelings for her."

If I have feelings for her, Gwen mused, thinking about how she'd been torturing herself with thoughts of Shelby.

Unfair and unreasonable: that's what Melissa always called

her when she voiced her opinion of people living in the closet. The possibility that she'd been too rigid reentered her mind. Was she overreacting because of what she'd been through in the past? Maybe it wasn't so bad that Shelby had taken her time coming out to her parents. Sometimes people needed help, like a supportive partner, to give them confidence and something to fall back on if it all goes wrong. It doesn't have to mean they're ashamed or even uncertain about who they are. Shelby had certainly not had a supportive partner before.

"I do have feelings for her," Gwen said sincerely.

"Oh, I'm glad to hear that!" Vivian sounded truly relieved. She smiled warmly, a genuine, unselfconscious smile that made her seem much more approachable. "So you'll make up with her?"

"I'll think about it," Gwen promised. "Do you want to ask me anything about myself?"

"No." Vivian shook her head. "Shelby loves you. That's all that matters to me. Besides, she's a better judge of character than I am."

Shelby loves me? Gwen thought. *How strange it should be her mother who tells me that.*

"She might still have a couple of beautiful children," Gwen pointed out, "if she wants them."

"I hadn't thought of that." Vivian laughed lightly. "You're right. Nowadays, there's nothing to prevent that."

"She might even have a lovely wedding some day. How do you think I'd look in a white tuxedo?"

Vivian's face broke into a delighted smile. "Oh! A whole lot better than you looked in that Uncle Sam costume, I'm sure."

She wasn't quite the lunatic Gwen had imagined based on Shelby's few details. *I could cope with her as a mother-in-law,* Gwen thought. *Not on a daily basis, but maybe once a week. Or twice a month. Yes, that was certainly doable.*

CHAPTER THIRTY-FIVE

When Shelby realized it was Gwen on the front porch, she couldn't get the door open fast enough. Gwen smiled broadly, then held her arms out. Shelby ran into them, hugging her as tightly as she could, overjoyed to be enveloped in the tender comfort of her body. Gwen's hand caressed the back of her head.

"Come in," Shelby said, pulling Gwen by the hand. "I'm so glad to see you."

"Just to be clear," Gwen cautioned, her wide mouth suppressing a grin, "I'm not here because you saved the museum."

"No?"

"No, even though I'm thrilled about that and totally grateful. You're an angel!" Gwen looked fondly down at Shelby, holding her hand. "Nor am I here because your mother pleaded with me to take you to bed."

"*What?*"

Gwen laughed. "The women in your family are complicated. Never mind. I'll explain later. I'm here because I want to be with you." Gwen slipped her arms around Shelby's waist and pulled her close. She kissed her slowly and sensuously before pulling away and saying, "You're not expecting your mom tonight, are you?"

Shelby shook her head.

"And they're still holding Lucy in that hellhole?" Gwen stroked Shelby's face, pushing a strand of hair off her forehead.

"For a few more days. Besides, she may not be coming back here to live after all."

"Oh?"

"Mom and Aunt Vickie are taking her to see Cypress Villas tomorrow. She's thinking of moving there."

Gwen's mouth fell open. "That's too cool! She's moving in with Marjorie?"

"Well, she'd have her own apartment, but I'm guessing they'd be pretty friendly neighbors."

"Wow." Gwen looked overwhelmed.

"It'd be nice if this story had a happy ending, don't you think?"

Gwen looked down, her eyes flashing. "I do." She bent her head to kiss Shelby again.

As their tongues touched, Shelby felt a spark shoot through her chest and out through her arms and legs. Gwen's lips moved lightly across her neck and the hard ridge of her collarbone. Their mouths came together again and she felt herself falling into a soft emptiness, falling smoothly as through warm water.

Gwen's arms held her up, transported her, while their mouths created both fulfillment and greater longing, and before she knew what had happened, she was lying on her bed with Gwen kneeling above her, looking down with her eyes ablaze with passion.

They removed one another's clothes slowly, letting their fingers and tongues savor each revealed curve of flesh—a bare shoulder, a silky arm, smooth muscles of a back, the hollow behind a knee and the pale secret skin of the inner thigh.

Shelby had never been touched like this, not in her body or her mind, not by someone who desired her so completely, whose breath quavered at the sight of her exposed breasts and the sensation of belly against belly. Gwen's arms enfolded her with the certainty of need. Her mouth possessed her with a craving that trembled as she held it back, like a horse straining to gallop.

Gwen was on top of her, inside her, all around her, leading her body gradually into that gallop, and then with straining muscles, into a full run—running blindly—harder, faster, running unstoppable toward home like a wild beast who has never known a bridle or a bit.

CHAPTER THIRTY-SIX

They drove across the Richmond bridge in a gray drizzle with a thick layer of coastal fog choking out the summer sun. There was nothing but a solid wall of bright white between the spires of the Golden Gate. This wasn't a day for sightseeing. Nana sat in the passenger seat of her car while Shelby drove. Gwen sat in back with Oscar. Shelby snuck a look at her every time she glanced in the rearview mirror. A couple of times Gwen caught her looking and made a face at her. This time, she puckered her lips.

"The worst part," Nana said, "is having some strangers living in my house. Practically my whole life happened in that house. The girls were born there, grew up there. Marjorie and I spent that incredible fall and winter there. Just so much of me is there. Of all of us. The family."

"Right," Shelby said. "That's the sad part of this. I wish I could afford to rent it myself."

"Where are you going to live?" Nana asked.

"She's moving in with me," Gwen said.

"Oh!" Nana responded, clapping her hands together spontaneously. "How wonderful!"

"So you think Gwen's okay, do you?"

Nana laughed. "She's a doll."

"Why, thank you," Gwen said, fluttering her lashes.

"When?" Nana asked.

"Right away," Shelby said. "We can't stand living apart another day. Well, maybe a couple of days longer."

"Is it a nice place?"

"Not particularly," Gwen said. "But we won't mind. It'll be fine for now. It's all we can afford at the moment."

Shelby nodded. "Money's going to be tight for a while. Gwen doesn't make much at the museum and I'm sure whatever job I find will be near minimum wage."

Nana was silent for a moment before saying, "Why can't you two stay at my place?"

"Because the rent you're asking is way beyond our means," Shelby pointed out.

"What if I lowered the rent?"

"That wouldn't be smart, would it, especially since your own cost of living is about to go sky-high."

"Oh, Shelby, you know I have enough savings to last the rest of my life. I could charge you nothing but utilities and it wouldn't cause me any trouble at all. In fact, that's a fantastic idea." Nana's voice rose as she warmed up to her new plan. "You two can live there and take care of the place for me. Keep it in the family. We'll set it up so you're leasing it. When I die, it's yours free and clear. Whatever you've paid by then is the purchase price. What do you say?"

Shelby glanced in the rearview mirror to see Gwen's expression. She looked back with astonishment.

"I don't think Mom'll like that," Shelby said. "Or Aunt Vickie either."

"So what? It's not their house."

"Well, they think it is. I mean, it's theirs to inherit."

"Not their decision," Nana said with finality. "There's nothing that would make me happier than to see the two of you living there. Then when I come to visit, I can stay in my own house and won't have to stay with those two crabby daughters of mine."

Shelby and Gwen looked at each other in the mirror, then Shelby said, "Thank you, Nana. We'll take good care of it."

"Woo hoo!" Gwen hollered.

Nana nodded, then sat quietly with a satisfied smile on her face.

"I talked to Marjorie on the phone yesterday," she said as they neared their destination. "Vivian and Vickie have been down there fussing in my new place."

"They're fixing it up for you, making it homey."

"Marjorie said it was looking very nice."

Nana went back to looking out the window. It was understandable that she was nervous and uncertain. She hadn't even seen her new apartment, after all, but Shelby was confident Vivian and Aunt Vickie had made it lovely and inviting for her.

They fell silent, then, until they reached Cypress Villas. Shelby didn't know what to expect, so when it came into view like an oasis plunked down in a stretch of sparse vegetation and coastal scrub, it made quite an impression. It was a complex of several white buildings with red tile roofs: Spanish Colonial Revival. As they approached from the north, a verdant green golf course stretched out over gentle undulations in the landscape. A tall iron fence surrounded the buildings and a huge double gate stood open at the entrance to the grounds. Must be a whole crew of gardeners, she imagined, appreciatively scanning the meticulous landscaping with its rainbow of blooming plants, shade trees, intriguing sculptures and fountains.

"Wow," Gwen said, peering out the window. "This is some classy resort."

When they reached the parking area, Shelby pulled the walker out of the car and unfolded it, clamping it into place. Then she helped Nana through their learned routine of getting out of the car: *swing both legs out, then stand.*

She called her mother to report they had arrived.

"We're here in the apartment," said Vivian, sounding excited.

Inside, the main building was just as impressive as the grounds, opulent, but expansive and light. A grouping of sofas, chairs and tables made the reception area look like a large living room. The clatter of dishes from the nearby dining room heralded the midday meal. An elderly man was sitting in one of the plush chairs reading a newspaper. A couple of other residents were traveling past with walkers. One woman had her Pomeranian leashed to her walker and it pranced beside her.

Gwen went to the front desk to get directions while Shelby and Nana took in the surroundings. Then they made their way out of the main building and into one of the satellite buildings. Gwen led Oscar as they all traveled at the slow pace of the walker's wheels. They passed a placid pond with reeds and water lilies and an assortment of boulders on its borders that made it look almost natural.

"I think I'd like to live here," Gwen remarked.

"Not what you expected, is it?" Shelby asked.

"Well, it's nothing like the place they dumped Aunt Peggy," Nana said. "That's for sure."

Gwen pointed out the sparkling swimming pool in the distance. "It's all a matter of what you can afford, I guess."

Finally they arrived at Nana's new place where streamers were hung in the open doorway. Nana rolled in first, then Shelby and Gwen followed. Inside, Marjorie and Vivian stood in the middle of the living room, waiting to see Nana's reaction. Shelby noticed that Marjorie had had her hair done and was wearing a smart suit of purple slacks and a brocade jacket. She had on earrings and a necklace of colored beads.

The apartment looked inviting and bright. There were large windows and a skylight. Vivian and Vickie had obviously put a huge effort into making Nana comfortable and happy with her new home. Nana's pictures hung on the walls and her favorite plant, the weeping fig, stood in one corner. Familiar furniture had been strategically arranged into a functional scheme. Some of Nana's dishes were in the kitchen and her curios were on the shelves. There was a large vase of flowers on the table. It was gorgeous.

"Oh, this is beautiful!" Nana said, rolling inside. "Look at all my stuff! Look at the flowers."

"Welcome home!" Marjorie announced, flinging her arms wide to hug Nana.

"Of course, you can change anything you want," Vivian said, "if it doesn't suit you. Some of your things wouldn't fit and I bought some new things to fill in."

Nana rolled over to the living room wall where her stereo was set up and peered through the rack of CDs. "All my music," she said, delighted. Then she abandoned her walker and limped toward the kitchen, a small open area with a refrigerator, sink, cupboards and a table large enough for a comfortable twosome.

"Shouldn't you be using your walker?" Vivian asked.

"Oh, I don't need that thing just to walk around my own place." She opened the refrigerator to see it stocked with essentials and nodded approvingly. She looked around, wrinkling her brow, then asked, "Where's the oven?"

"No oven," Vivian said. "No stove, no oven. They cook for you. You go to the dining room to eat. But you've got a microwave." Vivian stepped over to indicate the small, under-cabinet microwave.

"What if I want to roast a chicken?" Nana asked.

"What do you think you're gonna do, Lou?" asked Marjorie, jovially. "Gonna go find yourself a chicken and wring its neck?"

They both laughed, then held one another's gazes meaningfully.

"Come see the rest of the place," Vivian said. "The bedroom's darling."

"I think she likes it," Marjorie confided to Shelby as Nana followed Vivian into the next room.

"I think she does," Shelby agreed. "Did you help with all of this?"

"A little. It was mostly your mother and your aunt Vickie, though. Vickie had to work today, so she didn't get to see this. Too bad."

"I want to see the bedroom too," Shelby said, joining her

mother and Nana in the back. Nana's bed was in place with a new comforter. Her pictures were on the walls and her dresser was across from the bed. A chair and a lamp had come over from the old house. New sheers covered the window.

"Oh, my ballerina!" Nana exclaimed as she examined the contents of the dresser. "Marjorie, do you remember this?"

Marjorie, who was behind Shelby, edged into the room to take a look. "Of course I remember it. Does it still work?"

Nana picked up the ballerina and wound it with deliberate care, then set it down. All of them gathered around the dresser watching her twirl, lifting her arms above her head. Marjorie clapped her hands together, looking delighted.

"Where do you want this?" Shelby asked, showing Nana the 1944 photo of herself and Marjorie, which she'd had enlarged and framed.

"Oh, look at that," Nana said, taking it in both hands.

Marjorie looked over her shoulder. "I haven't seen that in a long time."

Nana set the photo beside the ballerina. "Right here, I think."

"We've got a bunch of stuff in the car to bring in," Shelby announced.

"I'm going to run over to the front desk," Vivian said. "There's still some business to take care of. You do like it, don't you, Mom?"

"I love it!" Nana said, her face looking rosy and flushed. She was excited. "You've done a marvelous job, Viv."

Gwen and Shelby walked out to the parking lot to unload the boxes from the trunk. Shelby stood looking at the bay under its thinning blanket of fog. The distant sound of sea lions barking and the groan of a foghorn reached her ears. She leaned against Gwen, who slipped her arms around her waist and nuzzled her face against Shelby's neck.

"I know she'll like being here," Shelby said. "Still on the bay."

She watched as the fog grew thinner, swirling above like a sheet billowing in the wind and slowly fading into nothing. The San Francisco skyline gradually came into view and the Golden

Gate Bridge grew more and more solid as they watched. And suddenly there was sunshine and a bright blue sky as the last wisps of fog just seemed to vanish all at once.

"Let's get this stuff in." Shelby opened the trunk and they each took a box.

"It's so cool how all of this worked out," Gwen said.

"I'm really glad we can keep the house in the family. When do you think you'll want to move in?"

"Two or three weeks. That'll give us time to take the rest of Lucy's stuff to Goodwill and straighten up. Maybe we can paint a couple of rooms."

They carried the boxes back to the apartment, hearing music as they neared the open door. Inside, Marjorie and Nana were dancing, slow and close, in the center of the living room. "For Me and My Gal" played on the stereo. Shelby put her box on the floor and Gwen put hers on top of that, then they stood watching as the two old women swayed together to the music, their feet barely moving. Nana had a hand on one of Marjorie's shoulders and her head on the other. As they turned, Marjorie caught Shelby's eye and winked.

Gwen reached over and took hold of Shelby's hand, squeezing it tightly.

"Want to cut a rug?" she asked, her mouth spreading into its familiar wide grin.

Shelby nodded. Gwen led her into the room where the two young women joined their elders in a dance of timeless love.

**Publications from
Bella Books, Inc.
Women. Books. Even Better Together.
P.O. Box 10543
Tallahassee, FL 32302
Phone: 800-729-4992
www.bellabooks.com**

CALM BEFORE THE STORM by Peggy J. Herring. Colonel Marcel Robicheaux doesn't tell and so far no one official has asked, but the amorous pursuit by Jordan McGowen has her worried for both her career and her honor.
978-0-9677753-1-9

THE WILD ONE by Lyn Denison. Rachel Weston is busy keeping home and head together after the death of her husband. Her kids need her and what she doesn't need is the confusion that Quinn Farrelly creates in her body and heart.
978-0-9677753-4-0

LESSONS IN MURDER by Claire McNab. There's a corpse in the school with a neat hole in the head and a Black & Decker drill alongside. Which teacher should Inspector Carol Ashton suspect? Unfortunately, the alluring Sybil Quade is at the top of the list. First in this highly lauded series.
978-1-931513-65-4

WHEN AN ECHO RETURNS by Linda Kay Silva. The bayou where Echo Branson found her sanity has been swept clean by a hurricane—or at least they thought. Then an evil washed up by the storm comes looking for them all, one-by-one. Second in series.
978-1-59493-225-0

DEADLY INTERSECTIONS by Ann Roberts. Everyone is lying, including her own father and her girlfriend. Leaving matters to the professionals is supposed to be easier! Third in series with *PAID IN FULL* and *WHITE OFFERINGS*.
978-1-59493-224-3

SUBSTITUTE FOR LOVE by Karin Kallmaker. No substitutes, ever again! But then Holly's heart, body and soul are captured by Reyna... Reyna with no last name and a secret life that hides a terrible bargain, one written in family blood.
978-1-931513-62-3

MAKING UP FOR LOST TIME by Karin Kallmaker. Take one Next Home Network Star and add one Little White Lie to equal mayhem in little Mendocino and a recipe for sizzling romance. This lighthearted, steamy story is a feast for the senses in a kitchen that is way too hot.
978-1-931513-61-6

2ND FIDDLE by Kate Calloway. Cassidy James's first case left her with a broken heart. At least this new case is fighting the good fight, and she can throw all her passion and energy into it.
978-1-59493-200-7

HUNTING THE WITCH by Ellen Hart. The woman she loves — used to love — offers her help, and Jane Lawless finds it hard to say no. She needs TLC for recent injuries and who better than a doctor? But Julia's jittery demeanor awakens Jane's curiosity. And Jane has never been able to resist a mystery. #9 in series and Lammy-winner.
978-1-59493-206-9

FAÇADES by Alex Marcoux. Everything Anastasia ever wanted — she has it. Sidney is the woman who helped her get it. But keeping it will require a price — the unnamed passion that simmers between them.
978-1-59493-239-7

ELENA UNDONE by Nicole Conn. The risks. The passion. The devastating choices. The ultimate rewards. Nicole Conn rocked the lesbian cinema world with *Claire of the Moon* and has rocked it again with *Elena Undone*. This is the book that tells it all...
978-1-59493-254-0

WHISPERS IN THE WIND by Frankie J. Jones. It began as a camping trip, then a simple hike. Dixon Hayes and Elizabeth Colter uncover an intriguing cave on their hike, changing their world, perhaps irrevocably.
978-1-59493-037-9

WEDDING BELL BLUES by Julia Watts. She'll do anything to save what's left of her family. Anything. It didn't seem like a bad plan...at first. Hailed by readers as Lammy-winner Julia Watts' funniest novel.
978-1-59493-199-4

WILDFIRE by Lynn James. From the moment botanist Devon McKinney meets ranger Elaine Thomas the chemistry is undeniable. Sharing—and protecting—a mountain for the length of their short assignments leads to unexpected passion in this sizzling romance by newcomer Lynn James.
978-1-59493-191-8

LEAVING L.A. by Kate Christie. Eleanor Chapin is on the way to the rest of her life when Tessa Flanagan offers her a lucrative summer job caring for Tessa's daughter Laya. It's only temporary and everyone expects Eleanor to be leaving L.A...
978-1-59493-221-2

SOMETHING TO BELIEVE by Robbi McCoy. When Lauren and Cassie meet on a once-in-a-lifetime river journey through China their feelings are innocent...at first. Ten years later, nothing—and everything—has changed. From Golden Crown winner Robbi McCoy.
978-1-59493-214-4

DEVIL'S ROCK by Gerri Hill. Deputy Andrea Sullivan and Agent Cameron Ross vow to bring a killer to justice. The killer has other plans. Gerri Hill pens another intriguing blend of mystery and romance in this page-turning thriller.
978-1-59493-218-2

SHADOW POINT by Amy Briant. Madison McPeake has just been not-quite fired, told her brother is dead and discovered she has to pick up a five-year old niece she's never met. After she makes it to Shadow Point it seems like someone—or something —doesn't want her to leave. Romance sizzles in this ghost story from Amy Briant.
978-1-59493-216-8

JUKEBOX by Gina Daggett. Debutantes in love. With each other. Two young women chafe at the constraints of parents and society with a friendship that could be more, if they can break free. Gina Daggett is best known as "Lipstick" of the columnist duo Lipstick & Dipstick.
978-1-59493-212-0

BLIND BET by Tracey Richardson. The stakes are high when Ellen Turcotte and Courtney Langford meet at the blackjack tables. Lady Luck has been smiling on Courtney but Ellen is a wild card she may not be able to handle.
978-1-59493-211-3